MURDER IN THE MANOR

MURDER IN THE MANOR

A Lacey Doyle Cozy Mystery—Book 1

FIONA GRACE

FIONA GRACE

Debut author Fiona Grace is author of the LACEY DOYLE COZY MYSTERY series which includes MURDER IN THE MANOR (Book #1), DEATH AND A DOG (Book #2) and CRIME IN THE CAFE (Book #3). Fiona would love to hear from you, so please visit www.fionagraceauthor.com to receive free ebooks, hear the latest news, and stay in touch.

TABLE OF CONTENTS

CHAPTER ONE

No-fault.

That's what the divorce papers stated, in black ink and bold text, stark against the white of the paper.

No-fault.

Lacey sighed as she looked down at the documents. The innocuous-looking manila envelope had just been hand delivered to her door by a pimple-faced teenager with a blasé attitude, as if it were nothing more significant than a takeout pizza. And though Lacey had immediately known the reason she was receiving a couriered letter, she'd felt nothing in the moment. It was only after she'd flopped onto the living room couch—where the cappuccino she'd abandoned at the sound of the door buzzer was on the coffee table still spewing little coils of steam—and slid the documents from the envelope that it actually hit her.

Divorce papers.

Divorce.

Her reaction had been to scream and throw them to the ground, like she was an arachnophobic who'd just been mailed a live tarantula.

And there they now lay, spread across the fashionable and extremely expensive rug she'd been gifted by her boss, Saskia, at the interior design firm where she worked. The words *David Doyle vs Lacey Doyle* stared up at her. From the nonsensical mass of letters, words began to form before her eyes: dissolution of marriage, irreconcilable differences, no-fault...

She picked the papers up tentatively.

1

Of course, this wasn't a surprise. David had ended their fourteen-year marriage with the exclamation, "You'll be hearing from my lawyer!" after all. But that still hadn't prepared Lacey for the emotional fallout of actually being in physical possession of the documents. Of feeling their weight, their solidness, and seeing that horrible, bold, black text declaring faultlessness.

It was how New York did things—*blameless divorces are less messy, right?*—but "no-fault" seemed a bit rich, as far as Lacey was concerned. The fault, according to David anyway, was all hers. Thirty-nine and no baby. Not even the slightest itch of broodiness. No hormonal surges at the sight of their friends' newborns—of which there had been many, materializing into being in an endless stream of nice little squidgy things that made precisely nothing stir within her.

"You're a ticking clock," David had explained over a glass of merlot one night.

Of course, what he really meant was, "Our marriage is a ticking time bomb."

Lacey let out a deep sigh. If only she'd known when she'd married him at twenty-five, in a blissful whirlwind of white confetti and champagne bubbles, that prioritizing her career over motherhood would come back to bite her so spectacularly in the ass.

No-fault. Ha!

She went to find a pen—her limbs suddenly made of steel—and found one in the pot of keys. At least things were *organized* now. No more David running around searching for lost shoes, lost keys, lost wallets, lost sunglasses. These days, everything was where she'd left it. But in this moment, that didn't feel like much of a consolation prize.

She returned to the couch, pen in hand, and positioned it over the dotted line she was supposed to sign. But instead of touching it to paper, Lacey paused, the pen hovering, poised barely a millimeter above the line, as if there were some kind of invisible barrier between the ballpoint and the paper. The words "spousal support clause" had caught her attention.

Frowning, Lacey turned to the appropriate page and scanned the clause. As the highest earner of the pair, and the sole proprietor of the Upper Eastside apartment in which she was currently sitting, Lacey would have to pay David a "fixed sum" for "no more than two years," in order for him to "set up" his new life in a "manner consistent with that of which he lived before."

Lacey couldn't help but let out a rueful laugh. How ironic that David was profiting from her career, the very thing that had ended their marriage in the first place! Of course, he wouldn't see it that way. David would call it something like "recompense." He was a stickler for balance, for fairness and equilibrium. But Lacey knew what that money really was. Retribution. Vengeance. Retaliation.

Way to get bit in the ass twice, she thought.

Suddenly, Lacey's vision blurred and a splotch appeared on her surname, making the ink distort and the paper crinkle. A rogue tear had fallen from her eye. She wiped the offending eye aggressively with the back of her hand.

I'll have to change my name, she thought as she stared at the now deformed word. *Return to my maiden name.*

Lacey Fay Bishop was no more. Erased. That name belonged to David Bishop's wife, and once she signed on the dotted line, she would no longer be that woman. She'd become Lacey Fay Doyle once again, a girl she hadn't inhabited since her twenties and one she hardly even remembered.

But the Doyle name meant even less to Lacey than the one she'd had on loan from David for the last fourteen years. Her father had left when she was seven, immediately after an otherwise charming family holiday to the idyllic seaside town of Wilfordshire, England. She hadn't seen him since. There one day—eating ice cream on a rugged, wild, windswept beach—gone the next.

And now she was as much of a failure as her parents! After all those childhood tears she had shed for her missing father, all those angry teenage insults she'd thrown at her mom, she'd only gone and repeated the very same mistakes! She'd failed at marriage, just as they had. The only difference, Lacey reasoned, was that her failure had no collateral damage. Her divorce wouldn't leave two distraught, damaged daughters in its wake.

She stared down again at that blasted line. It was demanding to be signed. But still, Lacey dithered. Her mind seemed stuck on her new name.

Maybe I'll just drop my surname altogether, she thought, wryly. *I could be Lacey Fay, like some kind of pop star.* She felt a bubbling sense of hysteria rising in her chest. *But then why stop there? I could change my name to anything I wanted for a few dollars. I could be*—she glanced around the room for inspiration, her eyes settling on the coffee mug still untouched on the table before her—*Lacey Fay Cappuccino. Why not? Princess Lacey Fay Cappuccino!*

She burst into laughter, throwing back her head of glossy dark curls and barking at the ceiling. But the moment was short-lived, the laughter stopping as soon as it had started. Silence fell in the otherwise empty apartment.

Quickly, Lacey scribbled her signature on the divorce papers. It was done.

She took a sip of coffee. It was cold.

Business as usual, Lacey boarded the busy subway, heading to the office where she worked as an interior designer's assistant. Heels, handbag, no eye contact, Lacey was just like any other commuter. Except, of course, she wasn't. Because out of the half million people currently riding the New York subway during morning rush hour, she was the only one who'd been served with divorce papers that morning—or at least that's how she felt. She was the newest member of the Sad Divorcées Club.

Lacey could feel the tears coming. She shook her head and forced her mind to think of happy things. It went straight to Wilfordshire, to that peaceful, wild beach. In a sudden, vivid memory, Lacey recalled the ocean and the salty air. She remembered the ice cream truck with its creepy, chiming jingle, and the hot fries—*chips, Dad said they were called over there*—that came in a little Styrofoam tub with a small wooden fork, and all the seagulls that tried to steal them the second her attention wandered. She thought of her parents, of their smiling faces that holiday.

Had it all been a lie? She'd only been seven, Naomi four, neither old enough to really pick up on the nuances of adult emotion. Her parents had evidently been good at hiding things, because everything was perfectly fine until, overnight, it was devastating.

They really had seemed happy back then, Lacey thought, but to the outside world, she and David probably looked like they had it all, too. And they had. A nice apartment. Well-paying, satisfying jobs. Good health. Just not those blasted babies that had abruptly become so important to David. In fact, it had almost been as abrupt as her father leaving. Maybe it was a male thing. A sudden eureka moment in which there could be no coming back once the decision had been made, and so everything that stood in its way was burned to the ground because why leave anything intact?

Lacey exited the subway and joined the throngs of people jostling through the streets of New York City. She'd called New York home her whole life. But now it seemed stifling. She'd always loved the busyness, not to mention the businesses. New York was her all over. But now she felt overwhelmed with a desire for a radical change. For a fresh start.

As she walked the last couple of blocks to her office, she took her cell from her purse and called Naomi. Her sister answered on the first ring.

"Everything okay, hon?"

Naomi had been anxiously waiting for the divorce papers, hence the immediate pickup despite the early hour. But Lacey didn't want to discuss the divorce.

"Do you remember Wilfordshire?"

"Huh?"

Naomi sounded sleepy. As a single mother to Frankie, the world's most rambunctious seven-year-old boy, that was to be expected.

"Wilfordshire. The last vacation we had with Mom and Dad together."

There was a moment of silence.

"Why are you asking me that?"

Like their mother, Naomi had taken a vow of silence in regards to all things Dad. She'd been younger when he left, and proclaimed that she had no memories of him whatsoever so why waste the energy on caring about his absence? But after one too many shots on a Friday night, she'd confessed to remembering him vividly, dreaming of him often, and devoting three whole years of weekly therapy sessions furiously blaming his abandonment on the failure of every one of her adult relationships. Naomi had jumped onto the carousel of passionate, tumultuous relationships at the age of fourteen and never gotten off. Naomi's love life made Lacey dizzy.

"They came. The papers."

"Oh, hon. I'm so sorry. Are you—FRANKIE PUT THAT DOWN OR SO HELP ME GOD!"

Lacey winced, moving the cell phone from her ear while Naomi barked a threat of death at Frankie if he continued doing whatever activity it was he wasn't supposed to.

"Sorry, hon," Naomi said, her voice back to indoor volume. "Are you okay?"

"I'm fine." Lacey paused. "No, actually I'm not. I'm feeling impulsive. On a scale of one to ten, how crazy would it be to skip work and catch the next flight to England?"

"Er, how about eleven? They'll fire you."

"I'll ask for some personal time."

Lacey could practically hear Naomi roll her eyes.

"From Saskia? Really? You think she'll give you a personal day? The woman who made you work Christmas last year?"

Lacey twisted her lips in consternation, a gesture she'd inherited from her father, according to her mom. "I need to do something, Naomi. I feel stifled." She tugged the collar of her turtleneck, which suddenly felt like a noose.

"Of course you do. No one blames you for that. Just, don't do anything rash. I mean, you chose your career over David. Don't risk it."

Lacey paused, confusion forcing her eyebrows together. Was that how Naomi interpreted the situation?

"I didn't *choose* my career over him. He gave me an ultimatum."

"Spin it how you want, Lace, just…FRANKIE! FRANKIE I SWEAR—"

Lacey had reached her office. She sighed. "Bye, Naomi."

She ended the call and stared up at the tall brick building she'd given fifteen years of her life to. Fifteen to the job. Fourteen to David. Surely it was time she gave herself something? Just one little vacation. A trip down memory lane. A week. A fortnight. A month at the most.

With a sudden sense of resolve, Lacey marched inside the building. She found Saskia standing over a computer, barking orders at one of the terrified-looking interns. Before her boss even had a chance to say a word to Lacey, Lacey held a hand up to stop her in her tracks.

"I'm taking some personal time off," she said.

She just had time to see Saskia frown before spinning on her heel and marching out the way she'd come.

Five minutes later, Lacey was on the phone booking a flight to England.

CHAPTER TWO

"You've officially gone crazy, sis."

"Darling, you're acting irrationally."

"Is Auntie Lacey okay?"

The words from Naomi, Mom, and Frankie repeated in Lacey's mind as she stepped from the plane onto the tarmac of Heathrow Airport. Maybe she was crazy, jumping on the first flight out of JFK, spending seven hours on a plane with nothing but her purse, her thoughts, and a tote bag full of clothes and toiletries she'd purchased from the chain stores in the airport. But turning her back on Saskia, and New York, and David, had felt *exhilarating*. It had made her feel young. Carefree. Adventurous. Brave. In fact, it had reminded her of the Lacey Doyle she'd been BD (*Before David*).

Breaking the news to her family that she was swanning off to England without warning—over speakerphone, no less—had been less exhilarating, since none of them seemed to possess a filter, and all three shared the same bad habit of expressing aloud whatever was on their mind.

"What if you get fired?" Mom had wailed.

"Oh, she'll definitely get fired," Naomi had agreed.

"Is Auntie Lacey having a breakdown?" Frankie had asked.

Lacey could picture the three of them sitting around a conference table, doing their best to burst her bubble. But of course that wasn't the reality of the situation. As her nearest and dearest, it was their job to dish out the hard truths to her. In this new, unfamiliar era, AD—*After David*—who else was going to?

8

Lacey crossed the concourse, following the rest of the bleary-eyed passengers. The famed English drizzle hung in the air. So much for spring. With the moisture frizzing her hair, Lacey was finally given pause for thought. But there was no turning back now, not after a seven-hour flight and several hundred bucks being docked from her bank account.

The terminal was an enormous greenhouse-esque building, all steel and sleek blue-tinted glass, topped with a state-of-the-art curved roof. Lacey entered into the shiny, tiled room—decorated with Cubist murals sponsored by the quaint-sounding British Building Society—and joined the queue for passport control. When her turn arrived, the guard at the kiosk was a scowling blond woman with black, block-drawn eyebrows. Lacey handed her passport over.

"Reason for your visit? Business or pleasure?"

The guard's accent was harsh, far from the soft-spoken British actors who charmed Lacey on her favorite late-night talk shows.

"I'm on vacation."

"You don't got a return ticket."

It took Lacey's brain a moment to work out what the woman was actually saying, due to her unorthodox grammar. "It's an open-ended vacation."

The guard raised her big, black brows, her scowl turning to suspicion. "You need a visa if you're planning on working."

Lacey shook her head. "I'm not. The last thing I'm here to do is work. I just got divorced. I need a bit of time and space to clear my head and eat ice cream and watch bad movies."

The guard's features instantly softened with empathy, giving Lacey the distinct impression she was also a fellow member of the Sad Divorcées Club.

She handed Lacey back her passport. "Enjoy your stay. And chin up, yeah?"

Lacey swallowed the little lump that had formed in her throat, thanked the guard, and went on through to arrivals. There, several distinct huddles of people stood waiting for their loved ones to appear. Some were holding balloons, others flowers. One group of very blond children held a sign that read, "Welcome Home Mummy! We missed you!"

Of course, there was no one to greet Lacey, and as she crossed the busy concourse, heading for the exit, she thought about how she would never be greeted by David at an airport ever again. If only she'd known when she'd returned from that business trip—antique vase shopping in Milan—that it would be the last time David would surprise her at the airport with a grin on his face and a big bunch of colorful daisies in his arms. She would have savored it more.

Outside, Lacey hailed a cab. It was a black hackney carriage, the sight of which immediately caused a pang of nostalgia to hit her. She, Naomi, and their parents had traveled in a black cab all those years ago, during that fateful, final family vacation.

"Where you off to?" the tubby driver asked as Lacey slid into the back seat.

"Wilfordshire."

A beat passed. The driver turned fully in his seat to face her, a deep scowl furrowing his wiry brows. "Do you know that's a two-hour drive?"

Lacey blinked, unsure what he was trying to communicate to her.

"That's fine," she said, with a small shrug.

He looked even more perplexed. "You're a yank, right? Well, I dunno how much you're used to spending on fares over *there*, but on this side of the pond a two-hour drive will set you back a pretty penny."

His abrupt manner took Lacey by surprise, not just because it didn't match the image in her mind of a cheeky London cab driver, but because of his veiled suggestion that she couldn't afford such a journey. She wondered if it was something to do with her being a solo female traveler. No one ever questioned David when they took long cab journeys together.

"I can pay," she assured the cabby, her tone a little frosty.

The driver turned back to face the front and pressed the start button on the fare machine. It beeped and flashed up a pound symbol in green, the sight of which prompted another wave of nostalgia in Lacey.

"As long as you can," he said thinly, pulling away from the curb.

So much for British hospitality, Lacey thought.

They arrived at Wilfordshire the promised two hours later, Lacey "two hun'erd 'n' fifty quid" worse off for it. But the steep fare—and the less than friendly cabby—paled into insignificance the moment Lacey exited the vehicle and took a deep inhalation of that fresh, seaside air. It smelled just as she remembered.

It had always struck Lacey as remarkable the way smells and tastes could evoke such strong memories—and now was no different. The salty air caused a sudden surge of carefree delight to rise inside of her, one she hadn't felt since before her father had left. It was so strong she was almost bowled over. The anxiety her family's reaction to the impromptu trip had instilled in her simply melted away. Lacey was exactly where she needed to be.

She headed down the main street. The drizzle that had surrounded Heathrow Airport was nowhere to be found, and the last dregs of sunset bathed everything in a golden light, making it look magical. It was just as she remembered—two parallel rows of ancient stone cottages, built right up to the cobblestone sidewalks, their original glass bay windows bulging into the streets. None of the storefronts had modernized since she'd last been here. Indeed, they all still had what looked like their original wooden signs swinging above them, and each store was unique, selling everything from children's boutique clothing to haberdashery, to baked goods and small batch coffee. There was even an old-style "sweet shop" filled with large glass jars of colored candy, where everything could be bought individually for "a penny."

It was April, and the town was decorated with colored bunting for the upcoming Easter celebrations, all strung up between the stores and crisscrossing overhead. And there were plenty of people about—the post-work crowd, Lacey presumed—sitting outside pubs on picnic benches drinking pints, or outside cafes on bistro tables eating desserts. Everyone seemed to be in good spirits, their merry chatter providing a comforting backdrop like white noise.

Feeling a calming surge of rightness, Lacey took out her cell phone and snapped a picture of the main street. With the silver band of sea glittering on the horizon and the gorgeous pink-streaked sky, it looked just like a postcard, so she shared it to the *Doyle Girlz* family thread. Naomi had named it, much to Lacey's chagrin at the time.

It's just as I remembered, she added beneath the picture-perfect image.

A moment later, her phone pinged in response. Naomi had replied.

Looks like you ended up in Diagon Alley by accident, sis.

Lacey sighed. It was a typically sarcastic response from her younger sister and she ought to have expected it. Because *of course* Naomi couldn't just be happy for her, or proud of the way she'd taken command of her own life.

Did you use a filter? came Mom's response a moment later.

Lacey rolled her eyes and put her phone away. Determined not to let anyone bring down her mood, she took a deep, calming breath. The difference in the air quality compared to the polluted New York City air she'd been breathing earlier that morning was truly astounding.

She continued along the street, her heels click-click-clicking against the cobblestones. Her next goal was to find a hotel room for the open-ended number of nights she'd was going to be staying here. She stopped outside the first B&B she came across, The Shire, but saw the flip sign in its window had been turned to "No vacancies." Not to worry. The main street was long, and if Lacey's memory served her correctly, there'd be plenty more places to try.

The next B&B—Laurel's—was painted cotton-candy pink, and its sign proclaimed, "Fully booked." Different words, same sentiment. Only this time, it provoked a flicker of panic in Lacey's chest.

She forced it away. It was just the worm her family had put in her ear. There was no need to fret. She'd find a place soon enough.

She carried on. Between a jewelry store and a bookshop, The Seaside Hotel was fully booked, and on past the camping supplies store and beauty salon, Carol's B'n'B also had no vacancies. It went on and on that way until Lacey found herself at the end of the street.

Now the panic truly did set in. How had she been so foolish as to come here without anything prepared? Her whole career involved *organizing* things, yet she'd failed to organize her own vacation! She didn't have any of her belongings and now she didn't have a room either. Was she going to have to turn back around the way she'd come, shell out another "two hun'red quid" for a taxi back to Heathrow, and catch the next flight home? No wonder David had included a spousal support clause—she couldn't be trusted with her money at all!

As Lacey's mind swirled with anxious thoughts, she turned on the spot, as if by glancing helplessly up the way she'd come she could magic another B&B out of thin air. It was only then that Lacey realized the final corner building she was standing outside of was an inn. The Coach House.

Feeling foolish, Lacey cleared her throat and collected her senses. She went inside.

The interior was typically pub-like; large wooden tables, a black-board with that evening's menu written in cursive white chalk, a gambling machine in the corner with gaudy flashing lights. She went up to the bar, where glass shelves were crammed with bottles of wine, and a row of glass optics hung, filled with a variety of dif-ferent-colored spirits. It was all very quaint. There was even an old drunk dozing at the bar, using his arms as his pillow.

The barmaid was a slight girl with pale blond hair piled into a messy bun at the crown of her head. She looked far too young to be working in a bar. Lacey decided it was because of the lower drink-ing age in England rather than the fact that the older she got, the more baby-faced everyone else seemed to become.

"What can I get you?" the barmaid asked.

"A room," Lacey said. "And a glass of prosecco."

She felt like celebrating.

But the barmaid shook her head. "We're all booked up for Easter." She spoke with such a wide mouth Lacey could see the gum she was chewing. "The whole town is. It's the school holidays and a whole lotta folks like to take their kids to Wilfordshire. There won't be anything for a least a fortnight." She paused. "So, just a prosecco then?"

Lacey grabbed the bar to steady herself. Her stomach flipped. Now she really did feel like the silliest woman in the world. No wonder David had left her. She was a disorganized mess. A sorry excuse for a person. Here she was, pretending she could be an independent adult abroad, when in reality she couldn't even get a hotel room for herself.

At that moment, Lacey saw a figure in her peripheral vision. She turned to see a man coming toward her. He was sixty-odd, wearing a gingham shirt tucked into blue jeans, sunglasses perched on his bald head and a cell phone holster at his hip.

"Did I hear you say you're looking for a place to stay?" he asked.

Lacey was about to say no—she might be desperate, but shacking up with a man double her age who'd approached her in a bar was a bit too *Naomi* for her tastes—when the man clarified, "'Cos I rent holiday cottages."

"Oh?" she replied, taken aback.

The man nodded and produced a little business card from his jean pocket. Lacey's eyes scanned it.

Ivan Parry's cozy, rustic, charming holiday cottages. Ideal for all the family.

"I'm booked up, like Brenda said," Ivan continued, nodding to the barmaid. "Apart from one cottage I just snapped up at auction. It's not really ready to be rented yet, but I can show it to you if you're really stuck? Offer it at a discounted rate, since it's a bit of a tip? Just to tide you over until the hotels become available again."

Relief flooded through Lacey. The business card looked legit, and Ivan hadn't set off any Creep Alerts in her head. Her luck was turning! She was so relieved she could have kissed that bald head of his!

"You're a lifesaver," she said, managing to restrain herself.

Ivan blushed. "Maybe wait until after you've seen it before you make that judgment."

Lacey chuckled. "Honestly, how bad can it be?"

Lacey sounded like a woman in labor as she trudged up the cliffside beside Ivan.

"Is it too steep?" he asked, sounding concerned. "I should've mentioned it was on the cliff."

"It's no problem," Lacey wheezed. "I—love—sea views."

Throughout their whole walk here, Ivan had shown himself to be the opposite of a shrewd businessman, reminding Lacey of the promised discount (despite the fact they hadn't even discussed the price) and repeatedly telling her not to get her hopes up. Now, with her thighs aching from the trek, she was starting to wonder whether he was right to downplay it.

That was, until the house appeared at the crest of the hill. Silhouetted black against the fading pink sky was a tall stone building. Lacey gasped aloud.

"Is that it?" she asked breathlessly.

"That's it," Ivan replied.

Strength that came from nowhere suddenly powered Lacey up the rest of the cliff. Each step that drew her closer to that captivating building revealed another stunning feature: the charming stone façade, the slate roof, the twisting rose plant coiling up the wooden columns of a veranda, the ancient, thick, arched door like something from a fairytale. And framing the whole thing was the glittering, sweeping ocean.

Lacey's eyes bulged and her mouth dropped open as she hurried the last few paces toward it. A wooden sign beside the door read: *Crag Cottage.*

Ivan came up beside her, a large key chain jangling in his hands as he searched through the bundle. Lacey felt like a kid at the ice-cream truck, impatiently waiting for the soft serve machine to do its thing, bouncing on eager toes.

"Don't get your hopes up too high," Ivan said for the umpteenth time, finally finding the key—an aptly large, rusty bronze one that looked like it should open Rapunzel's castle—before twisting it in the lock and shoving the door open.

Lacey stepped eagerly inside the cottage and was hit with the sudden, powerful feeling of coming home.

The corridor was rustic to say the least, with untreated wooden floorboards and faded chintzy wallpaper. Running down the middle of the staircase to her right was a plush red carpet with gold runners, as if the original owner thought it was a stately home rather than a quaint little cottage. A wooden door to her left stood open, as if beckoning her to enter.

"Like I said, it's a bit on the shabby side," Ivan said, as Lacey tiptoed inside.

She found herself in a living room. Three of the walls were papered with fading peppermint-and-white-striped paper, the other showing off the exposed stone blocks. A big bay window overlooked the ocean, with a fitted window seat beneath it. A wood-burning stove with a long black flume took up the entirety of one corner, a silver bucket beside it filled with chopped wood. A large wooden bookcase took up most of one wall. The matching couch, armchair, and foot-stool looked like originals from the 1940s. Everything was in need of a good dusting, but for Lacey, it only made it all the more perfect.

She swirled to face Ivan. He looked apprehensive as he waited for her assessment.

"I love it!" she gushed.

Ivan's expression turned to surprise (with a hint of pride, Lacey noted).

"Oh!" he exclaimed. "What a relief!"

Lacey couldn't stop herself. Filled with excitement, she rushed about the living room, taking in all the little details. On the ornate, carved wooden bookshelf were a couple of mystery books, their pages crinkled from age. A porcelain money box of a sheep and a clock that was no longer ticking were displayed on the next shelf down, and at the bottom was a collection of delicate china teapots. It was an antique lover's dream come true.

"Can I see the rest?" Lacey asked, feeling her heart swell.

"Help yourself," Ivan replied. "I'll go down into the cellar and sort out the heating and water."

They headed out into the small, dark corridor, Ivan disappearing through a doorway beneath the stairs while Lacey continued on to the kitchen, her heart beating with nervous anticipation.

As she stepped in through the door, she gasped aloud.

The kitchen looked like something from a living museum of the Victorian era. There was a genuine black Arga, brass pots and pans that hung from hooks screwed into the ceiling, and a large square butcher's block right in the middle. Through the windows, Lacey could make out a large lawn. On the other side of the elegant French doors was a patio, where a rickety table and chair set had been put out. Lacey could just picture herself sitting there, eating freshly baked croissants from the patisserie while drinking organic Peruvian coffee from the independent coffee shop.

Suddenly, a huge banging sound rudely jerked her from her reverie. It came from somewhere beneath Lacey's feet; she'd felt the floorboards vibrate.

"Ivan?" Lacey called, pacing back into the corridor. "Is everything okay?"

His voice came up through the open cellar door. "That's just the pipes. I don't think they've been used for years. It might take a while for them to settle."

Another huge bang made Lacey jump. But knowing the innocent cause, this time she couldn't help but laugh.

Ivan reemerged from the cellar staircase.

"That's all sorted. I really hope the pipes don't take too long to settle," he said, in his fretful manner.

Lacey shook her head. "It only adds to the charm."

"So, you can stay here as long as you need," he added. "I'll keep my ear to the ground and let you know if any of the hotels become available."

"Don't worry," Lacey told him. "This is exactly what I didn't realize I was looking for."

Ivan flashed her one of his shy smiles. "So is a tenner a night okay?"

Lacey's eyebrows shot up. "A tenner? That's, like, twelve dollars or something?"

"Too high?" Ivan interjected, his cheeks flaming red. "Would a fiver be okay?"

"Too *low!*" Lacey exclaimed, aware she was negotiating him *up* rather than down. But the ridiculously underpriced fee he was suggesting was tantamount to stealing, and Lacey wasn't going to take advantage of this sweet, bumbling man who'd saved her from her damsel in distress moment. "It's a two-bedroom period cottage. Fit for a family. Once it's had a dust and polish, you could easily make hundreds of dollars a night for this place."

Ivan didn't seem to know where to look. Clearly, money talk made him uncomfortable; more evidence, Lacey thought, that he wasn't suited to the life of a businessman. She hoped none of his tenants were taking advantage of him.

"Well, how about we say fifteen a night?" Ivan suggested, "And I'll send someone round to do the dusting and polishing."

"Twenty," Lacey replied. "And I can dust and polish it myself." She smirked and held out her hand. "Now give me the key. I won't take no for an answer."

The red in Ivan's cheeks spread to his ears and all the way down his neck. He gave a small nod of agreement and placed the bronze key in Lacey's palm.

"My number's on the card. Call me if anything breaks. *When,* I should say."

"Thanks," Lacey said, gratefully, with a little chuckle.

Ivan left.

Now alone, Lacey went upstairs to finish exploring. The master was at the front of the house, with the ocean view and a balcony. It was another museum-style room, with a big, dark oak, four-poster bed and matching closet big enough to lead to Narnia. The second bedroom was at the back of the house, overlooking the lawn. The toilet was separate from the bathroom, in its own room barely the size of a closet. The bath was a white slipper tub with bronze feet. There was no separate shower, just an attachment on the taps of the tub.

Returning to the master bedroom, Lacey sank down onto the four-poster. It was the first time she'd really had a chance to reflect on the dizzying day, and she felt almost shell-shocked. This morning she'd been a married woman of fourteen years. Now she was single. She'd been a busy New York City career woman. Now she was in a cliffside cottage in England. How thrilling! How *exciting!* She'd never done anything so bold in all her life, and boy did it feel good!

The pipes let out a loud bang, and Lacey squealed. But a moment later she burst into laughter.

She lay back on the bed, staring up at the fabric canopy above her, listening to the sound of the high-tide waves crashing against the cliffs. The sound brought back a sudden, previously lost, childhood fantasy of living beside the ocean. How funny that she'd forgotten all about that dream. If she hadn't returned to Wilfordshire, would it have remained buried in her mind, never to be retrieved? She wondered what other memories might come to her while she was here. Perhaps, after she woke up tomorrow, she'd explore the town a little, and see what clues it may hold.

CHAPTER THREE

Lacey was awoken by a strange noise.

She sat bolt upright, confused momentarily by the unfamiliar room, which was lit only by a thin stream of daylight coming in through a crack in the curtains. It took a second to recalibrate her brain and remember she wasn't in her apartment in New York City anymore, but in a stone cottage on the cliffs of Wilfordshire, England.

The noise came again. It wasn't the banging of water pipes this time, but something else entirely, something that sounded animal in origin.

Checking her cell phone with bleary eyes, Lacey saw that it was five a.m. local time. With a sigh, she heaved her weary body out of bed. The effects of jet lag were immediately apparent in the heaviness of her limbs as she padded over to the balcony doors on bare feet and pulled open the curtains. There was the cliff edge, and the sea stretching into the horizon until it met a clear, cloudless sky that was only just starting to turn blue. She could see no animal culprit on the front lawn, and when the noise came again, Lacey was able to orientate the sound to the back of the house.

Wrapping herself up in the robe she'd remembered to purchase at the last second from the airport, Lacey trotted down the creaking stairs to investigate. She went straight to the back of the house, into the kitchen where the large glass windows and French doors provided her with an unspoiled view of the back lawn. And there, Lacey discovered the origin of the noise.

There was an entire herd of sheep in the garden.

Lacey blinked. There must've been at least fifteen of them! Twenty. Maybe more!

She rubbed her eyes, but when she opened them again, all the fluffy creatures were still there, grazing on her grass. Then one raised its head.

Lacey locked gazes with the sheep in a stare-down, until, finally, the sheep tipped its head back and let out one long, loud, mournful bleat.

Lacey dissolved into giggles. She couldn't think of a more perfect way to begin her new life AD. Suddenly, being here in Wilfordshire felt like less of a vacation and more of a statement of intent, a reclamation of her old self, or perhaps a whole new self, one she'd not yet met. Whatever the feeling was, it made bubbles burst in her stomach like someone had filled it up with champagne (or maybe that was jet lag—as far as her internal clock was concerned, she'd just given her body a generous sleeping-in). Either way, Lacey couldn't wait to face the day.

Lacey was filled with a sudden enthusiasm for adventure. Yesterday she'd awoken to the usual sounds of New York City traffic; today the sound of incessant bleating. Yesterday she'd smelled fresh laundry and cleaning products. Today; dust and ocean. She'd taken the old familiarity of her life and blown it wide apart. As a newly single woman the world suddenly felt like her oyster. She wanted to explore! Discover! Learn! Suddenly, she was filled with an enthusiasm for life she hadn't felt since … well, since before her father had left.

Lacey shook her head. She didn't want to think of sad things. She was determined not to let anything bring down this newly found sense of joy. At least not today. Today she was going to grab hold of that feeling and not let go of it. Today she was *free*.

Trying to keep her mind off her grumbling stomach, Lacey attempted to shower in the big slipper bath. She used the odd hose-like attachment that was connected to the taps to spray herself down, like one might with a muddy dog. The water turned from warm to frigid at a moment's notice, and the pipes went *clang-clang-clang* the whole time. But the immediate softness of the water compared to the harsh stuff she was used to in New York City was the equivalent of slathering an expensive moisturizing balm all over her body, and Lacey reveled in it, even when a sudden blast of cold made her teeth chatter.

Once all that airport grime and city pollution was off her skin— leaving it, quite literally, shiny—she dried and dressed in the outfit she'd purchased at the airport. There was a large mirror on the inner door of the Narnia wardrobe which Lacey used to assess her appearance. And it was *not* cute.

Lacey grimaced. She'd picked the clothes up from a beachwear store in the airport, reasoning casual wear was the most appropriate for her seaside vacation. But though beach casual had been her intention, this assemble was more thrift store casual. The beige slacks were a little too tight, the white muslin shirt swamped her frame, and the flimsy boat shoes were even less suited for the cobblestones than her work heels had been! She'd have to make investing in some decent clothes today's highest priority.

Lacey's stomach grumbled.

Second priority, she thought, tapping her stomach.

She headed downstairs, wet hair dripping down her back, and into the kitchen, seeing out the window that only a couple of stragglers from that morning's gang of sheep were still in the garden. Checking the cupboards and fridge, Lacey found both were empty. It was still too early to head into town to get her freshly baked breakfast treats from the patisserie on the main street. She'd have to kill some time.

"Kill some time!" Lacey exclaimed aloud, her voice filled with joy.

When was the last time she'd had any time to kill? When had she ever even allowed herself the freedom to waste time? David was always so regimented with what little spare time they had. Gym. Brunch. Family commitments. Drinks. Every "free" moment had been scheduled. Lacey had a sudden epiphany; the very act of *scheduling* free time negated the freedom of it! By allowing David to plan and dictate what they did with their time, she'd effectively wrapped herself up in a straitjacket of social obligation. The moment of clarity struck her in an almost Buddhist-like moment of realization.

The Dalai Lama would be so proud of me, Lacey thought, clapping her hands with delight.

Just then, the sheep in the garden bleated. Lacey decided she was going to use her newly acquired freedom to play amateur sleuth and find out where that herd of sheep had come from.

She opened the French doors and headed out onto the patio. Fresh morning ocean spray misted her face as she strolled along the garden path, heading toward the two puff balls still eating her grass. When they heard her coming, they trotted away clumsily, with zero grace, and disappeared through a gap in the hedges.

Lacey went over and peered through the gap, seeing another garden beyond the thicket of shrubbery, filled with bright flowers. So she had a neighbor. In New York City, her neighbors had been aloof, other professional couples like her and David whose lives consisted of leaving their apartments before sunrise and returning after sunset. But this neighbor, by the looks of their beautifully honed garden, enjoyed the good life. And owned sheep! There wasn't a single pet or animal in Lacey's old apartment block—busy business types had no time for pets, nor the inclination to deal with their shedding hair or farmyard smells. How delightful to now be living so close to nature! Even the smell of sheep manure was a welcome contrast to her hyper-clean apartment block back in NYC.

As she straightened up again, Lacey noticed a weathered patch of grass, like a pathway trod by many feet. It led along the shrubbery toward the cliffside. There was a small gate there, practically consumed by the plants. She went over and opened it.

A series of steps had been cut into the cliffside, and they headed all the way down to the beach. It was like something from a fairytale, Lacey thought, delighted as she carefully began to make her way down them.

Ivan hadn't even mentioned that she had a direct route down to the beach, that if she got the hankering for the feel of sand between her toes, she could get it within a matter of minutes. And to think back in New York, she'd been so smug about her two-minute walk to the subway.

Lacey made her way down the higgledy-piggledy steps until they stopped a couple of feet from the beach. Lacey leapt down. The sand was so soft, her knees absorbed the shock in spite of the complete lack of cushion provided by her cheap airport boat shoes.

Lacey took a deep breath, feeling totally wild and carefree. This part of the beach was deserted. Unblemished. It must be too far from the shops in town for people to venture, she thought. It was almost like her own private bit of beach.

Looking over in the direction of town, Lacey saw the pier jutting out into the ocean. She was struck immediately by a memory of playing fair games, and the loud arcade her father had allowed them to spend their 2ps in. There was a cinema on the pier as well, Lacey recalled, excited by the fragments of memory returning to her. It was a tiny eight-seater, barely changed since it had been built, with plush red velvet seats. Dad had taken her and Naomi to watch an obscure Japanese cartoon there. She wondered how many more memories her trip to Wilfordshire would produce. How many more blanks in her memory would be filled in by coming here?

The tide was out, so a lot of the pier's structure was visible. Lacey could see some dog walkers and a couple of joggers. The town was starting to wake up. Maybe there'd be a coffee shop open now. She decided to take the long sea route to town and began to stroll along in that direction.

The cliff receded the closer she got to town, and soon there were roads and streets. The second she stepped onto the promenade, Lacey was hit by another sudden memory, of a market with tarpaulin stalls, selling clothes and jewelry and sticks of rock. A series of spray-painted numbers on the floor indicated their specific plots. Lacey felt a surge of excitement.

Turning off the beach, Lacey headed toward the main street— or high street as the British called it. She noted the Coach House on the corner where she'd first met Ivan, before turning along the bunting-clad street.

It was so different from being in New York. The pace was slower. There were no honking cars. No one shoved anyone else. And, to her surprise, some of the coffee places were indeed open.

She entered the first one she came to—no queue in sight—and got herself a black Americano and croissant. The coffee was perfectly roasted, rich and chocolaty, the croissant a crumbly mouthful of flaky pastry and buttery yumminess.

With her stomach satisfied at last, Lacey decided it was time to find herself some better clothes. She'd seen a nice boutique fashion store at the other end of the high street and had started walking that way when the smell of sugar assaulted her nostrils. She looked over to see a homemade fudge store had just opened its doors. Unable to resist, she went inside.

"Want to try a free sample?" the man in a stripy white and pink apron asked. He gestured to a silver tray filled with cubes in different shades of brown. "We've got dark chocolate, milk chocolate, white chocolate, caramel, toffee, coffee, fruit medley, and original."

Lacey's eyes bulged. "Can I try them all?" she asked.

"Of course!"

The man cut little cubes of each flavor and presented them to Lacey to try. She popped the first one in her mouth and her taste buds exploded.

"Amazing," she said through her mouthful.

She moved onto the next. Somehow, it was even nicer than the last.

She tried one sample after another, and they seemed to get progressively more delicious as she went.

When Lacey swallowed her final mouthful, she barely gave herself time to take a breath before exclaiming, "I have *got* to send some of this to my nephew. Will it keep if I mail it to New York?"

The man grinned and produced a flat cardboard box lined with foil paper. "If you use our special delivery box, it will," he said with a laugh. "It became such a common request, we had these designed especially. Slim enough to fit through the letter box, and lightweight enough to keep the postage costs down. You can also buy the stamps here."

"How innovative," Lacey said. "You've thought of everything."

The man filled the box with a cube of each available flavor, secured the flat box with packing tape, and stuck the correct postage stamps onto it. After paying and thanking the man, Lacey took her little parcel, wrote Frankie's name and address on the front, and posted it through the slit in the traditional red letter box across the street.

Once it had disappeared through the hole, Lacey remembered she was getting distracted from her actual task—to find some better clothes. She was about to head off in search of a boutique store when she was distracted by the window display in the store beside the post box. It depicted a scene of Wilfordshire beach, with the pier stretching into the sea, but the whole thing was made from pastel-colored macarons.

Lacey immediately regretted the croissant she'd eaten and all the fudge she'd sampled because the delicious sight made her salivate. She snapped a photo for the Doyle Girlz thread.

"Can I help?" a male voice came from somewhere beside her.

Lacey straightened up. Standing in the doorway stood the shop's owner, a very handsome man in his mid-forties, with thick, dark brown hair and a well-defined jawline. He had sparkling green eyes, with laugh lines beside them that immediately told her he was someone who enjoyed life, and a tan that suggested he took frequent trips to warmer climates.

"I'm just window shopping," Lacey said, her voice sounding as if someone was squeezing her vocal cords. "I like your display."

The man smiled. "I made it myself. Why don't you come in and try some of the cakes?"

"I'd love to, but I've already eaten," Lacey explained. The croissant and coffee and fudge seemed to be swilling in her stomach, churning around and making her feel a bit nauseous. Lacey suddenly realized what was happening—it was that long-lost feeling of physical attraction giving her butterflies in her stomach. Her cheeks immediately flooded with warmth.

The man chuckled. "I can tell from your accent you're American. So you might not know that here in England, we have this thing called elevenses. It comes after breakfast and before lunch."

"I don't believe you," Lacey replied, feeling her lips twitching up at the sides. "Elevenses?"

The man pressed his hand to his heart. "I promise you, it's not a marketing gimmick! It's the perfect time for tea and cake, or tea and sandwiches, or tea and biscuits." He gestured with his arms in through the open doorway, toward the glass display cabinet filled with creatively designed sweet treats in all their delicious-looking glory. "Or all of them."

"As long as you have it with tea?" Lacey quipped.

"Exactly," he replied, his green eyes twinkling with mischief. "You can even try before you buy."

Lacey couldn't resist anymore. Whether it was the addictive effects of sugar luring her in or, more likely, the magnetic pull of this gorgeous specimen of a man, Lacey went inside.

She watched eagerly, her mouth watering, as the man took a round cakey bun thing from the glass chill cabinet, filled it with butter, jam, and cream, and cut it neatly into quarters. The whole thing was done in a casually theatrical manner, like he was performing a dance routine. He placed the pieces onto a small china plate and held it out to Lacey balanced on his fingertips, finishing the thoroughly unself-conscious display with a flourishing, "Et voilà."

Lacey felt warmth flooding into her cheeks. The whole performance had been distinctly flirty. Or was that just wishful thinking?

She reached up and took one of the quarters from the plate. The man did the same, tapping his piece against hers.

"Cheers," he said.

"Cheers," Lacey managed.

She popped it into her mouth. It was a taste sensation. Thick, sweet clotted cream. Strawberry jam so fresh the sharpness made her taste buds tingle. And the cake! Dense and buttery, somewhere between sweet and savory, and oh-so-comforting.

The flavors suddenly sparked a memory in Lacey's mind. Her and Dad, Naomi, and Mom, all sitting around a white metal table in a bright cafe, tucking into cream- and jam-filled pastries. She was struck by a bolt of comforting nostalgia.

"I've been here before!" Lacey exclaimed before she'd even finished chewing.

"Oh?" came the man's amused reply.

Lacey nodded enthusiastically. "I came to Wilfordshire as a child. This is a scone, isn't it?"

The man's eyebrows rose with genuine intrigue. "Yes. My father owned the patisserie before I did. I still use his special recipe to make the scones."

Lacey glanced toward the window. Though there was now a built-in wooden seat with a baby blue cushion atop and a rustic matching wooden table, she could just about picture how it had looked thirty years earlier. Suddenly, she felt herself transported back to that moment. She could almost recall the breeze on the back of her neck, and the sticky feel of the jam on her fingers, the sweat in the creases on the backs of her knees... She could even remember the sound of laughter, of her *parents'* laughter, and the carefree smiles on their faces. They had been so happy, hadn't they? She was certain it had been genuine. Then why had it all fallen apart?

"Are you okay?" came the man's voice.

Lacey snapped back to the moment. "Yes. Sorry. I was lost in my memories. Tasting that scone brought me back about thirty years."

"Well, you'll have to have elevenses now," the man said, chuckling. "Can I tempt you?"

The tingles racing all through Lacey's body gave her the distinct impression that *anything* he suggested in that gentle accent with those alluring, kind eyes, she'd agree to. So she nodded, finding her throat suddenly too dry to actually formulate words.

He clapped his hands. "Excellent! Let me fix you up the whole works. Give you the full English experience." He went to turn around then paused and looked back. "I'm Tom, by the way."

"Lacey," she replied, feeling as giddy as a teenager with a crush.

As Tom busied himself in the kitchen, Lacey took the seat in the window. She tried to evoke more memories of the time she'd spent here before, but alas there was nothing more to recall. Just the taste of scones and the laughter of her family.

A moment later, the handsome Tom appeared with a cake stand filled with crustless sandwiches, scones, and a selection of multicolored fairy cakes. He set a teapot down on the table beside it.

"I can't eat all that!" Lacey cried.

"It's for two," Tom replied. "On the house. It's not polite to make a lady pay on the first date."

He took a seat right beside her.

His forthrightness took Lacey by surprise. She felt her pulse begin to flutter. It had been so long since she'd talked to another man in a flirty manner. It made her feel like a giddy teenager again. Awkward. But maybe it was just a British thing. Perhaps all Englishmen behaved this way.

"First date?" she repeated.

Before Tom could answer, the bell over the door tinkled. A group of about ten Japanese tourists bustled into the store. Tom jumped up.

"Uh-oh, customers." He looked down at Lacey. "We'll take a rain check on that date, okay?"

With that same self-assured confidence, Tom headed for the counter, leaving Lacey with her words stuck in her throat.

With the shop now crowded with tourists, it became loud and busy. Lacey tried to keep one eye on Tom while she wolfed down her elevenses but he was busy making up orders for the gaggle of customers.

When she was done, she tried to wave goodbye but he'd retreated into the kitchen area and didn't see her.

Feeling a little disappointed, and extremely full, Lacey headed out of the patisserie and back onto the street.

Then she paused. An empty storefront across the street from the patisserie had caught her eye. It stirred such deep emotion within her, it literally took her breath away. The store had been something before, something the deepest recesses of her childhood memories wanted to recall. Something that demanded she take a closer look.

CHAPTER FOUR

L acey peered in through the window of the vacant storefront, searching her mind for the memories it had stirred within her. But nothing concrete came to her. It was more a feeling that had been awoken, deeper than just the feeling of nostalgia, closer to falling in love.

Peering through the windows, Lacey could see that inside, the store was empty and unlit. The floors were made of pale wooden boards. There was a lot of built-in shelving in the various alcoves, and a large wooden desk against one wall. The light fixture hanging down from the ceiling was an antique brass one. *Expensive,* Lacey thought. *Surely it must've been left behind accidentally.*

The storefront door, Lacey noticed then, was unlocked. She couldn't help herself. She went inside.

A metallic smell, tinged with dust and mildew, wafted out. Immediately, Lacey was hit by another bolt of nostalgia. The smell was exactly the same as her father's old antiques store.

She'd loved that place. As a child, she'd whiled away many an hour in that labyrinth of treasures, playing with the creepy old china dolls, reading all manner of children's collectible comics, from Bunty to The Beano, to exceptionally rare and valuable Rupert the Bear originals. But her favorite thing to do was just peruse the trinkets and imagine the lives and personalities of the people they'd once belonged to. There was an endless supply of odds and ends, gadgets and gizmos, and every item had that same strange metal-dust-mildew aroma she could smell right now.

31

Just like seeing Crag Cottage beside the ocean had awakened an old childhood dream of hers to live beside the sea, now too, she found an old childhood desire to run her own store come flooding back at her.

Even the layout reminded her of her dad's old shop. As she looked around, images from the deepest recesses of her memory transposed themselves upon the view through her eyes, like a sheet of tracing paper laid on top of a drawing. Suddenly, she could see the shelves stocked with beautiful relics—mainly Victorian kitchenware items, as was her father's particular interest—and there, on the counter, Lacey visualized the big brass cash register, the cumbersome old-fashioned one with the stiff keys that her father had insisted on using because it "keeps your mind sharp" and "hones your skills in mental mathematics." She smiled dreamily to herself as her father's words sounded in her ears and as the images and memories played out in front of her eyes.

She was so lost in her daydream, Lacey didn't hear the footsteps coming from the back room toward her. Nor did she notice the man the footsteps belonged to as he emerged through the door—a frown on his face—and marched right up to her. It was only when she felt a tapping on her shoulder that Lacey realized she was not alone.

Her heart jumped in her chest. Lacey almost screamed with surprise as she leapt out of her skin, swirled, then took in the face of the stranger. Elderly, thinning white hair, puffy purple bags beneath his bright blue eyes.

"Can I help you?" the man said, in an unfriendly and gruff way.

Lacey's hand flew to her chest. It took her a moment to realize that the ghost of her father had not just tapped her on the shoulder, and that she wasn't actually a child standing in his antiques store but a grown woman on vacation in England. A grown woman who was currently trespassing.

"Oh my goodness, I'm so, so sorry!" she exclaimed hurriedly. "I didn't realize there was anyone here. The door was unlocked."

The man glared at her with skepticism. "Can't you see the shop's vacant? There's nothing here to buy."

"I know," Lacey continued gushing, desperate to clear her name and wipe that frown of suspicion from the old man's face. "But I couldn't help myself. This place reminded me so much of my father's store." To Lacey's surprise, she found her eyes suddenly flood with tears. "I haven't seen him since I was a child."

The man's demeanor shifted in an instant. He went from frowning and defensive, to soft and gentle.

"Dear, dear, dear," he said, kindly, shaking his head as Lacey hurriedly wiped away her tears. "It's all right, my dear. Your father owned a store like this?"

Lacey felt immediately embarrassed to have dumped her emotions onto this man, not to mention guilty that instead of calling the cops to get her chucked off his private property he'd reacted like a skilled therapist, with non-judgmental compassion, encouragement, and interest. But Lacey couldn't help herself. She opened up and poured out her heart.

"He sold antiques," she explained, the smile playing across her lips again at the memories, even as the tears plopped from her eyes. "The smell in here made me nostalgic, and it all came flooding back to me. His store even had the same layout." She pointed toward the back room door the man must've entered through. "That back room was used for storage but he always wanted to turn it into an auction room. It was very long and opened out onto a garden."

The man began to chuckle. "Come and look. The back room here is long, too, and it opens out onto a garden."

Touched by his compassion, Lacey followed the man through the door into the back room. It was long and narrow, reminiscent of a train carriage, and almost identical to the room her father had dreamed of hosting auctions in. Passing straight through the room, Lacey stepped out into a wonderland of a garden. It was narrow and long, stretching back about fifty feet. There were colorful plants everywhere, and strategically placed trees and shrubbery providing just the right amount of shade. A knee-high fence was all that separated it from that of the neighboring store's garden—which, in contrast to the immaculate garden she was standing in, seemed to be used only for storage, with several large, ugly, gray plastic sheds and a row of trash cans blighting it.

Lacey returned her attention to the pretty garden.

"This is incredible," she gushed.

"Yes, it's a beautiful spot," the man replied, picking up a knocked over plant pot and righting it. "The folks who leased the place before used it as a home and garden store."

Lacey immediately noted the melancholy air in his tone. She realized then that the large glass greenhouse in front of her had its doors wide open, and several potted plants lay strewn all over the floor, their stems smooshed, the soil from their pots spilled across the floor. Her curiosity was suddenly piqued. The sight of the strewn plants in an otherwise carefully tended garden seemed odd. Her mind switched immediately from her father to the present moment.

"What happened here?" she asked.

The elderly man's expression was now downcast. "That's why I'm here. I got a call from the neighbor this morning saying it looked like the place had been emptied overnight."

Lacey gasped. "They were burglarized?" Her mind couldn't quite conflate the concept of crime with the beautiful, tranquil seaside town of Wilfordshire. To her, it felt like the sort of place where the closest anyone came to wrongdoing was the local scamp of a boy stealing a freshly baked pie off a window ledge where it had been placed to cool.

The man shook his head. "No, no, no. They left. Packed up their stock and cleared out. Didn't even give notice. Left me with all their debts, too. Unpaid utility bills. A mountain of invoices." He shook his head sadly.

Lacey was shocked to realize the store had only become vacant that morning, and that she'd inadvertently intruded into an unfolding scenario, inserting herself accidentally into a mysterious narrative that had only just begun.

"I'm so sorry," she said with genuine empathy for the man. Now it was her turn to play therapist, to pay back the kindness the man had shown her. "Are you going to be okay?"

"Not really," he said, glumly. "We'll have to sell to settle the bills, and honestly, me and the wife are far too old for this kind of stress." He tapped his breastbone, as if to indicate the fragility of his heart. "It will be a damn shame to say goodbye to this place though." His voice cracked. "It's been in the family for years. I love it. We've had some very *colorful* tenants in that time." He chuckled, his eyes misting over as he reminisced. "But, no. We can't go through that upheaval again. It's too much of a strain."

The sadness in his tone was enough to break Lacey's heart. What an awful predicament to have been left in. How terrible a situation. The deep empathy she felt for the man was only compounded by her own situation, by the way the life she'd built with David in New York City had been unjustly ripped away from her. She felt a sudden responsibility to fix the problem.

"I'll lease the store," she blurted, the words leaving her lips before her brain had even realized what she was saying.

The man's white eyebrows shot upward with evident surprise. "I'm sorry, what did you just say?"

"I'll lease it," Lacey repeated quickly, before the logical part of her mind had a chance to kick in and talk her out of it. "You can't sell it. It has too much history, you said so yourself. Too much sentimental value. And I'm super trustworthy. I have experience. Sort of."

She thought of the dark-eyebrowed border guard at the airport, telling her she needed a visa to work, and how she'd so confidently assured her the last thing she wanted to do in England was work.

And what about Naomi? Her job with Saskia? What about all of that?

Suddenly, none of it mattered. That feeling Lacey had been hit with when she'd seen the store was akin to love at first sight. She was throwing herself in at the deep end.

"So? What do you think?" she asked him.

The old man looked a little stunned. Lacey couldn't blame him. Here was this strange American woman dressed in thrift store couture asking him to lease her his store when he'd already decided to sell it.

"Well … I …" he began. "It would be nice to keep it in the family a little longer. Now isn't the best time to be selling either, with the market the way it is. But I'd need to speak to my wife, Martha, first."

"Of course," Lacey said. She quickly scribbled her name and number on a slip of paper and handed it to him, surprised by how certain she felt. "Take all the time you need."

She needed time to sort out her visa, after all, and work out a business plan and finances and stock, and well, *everything.* Maybe she should start by purchasing a copy of *The Dummies Guide To Running A Store.*

"Lacey Doyle," the man said, reading the paper she'd handed him.

Lacey nodded. Two days ago, that name had been so unfamiliar to her. Now it felt like hers again.

"I'm Stephen," he replied.

They shook hands.

"I look forward to your call," Lacey said.

She left the store, her heart soaring with anticipation. If Stephen did decide to lease it to her, she'd be staying in Wilfordshire on a much more permanent basis than she'd planned. The thought ought to scare her. But instead, it left her delighted. It felt so right. More than right. It felt like fate.

CHAPTER FIVE

"I thought this was a vacation!" Naomi's furious voice exploded through the cell phone wedged between Lacey's ear and her shoulder.

She sighed, tuning out her sister's tirade, as she tapped away at the keyboard of the Wilfordshire town library computer. She was checking on the status of her online application form to switch her vacation visa to a business start-up visa.

After her meeting with Stephen, Lacey had thrown herself into research and learned that as a fluent English speaker with a healthy amount of capital in the bank, the only other thing she required was a decent business plan, something she'd had plenty of experience with thanks to Saskia's penchant for offloading responsibilities onto Lacey's shoulders that were far beyond her pay grade. It had only taken Lacey a few evenings to compile the plan and submit it, a painless process that made her more than certain the universe was having a hand in her whole new life.

As the screen logged her into the official UK government portal, she saw that her application was still showing as "pending." She was so desperate to get going, she couldn't help but sag a little with disappointment. Then her focus tuned back into Naomi's voice in her ear.

"I CANNOT believe you're moving!" her sister was yelling. "Permanently!"

"It's not permanent," Lacey explained, calmly. She'd had plenty of practice over the years in not rising to Naomi's moods. "The visa's only for two years."

Oops. Wrong move.

"TWO YEARS?" Naomi yelled, her anger reaching a fever pitch.

Lacey rolled her eyes. She'd been fully aware her family wouldn't support her decision. Naomi needed her in NYC for babysitting duty, after all, and Mom basically treated her like an emotional support animal. The giddy message she'd typed onto the *Doyle Girlz* thread had been received with the gratitude of a nuclear bomb. Days later, Lacey was still dealing with the fallout.

"Yes, Naomi," she replied disappointedly. "Two years. I think I deserve it, don't you? I gave fourteen years to David. Fifteen to my job. New York City had me for thirty-nine. I'm hurtling toward forty, Naomi! Do I really want to have lived my whole life in one place? Had one career? Been with one man?"

Tom's handsome face flashed in her mind as she said it, and she felt her cheeks grow immediately warm. She'd been so busy organizing her potential new life, she hadn't returned to the patisserie again—her vision of languorous breakfasts on the patio temporarily replaced by a banana on the go and a pre-mixed frappuccino from the convenience store. In fact, it had only just occurred to her that if this deal went through with Stephen and Martha, she'd be renting the store opposite to Tom, and she'd be seeing him through her window *every day*. Her insides squirmed with delight at the thought.

"What about Frankie?" Naomi wailed, bringing her back to reality.

"I've mailed him some fudge."

"He needs his aunt!"

"He still has me! I'm not dead, Naomi, I'm just going to live abroad for a bit."

Her little sister hung up on her.

Thirty-six going on sixteen, Lacey thought wryly.

As she put her cell phone back in her pocket, Lacey noticed something on the computer screen flicker. The status of her application form had switched from "pending" to "approved."

With a squeal, Lacey jumped up from her seat and punched the air. All the senior citizens playing solitaire on the other library computers turned to look at her with alarm.

"Sorry!" Lacey exclaimed, trying to temper her excitement.

She sank back down, breathless with awe. She'd done it. She'd been given the green light to set her plan in motion. And it had all been so painless, Lacey couldn't help but suspect that fate had had a hand to play in it...

Except, there was one last hurdle. She needed Stephen and Martha to agree to lease her the store.

Lacey was anxious as she ambled around the town center. She didn't want to stray too far from the store, because the second she received Stephen's call, she was going to go straight back there with her checkbook and a pen and sign the blasted deal before her self-saboteur told her she couldn't do it. But Lacey was an exceptionally talented window-shopper, and got to work perusing everything the town had to offer. As she strolled, her cheap airport boat shoes caught on the cobblestones, making her stumble and twist her ankle. It was then that Lacey realized she needed to do away with her whole thrift store casual look if she wanted to be taken seriously as a potential new business owner.

She headed to the boutique clothing store that sat next to the vacant one she hoped would soon be hers.

May as well meet the neighbors, she reasoned.

She stepped inside and found that it was a very minimalist-looking place stocked with just a few select items. The woman behind the counter looked up as she entered, her nose rising snootily up as her gaze traveled across Lacey's attire. The woman was rake-thin and rather severe looking, but her wavy brown hair was styled in exactly the same way as Lacey's. Her black dress made her appear like a sort of evil clone version of herself, she thought with amusement.

"Can I help you?" the woman asked in a thin, unpleasant voice.

"No thank you," Lacey replied. "I know exactly what I want."

She selected a two-piece suit from the rack, the type that she was accustomed to wearing back in New York, then paused. Did she want to replicate herself? To dress as that woman who she'd been before? Or did she want to be someone new?

She turned back to the store clerk. "Actually, I may need a bit of help."

The woman's face remained impassive as she stepped out from behind the counter and approached Lacey. Evidently, she assumed that Lacey was a time waster—what sort of thrift store shopper could afford to be in a boutique like this?—and Lacey was looking forward to the moment she'd be able to flash her plastic in this woman's judgmental face.

"I need something for work," Lacey said. "Formal, but not too stiff, you know?"

The woman blinked. "And what is your work?"

"Antiques."

"Antiques?"

Lacey nodded. "Yup. Antiques."

The woman selected something from the rack. It was fashionable, kind of edgy, with a hint of androgyny in its cut. Lacey took it into the changing room and tried it on for size. The reflection that stared back at her made a grin burst onto her lips. She looked, dare she say it, *cool*. The store clerk, as shrew-faced as she was, had impeccable taste and an impressive eye for flattering a figure.

Lacey exited the changing room. "It's perfect. I'll take it. And four more in different colors."

The store clerk's eyebrows catapulted upward. "Excuse me?"

Lacey's phone began to ring. She looked at the screen and saw Stephen's number flashing at her.

Her heart leapt. This was it! The call she'd been waiting for! The call that would determine her future!

"I'll take it," Lacey repeated to the clerk, suddenly breathless with anticipation. "And four more in whatever colors you think will suit me."

The store clerk look bemused as she went out the back—to those ugly gray storage sheds, Lacey thought—to find her more suits.

Lacey answered her phone. "Stephen?"

"Hi, Lacey? I'm here with Martha. Would you like to come back to the store for a chat?"

His tone sounded promising, and Lacey couldn't help but smile. "Absolutely. I'll be there in five."

The store clerk returned with her arms laden with more suits. Lacey noted the impeccable color palette—nude, black, navy, and dust pink.

"Did you want to try them on?" the clerk asked.

Lacey shook her head. She was in a hurry now, and couldn't wait to finish her purchase and run next door. She kept looking over her shoulder at the exit.

"Nope. If they're the same as this one, I trust you that they'll be right. Can you ring them up, please?" She spoke quickly. Her waning patience was literally audible. "Oh, and I'm going to keep this one on, too."

The store clerk looked extremely unimpressed by the way Lacey was trying to speed her up. As if to spite her, she took her time ringing up each item and carefully folding it in tissue paper.

"Wait!" Lacey exclaimed, as the woman pulled out a paper bag to put the clothes into. "I can't carry a store bag. I'll need a handbag. A good one." Her eyes darted to the row of bags on a shelf behind the woman's head. "Can you choose one that'll go well with the suits?"

From the store clerk's expression, you'd be forgiven for thinking she was dealing with a madwoman. Still, she turned, considered each of the bags on sale, then took down an oversized black leather clutch with a gold buckle.

"Perfect," Lacey said, bouncing on her toes like a sprinter waiting for the starting gun. "Ring it up."

The woman did as she was commanded, and began to carefully fill the clutch with the suits.

"So that will be—"

"SHOES!" Lacey suddenly cried, interrupting her. What a scatterbrain. It had been her crappy boat shoes that had brought her into this store in the first place. "I need shoes!"

The store clerk looked somehow even more unimpressed. Maybe she thought Lacey was pranking her, and that she'd bolt at the end of all this.

"Our shoes are over here," she said coolly, gesturing with her arm.

Lacey looked at the small selection of beautifully crafted heels she would've worn back in New York City, where she'd considered sore ankles to be an occupational hazard. But things were different now, Lacey reminded herself. She didn't need to wear pain-inducing footwear.

Her gaze fell to a pair of patent black brogues. The shoes would perfectly complement the androgynous quality of her new suit collection. She beelined for them.

"These," she said, plonking them on the counter in front of the clerk.

The woman didn't bother asking Lacey whether she wanted to try them on, and so rang them up, letting out a cough into her fist at the four-digit price tag that flashed up on the till display.

Lacey pulled out her card, paid, slid on the new shoes, thanked the clerk, and hop-skipped out the store back into the vacant lot beside it. Hope blossomed in her chest that she was a matter of moments away from collecting the keys from Stephen and becoming neighbors of the unimpressed boutique store clerk she'd just purchased a whole new identity from.

When she entered, Stephen looked like he didn't recognize her.

"I thought you said she seemed a bit scatty?" the woman beside him, who must've been his wife, Martha, said out of the corner of her mouth. If she was trying to be discreet, she was failing miserably. Lacey could hear every word.

Lacey gestured to her outfit. "Ta-da. Told you I knew what I was doing," she teased.

Martha gave Stephen a look. "What were you worrying about, you old fool? She's the answer to our prayers! Give her the lease right away!"

Lacey couldn't believe it. What luck. Fate had definitely intervened.

Stephen hurriedly pulled some documents from his bag and placed them on the counter in front of her. Unlike the divorce papers she'd stared at with disbelief, in a moment of disembodied grief, these papers seemed to glow with promise, with opportunity. She took out her pen, the same one that had signed her divorce papers, and committed her signature to paper.

Lacey Doyle. Business owner.

Her new life was sealed.

CHAPTER SIX

With a broom in her hands, Lacey swept the floorboards of the store she was now the proud lease holder for, her heart fit to bursting.

She'd never felt like this before. Like she was in control of her whole life, her whole destiny, and that the future was hers for the taking. Her mind was racing a mile a minute, already formulating some pretty big plans. She wanted to turn the large back room into an auction room, in honor of the dream her father had never fulfilled. She'd been to a zillion auctions while working for Saskia (admittedly on the purchasing side rather than the selling one) but she was confident she'd be able to learn what it took to do it. She'd never run a store before, either, yet here she was. And besides, anything worth having required effort.

Just then, she saw a figure who'd been strolling past the store stop abruptly and face her through the windows. She looked up from her sweeping, hoping it would be Tom, but realized that the figure standing stock-still in front of her was a woman. And not just any random woman, one that Lacey recognized. Rake-thin, black dress, and that same long dark wavy hair as Lacey. It was her evil twin—the store clerk from next door.

The woman stormed into the store through the unlocked front door.

"What are you doing in here?" she demanded.

Lacey rested the broom against the counter and confidently held her hand out to the woman. "I'm Lacey Doyle. Your new neighbor."

The woman stared at her hand with disgust like it was covered in germs. "What?"

"I'm your new neighbor," Lacey repeated, with the same confident tone. "I just signed a lease on this place."

The woman looked like she'd just been slapped in the face. "But..." she murmured.

"Do you own the boutique, or just work there?" Lacey prompted, trying to bring the stunned woman back to her senses.

The woman nodded as if in a hypnotized trance. "I own it. I'm Taryn. Taryn Maguire." Then, suddenly, she shook her head as if overcoming her surprise, and forced a friendly smile onto her face. "Well, how lovely to have a new neighbor. It's a great space, isn't it? I'm sure the lack of light will work in your favor as well, it hides the tattiness."

Lacey stopped herself from raising her eyebrow. Years of dealing with her mother's passive-aggressiveness had trained Lacey not to rise to it.

Taryn laughed loudly, as if in an attempt to smother the backhanded compliment. "So, tell me, how *did* you get a lease for this place? Last I heard, Stephen was selling up."

Lacey just shrugged. "He was. But there was a change of plans."

Taryn looked like she'd sucked a lemon. Her eyes darted all around the store, the upturned nose Lacey had already had pointed at her once today seeming to reach even farther toward the heavens as Taryn's disgust became more and more apparent.

"And you're going to be selling antiques?" she added.

"That's right. My father was in the trade when I was a kid, so I'm following in his footsteps in his honor."

"Antiques," Taryn repeated. Evidently, the thought of an antiques store setting up next to her swanky boutique displeased her. Her eyes pinned Lacey like a hawk's. "And you're allowed to do that, are you? Hop over the pond and set up shop?"

"With the right visa," Lacey explained coolly.

"That's... interesting," Taryn replied, clearly choosing her words carefully. "I mean, when a foreigner wants a job in this country the company has to provide evidence there's no one British-born to fill the position. I'm just surprised the same rules don't apply to running a business..." The disdain in her tone was becoming more and more evident. "And Stephen just leased it to you, a stranger, like that? After the shop became vacant all of, what, two days ago?" The politeness she'd been forcing herself to express before seemed to be quickly fading away.

Lacey decided not to rise to it.

"It was a stroke of luck, really. Stephen happened to be in the store when I started nosing around. He was devastated by the old lessee's abandoning it and leaving him with loads of bills, and, I guess the stars just aligned. I'm helping him, he's helping me. It must be fate."

Lacey noticed that Taryn's face had turned red.

"FATE?" she screamed, passive-aggressiveness turning into straight out aggression. "FATE? I've had a deal with Stephen for months, that if the store became available he'd sell it to me! I'm meant to be expanding my store by taking on his!"

Lacey shrugged. "Well, I didn't buy it. I'm leasing it. I'm sure he still has that plan in mind, to sell to you when the time comes. The time just isn't now."

"I can't believe this!" Taryn wailed. "You swan in here and twist his arm into another lease? And he signs it over in a couple of days? Did you threaten him? Work some kind of voodoo on him?"

Lacey held her ground. "You'll have to ask him why he decided to lease to me rather than sell to you," she said, but in her mind she thought, *Maybe because I'm a nice person?*

"You stole my store," Taryn finished.

Then she stormed away, slamming the door behind her, her long dark hair swishing behind her as she went.

Lacey realized her new life wasn't going to be quite as idyllic as she'd hoped. And that her joke about Taryn being her evil twin had actually come true. Well, there was one thing she could do about that.

Lacey locked up the store front and waltzed with purpose down the road toward the hairdresser's, then marched right inside. The hairdresser, a redhead, was sitting idly flicking through a magazine in an evident lull between clients.

"Can I help?" she asked, looking up at Lacey.

"It's time," Lacey said with determination. "Time to go short."

It was another dream she'd never been brave enough to fulfill. David had loved her hair long. But there was no way she was going to resemble her evil twin for a second longer. The time had come. Time for the chop. Time to shed all of the old Lacey she'd been. This was her new life, and she was going to follow her own new rules.

"Are you sure you want to go short?" the woman asked. "I mean, you seem determined but I have to ask. I don't want you to regret it."

"Oh, I'm sure," Lacey said. "Once I do this, I'll have fulfilled three of my dreams in as many days."

The woman grinned and grabbed her scissors. "All right then. Let's score that hat-trick!"

CHAPTER SEVEN

"There," Ivan said, scooching out from the cupboard beneath the kitchen sink. "That leaky pipe shouldn't give you any more trouble."

He heaved himself to standing, self-consciously tugging at the hem of his crumpled gray T, which had ridden up over his lily-white pot belly. Lacey politely pretended not to have noticed.

"Thanks for repairing it so quickly," Lacey said, grateful he was a considerate landlord who fixed all the issues that arose with the house—of which there had already been a *lot*—and in such a timely manner. But she was also starting to feel guilty about the number of times she'd dragged him out to Crag Cottage; that cliff walk wasn't a breeze and he wasn't exactly a young guy.

"Do you want to stay for a drink?" Lacey asked. "Tea? Beer?"

She already knew the answer would be no. Ivan was shy, and he gave off the impression that he felt himself an imposition. She always asked anyway.

He chuckled. "No, no, you're fine, Lacey. I have business admin to do tonight. No rest for the wicked, as they say."

"Tell me about it," she replied. "I was at the store at five a.m. this morning, and didn't get home until eight."

Ivan frowned. "The store?"

"Oh," Lacey said, surprised. "I thought I mentioned it that time you were round unclogging the gutters. I'm opening an antiques store in town. I'm leasing the vacant lot from Stephen and Martha, the one that was a home and garden store before."

Ivan looked stunned. "I thought you were just here for a vacation!"

"I was. But then I decided to stay. Not in this exact house, of course. I'll find somewhere else as soon as you need it back."

"No, I'm thrilled," Ivan said, looking utterly delighted. "If you're happy here, I'm happy to have you. It's not too annoying having me fix the place up around you, is it?"

"I like it," Lacey replied with a smile. "I'm a bit lonely otherwise."

That had been the hardest part of leaving New York; it wasn't the place, or the apartment, or the familiar streets, but the people she'd left behind.

"I should probably get a dog," she added with a chuckle.

"You've not met your neighbor yet, I take it?" Ivan said. "Lovely lady. Eccentric. She has a dog, a Collie to round up the sheep."

"I've met the sheep," Lacey told him. "They keep coming into the garden."

"Ah," Ivan said. "There must be a gap in the fence. I'll see to that. But anyway, the lady next door is always up for a tea. Or beer." He winked in a paternal way that reminded her of her father.

"Really? She won't mind some random American turning up on her doorstep?"

"Gina? Not at all. She'll love it! Give her a knock. I promise you won't regret it."

He left, and Lacey did just as he'd suggested, heading over to the neighbor's house. Although "neighbor" was quite a loose description. The house was at least a five-minute trek across the clifftops.

She reached the cottage, a single-story version of her own, and knocked on the door. From the other side she heard an instant kerfuffle, of a dog scrabbling around and a female voice telling it to quiet down. Then the door opened several inches. A woman with long curly gray hair and exceptionally childlike features for a sixty-odd-year-old, peered out. She was wearing a salmon-colored woolen cardigan over a floor-length floral skirt. The muzzle of a black and white Border Collie could be seen urgently trying to push its way past her.

"Boudicca," the woman said down to the dog. "Get your sniffer out the way."

"Boudicca?" Lacey asked. "That's an interesting name for a dog."

"I named her after the vengeful pagan warrior queen who went on a rampage against the Romans and burnt London down to the ground. Now, how can I help you, dear?"

Lacey immediately warmed to the woman. "I'm Lacey. I'm living next door and thought I should introduce myself now that my stay is kind of permanent."

"Next door? Crag Cottage?"

"That's right."

The woman beamed. She threw the door wide open, throwing her arms open at the same time. "Oh!" she exclaimed with pure joy, pulling Lacey into a hug. Boudicca the dog went crazy, leaping up and barking. "I'm Georgina Vickers. George to my family, Gina to my friends."

"And to your neighbors?" Lacey quipped, as she was released finally from the woman's bone-crushing hug.

"Better go with Gina." The woman grabbed her hand and tugged her. "Now, come in! Come in! Come in! I'll put the kettle on."

Lacey had no choice but to be dragged inside the cottage. And though she didn't realize it at the time, "I'll put the kettle on," would become a phrase she heard a *lot*.

"Can you believe it, Boo?" the woman said as she bustled down the low-ceilinged corridor. "A neighbor at last!"

Lacey followed and they emerged into a kitchen. It was about half the size of hers, with dark red tiled floors and a big central island taking up the vast majority of the space. On the side with the sink, a large window looked out onto a lawn filled with flowers, the ocean view of crashing waves behind it.

"Do you garden?" Lacey asked.

"I do. It's my pride and joy. I grow all kinds of flowers and herbs for ailments. Like a witch doctor." She cackled at her own assessment of herself. "Would you like to try one?" She gestured to a row of amber-colored glass bottles crammed together on a makeshift, wonky wooden shelf. "I've got cures for headaches, cramps, toothache, rheumatism..."

"Uh...I think I'll stick with the tea," Lacey replied.

"Tea it is!" the eccentric woman exclaimed. She clattered to the other side of the kitchen and took two mugs out of a cupboard. "What kind? English Breakfast? Assam? Earl Grey? Lady Gray?"

Lacey hadn't realized there were so many types. She wondered what she'd drunk with Tom on their "date." That had been delightful. Thinking of it now brought back the memory.

"Which is the traditional one?" Lacey replied, at a loss. "The one you'd have with scones?"

"That would be English Breakfast," Gina said with an affirmative nod. She selected a tin from the cupboard, fished out two bags from inside it, and plonked them into the mismatched mugs. Then she filled the kettle and set it to boil, before turning back to Lacey with the sparkling eyes of genuine curiosity.

"So tell me," Gina said. "How are you finding Wilfordshire?"

"I've been here before," Lacey explained. "I came here on a vacation when I was a kid. I loved it then and wanted to know if it would feel just as magical a second time round."

"And?"

Lacey thought of Tom. Of the store. Of Crag Cottage. Of all the memories of her father that had been stirred up like dust left undisturbed for twenty-odd years. A smile turned the corners of her lips upward. "Definitely."

"And how did you end up in Crag Cottage?" Gina asked.

Lacey was about to explain the story of her chance meeting with Ivan in the Coach House, but the kettle was beginning to bubble loudly and her voice was drowned out. Gina held up a finger in a *hold-that-thought* kind of way, then went over to the kettle, Boudicca the Border Collie weaving herself around her legs as she went.

Gina poured steaming water into the mugs. "Milk?" she asked, looking over her shoulder with steamed up glasses.

Lacey recalled that Tom had given her a little pitcher of milk. "Please."

"Sugar?"

"If that's how you're supposed to take it."

Gina shrugged. "Well, that depends on the person. I do, but perhaps you're already sweet enough?"

Lacey giggled. "If you take sugar, I'll take it too."

"Righteo," Gina said. "One lump or two?"

Lacey's eyes widened with astonishment. "I had no idea so much went into making a cup of tea!"

Gina laughed with a witch's cackle. "It's a whole art form, my dear! One lump is considered quite genteel. Two is far less sophisticated. Three? Well, over here, we call that a builder's tea." She pulled a face, then cackled again.

"A builder's tea?" Lacey replied. "I'll have to remember that."

Gina finished making the tea, placing the squeezed bags on top of a mountain of other used bags sitting in a saucer next to the kettle, then brought them over to the rickety kitchen table. She sat down, plopped a sugar lump in Lacey's tea, stirred it in, then pushed the cup over to Lacey.

Lacey took it gratefully and sipped. It tasted pretty close to the tea Tom had made her, slightly stronger with a bit of a tang to it, but enough to fill her with tingling reminiscence.

Boudicca lay down at Gina's feet and wagged her tail happily.

"So, you were telling me about how you ended up in Wilfordshire," Gina prompted, bringing their conversation back to the point it had been before they'd been rudely interrupted by the kettle.

"Divorce," Lacey said. May as well rip the Band-Aid off.

"Oh, darling," Gina said, patting her hand tenderly. "I had one of those, too. Terrible times. But it was back in the nineties, mind you, so I've had plenty of time to process it."

"You never remarried?" Lacey asked, her eyes widening a little from the mental image of herself remaining single for the next thirty years, and turning into the next Gina.

"God, no! I was *relieved,* darling," Gina said. "My husband was like every other man; an immature little boy wearing a suit. If you ask me, you're better off out of it! What a load of shenanigans for nothing."

Lacey couldn't help but smile. "Did you have kids?"

"Just one, a son," Gina said, sighing deeply. "He chose to go the military route. Sadly we lost him during active duty."

Lacey gasped. "Oh, I'm so sorry."

Gina let out a mournful smile. "He was a cracking lad." Then she brightened. "But enough of that. How's your tea? Not quite what you're used to in the good old US of A?"

"It's delicious," Lacey said, taking another sip. "Comforting. I don't think I'm genteel though." She added a second sugar lump. "That's better."

Now it tasted just like the way Tom had made it. Lacey felt herself smile inwardly, wondering when the next chance would come for them to meet again.

"How long are you renting Ivan's cottage then?" Gina asked.

"Open ended at the moment," Lacey explained. "I'm opening a store in town. An antiques place."

"Really?" Gina exclaimed. She had a very personable way about her, like she was genuinely interested in knowing more about this strange American woman who'd shown up on her doorstep.

Lacey nodded. "It's an old dream of mine. My father had one when I was a kid. All the pieces sort of fell into place."

"That's the Universe, that is," Gina said. "Telling you what's what. Telling you you're right where you're meant to be."

Lacey smiled. She liked that idea.

"Where are you going to get your stock from?" Gina asked.

"I dealt a lot in antiques with my old interior designer firm," Lacey explained. "I've got a list of stores and contacts in the UK as long as my arm. All I need is a car, then I'll be cruising around the country and building up my stock list and specialty. I'm going to take an interior design angle, of course, since it's what I know."

Gina raised an eyebrow. "Did I hear that right? You're planning on buying from underneath your old company's nose?"

Lacey laughed. "It's not like that! Saskia had antiques contacts who could source her very specific items—certain vases, certain artwork, furniture pieces—all to fit in with her specific vision. I'm more interested in stocking items I love, cohesive pieces that the customer can put together on their own accord. Besides, I dealt with all of them personally. My old boss was such a dragon, she doesn't even know half of them by name. I think of them all as my own." She laughed again, this time with excitement at the thought of visiting them all in person, telling them her news of how she was now going alone. Even if her family were reticent, she knew most of the people in the business would be thrilled for her. None of them liked Saskia one bit!

Gina looked impressed. "If you ever want a companion on one of your London trips, I'd love to come. It's been a long time since I saw the city."

Lacey couldn't quite picture this Raggedy Ann–style woman in her patchwork clothing walking the streets of Mayfair. But she enjoyed her company, and having someone by her side was always nice.

"I'd like that," she said, smiling. "I'm going to the used car lot out of town tomorrow, then I'll be heading to London right away. Want to come?"

"I'd love to!" Gina said, looking thrilled.

"Then it's a date," Lacey replied.

"Now, drink up," Gina exclaimed. "I have to introduce you to the sheep."

Lacey couldn't help but laugh as she drained her tea and then followed the woman, who was already bustling toward the door. She really liked Gina and her carefree perspective on life and had the feeling they were going to get along famously.

Tea turned into drinks. Before Lacey knew it, it was the middle of the night.

"I'd better get to bed," she said, hurriedly, when she realized the time. "I have a *lot* to organize tomorrow. Pick you up at noon?"

"I'm looking forward to it," Gina replied.

Lacey left and returned back home, her head spinning a little from all the booze she'd consumed with the delightful Gina. She'd made a friend in the old woman, she was sure of it.

As she flopped into bed, Lacey heard her cell ping. To her surprise, it was an email from David.

She sat bolt upright, rubbing her eyes as if in disbelief. She hadn't had any direct contact with David since he stormed out of their apartment and slammed the door in her face.

Hands trembling slightly, she opened the message.

Lacey, it's come to my attention that you have fled the country and quit your job. I'm under no illusion that this is a childish attempt on your part to avoid paying spousal support. Please be aware that you will soon be hearing from my lawyer.

Lacey rolled her eyes and fell back into bed, falling into an exhausted, boozy sleep.

CHAPTER EIGHT

"Ta-da," Lacey said, placing down an orange glass vase in what she affectionately nick-named "Nordic Corner." She flopped down, exhausted, into the vintage 1960s Icelandic-designed armchair and rested her feet on the matching pouf. With a feeling of mounting pride, Lacey looked all around her. The store was so beautiful it looked like it belonged on the center page spread of an interior design magazine. The shelves were filled with gorgeous porcelain vases and delicate floral chinaware. It was a real achievement, how she'd transformed the store in such a short amount of time, especially considering that just a week earlier she'd not even known she wanted to run a shop! And now here she was, ready to open her doors to the public.

The last week had whizzed by for Lacey, filled with day trips up to London with Gina and Boudicca lasting from first light until whatever hour the stores closed—which in London, could be as late as eight p.m. They'd load themselves into the champagne-colored Volvo Lacey had purchased from a used-car lot (a stick-shift, which took some acclimatizing to, as did the whole driving on the left-hand side of the road thing, and the general London traffic jams), then drive up to London. There, they'd meet with one of Saskia's antiques-selling contacts (who, as Lacey had suspected, despised Saskia due to her habit of withholding invoice payments, and were thus extremely encouraging of Lacey's solo new business venture). Then they'd spend the day finding the best bargains, valuing them, purchasing them, and inventorying them. It didn't even feel like work; the whole process reminded Lacey of being a child in her father's store.

Now, seven days later, Lacey had filled the store to the brim.

From her position in the armchair, Lacey looked around at the store, filled with pride. She'd really transformed the place. The only thing that remained from the original store was the antique brass light fixture that had been there when Lacey first arrived, one she'd valued and discovered was indeed expensive and rare. The original tenants either must not have realized how valuable it was, or they'd left in such a hurry they'd forgotten to take it with them. Either way, it was perfectly suited for her store, and so it remained in pride of place.

With every shelf full and everything beautifully presented, Lacey took out her cell phone and snapped a final picture for the family *Doyle Girlz* thread.

She'd been sending pictures throughout the process, and though Mom had become somewhat supportive during the transformation, Naomi was still giving Lacey the digital equivalent of the cold shoulder. If it weren't for Naomi killing her buzz, Lacey probably would've felt a bit less trepidation about how the community would receive her new store. She still didn't know if Wilfordshire really wanted an antiques store, but she knew it fit perfectly nestled amongst the boutique clothing stores and delicatessens.

She headed toward the glass door—which she'd cleaned to sparkling perfection—and spun the *closed* sign to *open*. Then she clicked the lock and pulled the door wide open. She was officially open for business.

She stood in the doorway, looking out at the streets at the passersby. No one even looked her way. Obviously, she had not expected a stampede of customers the second she was open for business, but it still felt like a bit of a letdown to watch people walk by without paying her any heed.

She was about to head back inside when she noticed movement from across the street. Tom had come to the door of his patisserie, and he was watching her, arms folded across his white chef's apron, a big grin plastered across his face. Heart fluttering, Lacey met his eye and returned the smile. Despite the street between them, they held one another's gaze, and Lacey started to feel like the real world was melting away.

A sudden loud clatter coming from the back garden tore Lacey away from the moment. She broke the spell-binding gaze with Tom and hurried inside, through the main room, through the soon-to-be auction hall, and out into the garden.

She'd tried her best to keep the garden neat during the previous week, but she didn't exactly have a green thumb and it was starting to look a little worse for wear. The last thing Lacey wanted was her garden to turn out looking like the dreadful Taryn's, so decided she'd ask Gina whether she wanted to take on the project. Inject her magic into it.

Just then, Lacey saw the source of the loud bang. Her garbage cans were lying on their sides, the trash from inside spilling onto the lawn.

"Damn foxes," Lacey said as she went over to tidy them up.

There were lots of foxes in England, she'd discovered; looting through trash, scaring pet cats, making horrible barking noises like something from a horror movie.

But as she righted the cans and began to pick up the trash, she heard the unmistakable sound of a chuckle.

She stood, swirled on the spot, and just had time to catch the flash of light on glass as a door was closed with a click. The door was the back one of Taryn's store.

"You've got to be kidding me," Lacey said with astonishment.

Had a grown woman really just snuck into her garden and shoved over her trash cans?

Lacey was furious, and as she scooped up a handful of moldy coffee grains, she heard the bell over the door tinkle.

A customer! Lacey thought with excitement, straightening up. Her gaze fell to the coffee grains all over her hands, and the stains on the knees of her pants. It took everything in Lacey not to curse aloud.

She hurried back inside, grabbing a tea towel from the little kitchenette to clean her hands on as she raced back into the main room. But there was no one there.

Frowning, Lacey looked around. Was Taryn playing another trick on her? What was wrong with that woman? She was more childish than Naomi!

Just then, Lacey heard a scrabbling noise.

"Hello?"

She peered over the counter. To her surprise, a dog was lying on the floor. It was an English Shepherd, a bit scrawny but otherwise healthy and handsome. It looked up at her and made a whiny noise, like a mournful sort of greeting.

"Oh," Lacey said, her heart twitching at the sight of the lovely creature. "Who are you then?"

She came round the counter. The dog seemed friendly enough, letting her approach it and pet it. Lacey peered out the window to see if anyone in the street had lost their dog, but there did not appear to be anyone searching for it.

"Come on," she said to the creature. "Let's see if we can find your owners."

The dog immediately obeyed Lacey's command, standing up beside her legs as if it had understood her every word.

"You're a smart boy, aren't you?" Lacey commented.

She opened the door and headed outside, the dog trotting obediently at her heels.

Looking around, Lacey saw no sign of any distressed owners searching for their missing pooch. With a frown, she decided to speak to Tom—maybe he saw something. But as she headed toward his patisserie, she felt her palms begin to grow clammy.

Pull yourself together, she told herself sternly.

Swallowing the lump that had lodged itself in the back of her throat, she entered the store, the dog at her heels.

Tom was in the middle of decorating a cake, using a piping bag to make bright pink roses out of frosting. Lacey was awed by his artistic talents, by the way he could create art with the twirl of his hand—edible art, no less!—and immediately forgot what she was here to do. It was only when Tom looked up—evidently sensing he was being watched—that Lacey snapped back to the moment and approached. She thought she saw a glint in his eye at the sight of her, but wasn't sure if she was imagining it.

"Well, well, well, if it isn't Wilfordshire's newest antiques dealer," he said, placing the piping bag down onto the worktop. His apron was stained with pink streaks of frosting. "I was wondering when you'd come in and introduce yourself. And you brought a friend..." His voice trailed away then and a frown suddenly appeared between his eyebrows. "Chester!" he exclaimed. "What are you doing here?"

"You do know him," Lacey said, relieved. "He just wandered into my shop. Do you know where his owners are?"

Tom came out from behind the counter and crouched beside the dog. He rubbed it behind the ears and the dog wagged its tail with recognition. Tom peered up at Lacey. "He belonged to the people who leased the store before you! He must've wandered all the way back home."

Lacey gasped. She'd heard of dogs doing that before, of covering vast distances to get back to their old abodes.

"Wow, he *is* a clever dog," she said. "I'll phone Stephen and get the number of the old lessee. They must be besides themselves with worry."

She grabbed her cell and called her landlord.

"I'm sorry, Lacey," he said once she'd explained the situation to him. "But they didn't leave any contact details, and their phones just go to voicemail."

Lacey ended the call and looked at Tom. "There's no way to contact them."

She felt awful. She'd never had a pet herself, but she knew that people treated them like family. Chester's owners must be going nuts.

"We should try the RSPCA," Tom suggested. "If Chester has a microchip, they'll be able to read it and get his owners' contact details that way."

Lacey clicked her fingers. "That's some great detective work."

Tom shrugged. "Well, that's assuming they've updated them with their new address."

Lacey bit down on her bottom lip. "That's a good point. They left a lot of debt for Stephen. If Chester's microchip was a potential way for them to be traced, they might not have."

Just then, Chester started to whine sadly, almost as if he'd understood the meaning of Lacey's words.

She bent down and began to pet him. "I'm sorry, Chester. I'm sure that's not true. I'm sure we'll be able to get you reunited right away. Are you hungry, boy?"

"Here," Tom said, grabbing a cellophane-wrapped packet of what looked like chocolate drops off the shelf and handing it to Lacey. "Don't worry. It's carob, for people with chocolate allergies, so it won't poison him. I'll call the RSPCA."

While Tom spoke on the phone, Lacey fed Chester the carob treats. He ate them greedily, licking them right up from her palms. It looked like he hadn't eaten for a while and Lacey felt a huge responsibility to take care of him. Though he'd been in her life all of five minutes, Lacey felt like an instant bond had formed between them.

Tom came back in from the back room. "Okay, the alert's been put out to all local vets, and they'd like us to bring him in to them. I said we were both working, but that we'd come at the end of the day once we've closed up."

A tingly feeling ran across Lacey's skin every time Tom used the words, "we" and "our." She liked the idea of them being in this together.

"Is that okay?" Tom added.

Lacey nodded eagerly. "I can take care of Chester until then."

"Great," Tom said. "I'll pick you up at the end of the day. I owe you a date, after all."

Now Lacey really did blush, and tried to hide her face by busily rubbing Chester's neck.

"You'd better get back to your store," Tom added. "Looks like you have customers."

Lacey leapt up and swirled around. Sure enough, a tall, blond couple had wandered in through her open door. Her heart skipped a beat with excitement.

"A customer!" she cried.

Chester leapt up at the sound of her exclamation. Together, they hurried for the door. Just as she reached it, Lacey heard Tom calling to her.

"Oh, Lacey?"

She paused and looked back over her shoulder. "Yeah?"

"I love the new haircut."

Lacey grinned from ear to ear, then hurried away.

As Lacey saw to her first ever customers—a Danish couple on an anniversary vacation—Chester settled down in front of the desk and started to snore. Lacey tried to keep her mind focused on her business, but she kept seeing flashes of Tom through the window, and found her attention constantly drifting toward him.

"And how much would that be?" the Danish man asked, forcing Lacey back to the moment.

She glanced at the lamp he was gesturing to. "Oh, that one's fifty dollars. I mean, fifty pounds."

Get it together, Lacey, her mind chastised her.

"Great. I'll take it."

That was all Lacey needed to hear to bring her focus back to reality. She was about to make her first ever sale!

Doing her best to hide how giddy with joy she felt, she carried the lamp over to the counter and used the old analogue till machine to ring it up for the Danish couple. As the man handed over some notes, Lacey couldn't help the grin from spreading across her face. That fifty pounds represented independence, freedom, and new beginnings, and Lacey felt like all her Christmases had come early.

She bagged the lamp and held it out to the couple. "And that's for you. Have a great day, both of you. And congratulations."

The couple exchanged a glance as if Lacey was a little odd, before thanking her and leaving.

The second they were out of sight, Lacey jumped up and punched the air.

"Did you see that, Chester?" she asked the snoozy dog. "Did you see me make a sale?"

The dog lifted his head and whined, then let it drop back down and went back to snoring.

Lacey's eyes traveled through the window to the patisserie. There was Tom, watching her with a look of pride. He flashed her a thumbs-up.

Lacey felt like she was on top of the world.

The feeling lasted the rest of the morning. Everyone who came into the shop seemed very interested in the American expat who'd set up shop in a small seaside village in England. Those who were locals kept asking what had happened to the prior owners—prompted by the presence of Chester—of which Lacey could only explain that they'd left at short notice and their dog had wandered back a week later.

Then a man came in with his two young daughters. Both the girls had curly brown hair, and were about the ages of four and seven. It was just like when Lacey was a child, with Naomi and her dad, and the sight made a sudden flash of memory hit her.

They'd gone out shopping, the three of them, hunting for antiques to take back to his store in New York. Mom hadn't come on the shopping trip, though Lacey couldn't recall why. Then Naomi had dropped something. A porcelain trinket. She'd grabbed the broken item, cutting her finger open in the process, and it started bleeding profusely. The woman behind the counter had rushed over to help Naomi, showing her tender affection rather than being annoyed about the broken item. Dad and the store clerk had locked eyes, hadn't they? It had been like a romantic movie, the "meet cute" moment, where the hero and heroine merely brush one another's hands and fall instantly in love.

Coming back to reality, Lacey gasped. Had she invented the last bit of that memory, about the romantic tension between her father and the store clerk? She'd only been seven at the time, after all; there was no way she'd have picked up on any subtle romanticism at that age. Unless it had really been there, and she was able to understand it now. Was it relevant to her parents' subsequent divorce? Her father's disappearance? Lacey felt the hairs on her arms lift as goosebumps appeared across her skin.

Just then, the door tinkled. In waltzed Tom, a hamper in his arms.

"What are you doing here?" Lacey asked. Looking through the windows, she saw that his store had been locked up and a hand-drawn sign read: out for lunch. "Isn't this your busiest time?"

"I thought Chester might be hungry," Tom replied, opening up the basket and pulling out a packet of dog food, along with a delicate china bowl that he'd obviously taken from his cafe. "And I also thought you might be," he added, continuing to empty the contents of his basket onto the counter in front of a bewildered Lacey.

"Oh."

"Is that all right?" Tom asked, clearly picking up on her moment of hesitation.

"Yes, of course," Lacey gushed. "I just wasn't expecting it."

Which was quite the understatement. She'd been divorced for a matter of days. A gorgeous man showing sudden romantic interest in her was not something she'd ever expected. It had all happened so quickly she hadn't really had time to stop and work out if she wanted it.

She reminded herself that this was a new Lacey. The old Lacey had to be scheduled and organized and thorough and precise because *David* had wanted her to be. Perhaps the new Lacey was someone who threw caution to the wind. There was only one way to find out.

Tom set out the food for Chester, who began to eat greedily and happily. Then he unwrapped all the sandwiches and cakes he'd brought over for them to share. To Lacey's amusement, he produced a steaming hot tea pot from the basket.

"Really?" she laughed.

"Of course!" he replied, pouring her a cup.

Lacey couldn't even stop the muscles tugging her lips up at the corners; it was as if they had a mind of their own, as if her joy was untamable. And she loved the feeling.

"Cheers," Tom said, holding his cup up to chink against hers.

Lacey did the same. But instead of the soft clinking noise Lacey was expecting, the sound of a bell rang out. It was the door, tinkling as someone entered.

Lacey looked over Tom's shoulder to see Taryn strolling in, her shiny black heels clacking on the floorboards.

"Lacey, I'm out of change, can you switch me some for a tenner?"

Then Taryn paused, noticing that Lacey was sharing a pot of tea and lunch with someone. Lacey thought Taryn's face paled.

"Tom?" Taryn said with disbelief. Her head darted back over her shoulder as if to check that he wasn't in his store, as if she thought the only explanation for him being here with Lacey was if he were a replicant clone.

"Hello, Taryn," Tom said in his oh so easy-breezy way, which seemed very incongruous considering the way Taryn's face had completely blanched at the sight of him.

"You two know each other?" Lacey asked.

"Course we do," Tom said jovially, not picking up on the tension at all. "Taryn buys her morning coffee from me before work. And her evening coffee after."

He said it in his usual friendly manner, as if completely oblivious to Taryn's very obvious excuse to see him. But Lacey sure wasn't oblivious. Her nemesis's cheeks were pink, her eyes shifty. Taryn had a thing for Tom. A major thing.

Great, Lacey thought. *That's just what I need. Another reason for Taryn to hate me.*

CHAPTER NINE

As the clock ticked ever closer to five p.m., Lacey's excitement grew more and more pronounced. She couldn't wait for her adventure with Tom to begin. The last few hours she'd spent without him had felt too long.

But first she had to lock up on her first full day as a business owner.

As she balanced the till, Lacey was overcome with pride. She hadn't made enough to turn a profit, but considering most folk in town wouldn't even know she was open yet, she was thrilled by the stack of notes in her till. She'd logged every item that had sold—something she'd seen her father do—so she'd know exactly what kind of items she needed to stock up on.

Just as she'd finished writing a list of the London dealers she'd need to contact, she heard the sound of a honking car horn. She glanced up to see an iconic cherry-red VW van idling in the streets outside her store. Through its windows, Lacey saw Tom waving at her.

Lacey laughed with abandon. How fitting that Tom would drive a VW!

"Come on, Chester," she said, filled with girlish excitement.

The English Shepherd trotted alongside Lacey as she exited the store—closing up on her first ever day as a business owner—and skipped across the cobblestones toward the van. She hauled open the passenger side door and gestured for Chester to go in first. He leapt up into the passenger footwell, and Lacey hopped up after him. There was just enough room for her to squeeze her legs either side of him.

"Hi," Tom said, looking over from the driver's seat, flashing her one of his gorgeous smiles.

"Hey," Lacey replied, suddenly shy.

Tom pulled away from the curb and Lacey buckled up her seat belt. As she did, she heard her phone ping with an incoming message. She took it from her pocket, eager to see whether Naomi and Mom had finally gotten around to sending her congratulatory messages. Indeed, there was a notification on the *Doyle Girlz* thread, and she tapped with excitement. The message was from Naomi.

Are you sure this Tom guy isn't trying to recruit you into a cult? He seems suspiciously nice.

Disappointed, Lacey rolled her eyes. What did Naomi know? Her little sister had been in the most disastrous, unhealthy relationships Lacey had ever seen. If she thought the fact that Tom was *nice* was a red flag, well, that just showed how skewed her perspective really was.

Lacey turned to Tom. "Are you recruiting me into a cult?" she asked. "My sister wants to know."

"Nope," Tom said, laughing, completely unfazed by the question.

Before Lacey had a chance to reply, her phone buzzed again with another message from her sister.

I mean, what does RSPCA even mean? Sounds totally like a cult to me!

Lacey's thumbs tapped in overdrive. *It stands for the Royal Society for the Prevention of Cruelty to Animals, you numbskull!* Then she hit send and shoved her cell phone back into her pocket.

It buzzed again, but this time Lacey ignored it. She was determined not to let Naomi bring down her mood with her negativity and skepticism.

In the time it had taken for the back and forth messages to take place, the town of Wilfordshire had disappeared behind Lacey. She looked through the windshield to see that the VW was now cruising along the narrow roads of the open countryside, with rolling green hills either side. It was all very pretty, and very quaint.

"Look!" Lacey exclaimed, as she noticed a castle-like building nestled in a valley. It looked like something that belonged in the pages of a Bronte novel, and she couldn't help but let her jaw drop open in awe at its impressive architecture.

"That's Penrose Estate," Tom said, smiling at her astonishment. "It's the reason there's a town of Wilfordshire in the first place."

"Really?" Lacey asked, intrigued.

Tom nodded, his focus now back on the road. "Uh-huh. A lot of villages in England are like that. A whole economy grows around the home of a single aristocrat. A couple hundred years ago, if you weren't blue-blooded, your whole existence involved servicing someone who was."

"I was about to say it's gorgeous," Lacey said. "But I feel like I shouldn't now."

Tom laughed. "Oh, it's gorgeous, all right. Just important to remember its history."

He tapped on the left indicator and turned the van down a long, hilly road. There, as if springing up from nowhere, was a large red brick building that Lacey would've assumed was a boarding school if it hadn't been for the bright blue sign with the letters RSPCA embossed upon it.

Tom pulled the VW into the lot and parked up.

Lacey untangled herself from where Chester had curled up in the footwell, and coaxed the dog out of the van. As she'd come to expect from him, he obeyed her every word with a look of utter comprehension in his eye. Lacey wondered if other dogs were as sharp as this one, or if Chester was a rare genius.

"Oh, what a gorgeous dog," the receptionist said as the automatic double doors allowed Tom and Lacey inside.

The receptionist was a rather stout woman, short, with red, jolly cheeks and thick wiry gray hair that hung to her chin in the shape of a triangle.

"This is Chester," Tom said. "We called earlier about tracing his owner."

The receptionist checked her computer. "Oh yes. Mr. and Mrs. Forrester, is it?"

Lacey almost choked on nothing and was about to open her mouth to refute when Tom said merrily, "Yes, that's right."

Either he hadn't heard the receptionist's slip-up, or he didn't mind being mistaken for Lacey's husband. On the contrary, Lacey's heart had begun slamming against her ribcage at the thought of being Tom's wife.

"Go right on in," the receptionist said. "The vet's waiting for you."

Lacey couldn't even look at Tom as they walked side by side along the corridor and in through the vet's open door.

The veterinarian looked up and smiled as they entered. She was a short Asian woman, swamped by her dark green scrubs, and she had childlike features that made her look far too young to be a qualified veterinarian. *Another Brenda,* Lacey thought, thinking of the barmaid at the Coach House.

"This must be Chester?" the vet said, approaching them. "I hear he's lost."

"That's right," Lacey said. "He wandered into my store today. His owners were the prior tenants."

"Ah," the vet said as if this wasn't much of a surprise at all. "Dogs can have very strong homing instincts. Let's scan you, Chester, and see if we can get you reunited."

She got a black plastic device and held it to the back of Chester's neck. It beeped.

"He's microchipped," she said. "That's a good start."

She went over to the computer and began typing into it, leaving Lacey to stand awkwardly with her hands clasped, avoiding Tom's attempts to make eye contact.

"Oh," the vet said suddenly, looking up from her computer at the pair. By the look on her face, Lacey could tell there was some bad news coming.

"What is it?" she asked, concern fluttering inside of her.

"I'm afraid the owners are deceased."

Lacey and Tom gasped in unison.

"What? How?" Tom stammered. "We thought they moved away."

"There's a police report here," the vet explained, her gaze returning to the computer screen as she relayed aloud what it was showing her. "The registered owners were in a vehicle accident over a week ago. Both were declared dead at the scene."

Lacey was so shocked and saddened by the news, she didn't know what to do. She turned to Chester, petting him.

"My poor boy," she said, feeling tears welling in her eyes.

"That must've been why no one put out a missing alert on him," the vet added. "If he was in the vehicle when it happened, he might've just run straight away from the scene, heading back to somewhere that was familiar."

Lacey felt like her heart could break at the thought of Chester going through the trauma of a car wreck, then wandering, lost, for over a week until he made his way back home.

"Right," the vet said, standing up from the computer and coming over to Chester. "Let's get this lad registered into the rehoming process."

"Can't I keep him?" Lacey blurted, before her brain had even registered.

Tom and the vet turned to her, eyebrows raised in twin expressions of bemusement.

"That's not how it works," the vet explained.

"But I work in the store he's familiar with. It would be the least disruptive to him, wouldn't it? Rather than have him put in a kennel, to be gawped at by potential new owners, who'd take him somewhere he's never been before, when I'd be able to take him back to somewhere that was more or less home."

The vet looked bemused. "Huh. Well. I don't know. I'd have to find out. If he's been in an accident, we should probably keep him overnight to do checks anyway. I can call you in the morning once I know more?"

But Lacey felt very protective over the dog and didn't want to let go of him without confirmation he'd be returned to her the next day. Tom seemed to psychically pick up on this, because he said to the vet, "Can't we just skip the bureaucracy? If we hadn't brought him in, you'd never even have known he was missing in the first place."

The vet twisted her lips. But finally, she sighed. "You know what, you're right. Rather than add him onto the long list of dogs waiting for a home, I'll log you as his foster carers. After a few weeks you can phone up and say you'd like to adopt him."

Lacey's heart leapt with joy. She locked eyes with Tom, thrilled that he'd managed to get the vet to agree.

"That sounds great," she said to the vet.

The vet logged Lacey's contact details into the system, then they said goodbye to Chester, thanked the vet for bending the rules, and headed back to Tom's van.

"So, Lacey," Tom said as he gunned the van's engine to life. "How was that for a date? It must've been good, considering we're now supposedly married."

Lacey's cheeks hadn't even had a chance to cool down yet. Now they felt like raging infernos. "Yes, well, let's not joke about that. My sister would call the cops and declare you the next Jim Jones."

Tom laughed in that loud, unabashed, infectious way that Lacey was quickly coming to adore. But then her mind returned to the dog they'd left behind and her heart hitched.

"Poor Chester," she said. "To think he might have been in the car when it crashed. I know he's a dog but that must've been trau- matic for him!"

"Definitely," Tom said. "He's lucky you're adopting him. He'll need a lot of support and care to get over a thing like that. But what I'm wondering about is his owners. They left without notice, that's what Stephen said, right?"

"Yes," Lacey confirmed. "They packed up overnight and left all their unpaid utility bills and invoices."

She paused, suddenly thinking of the knocked over plants in the garden, evidence of haste. And the expensive brass light fixture they'd left behind. Lacey had assumed they'd been unaware of its value, but perhaps they'd just not had a chance to take it with them. A sudden chill ran up her spine.

"They were in a hurry," she said.

"Such a hurry they sped and crashed," Tom added. "Almost as if—"

"—they were running away from something," Lacey concluded.

The pair locked gazes, silent communication passing between them.

CHAPTER TEN

Through the walls, Lacey heard the familiar pounding music coming from Taryn's boutique. It had now become a staple backdrop. Her rival was clearly trying to rile her, but Lacey was floating on Cloud 9 these days and nothing would bring her down. Not even Taryn's sandwich board that Lacey suspected she purposefully placed to obscure the antiques store entrance.

Combining with the buzzing bass beat coming through Lacey's right-hand wall was the welcome sound of Chester snoring. Her "foster" dog had slotted right into Lacey's life like he was supposed to be there all along, and he was certainly helping her store garner more attention. These days, locals walking past would come in just to say hello to him, so Lacey had rearranged her stock so the cheaper, more useful items were right beside where he slept. Her ploy had worked—most people who came in to pet Chester would notice some kind of inexpensive trinket they wanted to purchase. She could count on at least £50 a day from Chester-petters alone!

Overall, Lacey was convinced she'd made the right decision coming to Wilfordshire. Not only did she have the store, which was thriving, and Chester, who was now her sidekick, but she had Gina, her neighbor, friend, and fellow antique-scouter, who had snapped up Lacey's offer to tend to the store's garden.

The only downside was that Lacey had been so busy, she hadn't had another chance to go on a "date" with Tom. He was busy, too; the Easter holiday brought many people to Wilfordshire and they all seemed to want to partake in his infamous pastel-colored macarons. But, Lacey realized with a little leap of excitement, today was the last day of the school holiday and the tourists would dwindle for another six weeks. Perhaps she and Tom would be able to steal a chance to hang out during the quieter season.

Lacey leaned her elbows against the counter and glanced down at the antique collector's magazine she was perusing. Her store was filled with treasures, but there were so many more she wanted to get her hands on. Saskia, her old boss, had always approached design with a minimalistic eye. But Lacey preferred the busy look of the Victorian era, where every pattern and color was celebrated—William Morris was her favorite designer—and where the most useless of items were invented—from special sugar bowls to special milk jugs and a special spoon for every different condiment. She loved all those things, and this magazine was a great resource. Besides, the more she read, the better she got at valuing items, and the closer she'd come to opening her own auction store out the back like her father had dreamed of doing.

She'd just spotted a collection of Victorian serving spoons for a steal when the bell above the door tinkled.

Lacey looked up from her magazine. An elderly woman had entered the store. As usual, Chester looked up to assess the visitor, sniffed the air, then went back to sleep.

"Hello," Lacey said, straightening up and smiling. "Let me know if you need any help."

"Oh, this is lovely," the woman said as she came in closer. "I like what you've done with the place."

Lacey realized that the woman must've known the store before, when it was for gardening and home supplies.

"You know the store?" she asked.

"I do," the woman smiled. "Though I never had a need to use it before."

"Do you have a need now?" Lacey asked.

"Now it's an antique dealer, I do."

"Oh?" Lacey said, her head quirking to the side with intrigue.

"You may recognize my name. Iris Archer."

Lacey drew a blank. "No, sorry, I don't. I'm not local."

The woman chuckled. "I can tell from your accent that you aren't."

She spoke without malice, and Lacey noted the woman's own accent was extremely regal sounding, like the dame from a British period drama.

"I live in the manor house on the outskirts of Wilfordshire," the woman continued, without even a hint of arrogance in her tone. "Penrose Estate."

Lacey's eyes widened. Penrose Estate! The miniature castle she'd gawked at on her road trip with Tom? It hadn't occurred to her that someone actually *lived* there!

"Oh yes, I know of the estate," Lacey said, trying her best to dispel her appearance as an ignorant foreigner.

"I have a collection of antiques," Iris continued. "I need to get them appraised. I've been far too nervous to remove them from my house and transport them, and I've not found someone yet who I trust enough to come over. You do valuations, I presume?"

"Absolutely," Lacey said, excited not only by the prospect of visiting a real-life English estate—Naomi would lose her mind when she showed her the photos—but for the opportunity to flex her brand knew valuation muscles. She grabbed the jotter pad beside the store telephone. "When would suit you?"

"The sooner the better," Iris told her. "It's a task I've been putting off for years and fear I may not have long left to see to it."

Morbid, Lacey thought, though she'd known elderly people in her time who spoke that way. Her grandmother had been one, her catch phrase having become "once I'm gone" a good decade before she'd finally passed.

"How about tomorrow?" Lacey suggested, enthusiasm making her rash. She could head out to Penrose Estate first thing in the morning, and get Gina to open up and cover for her a few hours in case the meeting overran.

"Why don't you come for breakfast?" Iris said. "I have it delivered to the house promptly for seven a.m."

"Sounds perfect," Lacey said, thinking about the half-hour drive and the fact she'd have to leave at six thirty.

She jotted it down in her pad, noting that her handwriting was a little shaky from her excitement.

"I have to ask though," she added, looking up at the regal-looking elderly woman. "Why do you trust me? I'm new to Wilfordshire, and to the antiques business."

"For that very reason," Iris Archer replied. "You don't know me. You don't know my history." Then she smiled such a tender, genuine smile, it made the decades of laugh lines brighten up her whole face. "And because you look just like Francis."

The sound of her father's name in her ears hit Lacey like gale force wind. "My dad?" she stammered. "You knew my dad?"

Just then, Taryn's loud bass music seemed to notch up in volume, loud enough to make the china on the shelves rattle. Lacey had to tear herself away from the woman, her question hanging in the air between them, and hurried over to the shelves to move the china pots apart so they didn't smash into one another from the vibrations. Even then, the vibrations seemed to make them jump up and down. It was perilous.

"Hold on one second," Lacey said to Iris. "Wait right there."

She hurried out of the store, anger making her heavy-footed, and bumped right into the purposefully placed sandwich board, bumping her hip bone. Irritated, she gave it a huge shove so it was out of her way, then marched into Taryn's boutique.

The place was super swanky and sparsely stocked with just a few select, expensive, beautifully displayed items. Two statuesque women were perusing one of the racks, and Taryn herself looked immaculate, standing innocently enough beside the counter. The sound system, Lacey noted then, was now placed next to their shared wall, when before it had been at the back of the store. Taryn had moved it purposefully.

It was evident to Lacey that she'd been expecting her, because her poised appearance, even tone, and look of expectation reminded Lacey of a badly acted daytime drama.

"Everything okay, Lace?" Taryn said.

"Okay?" Lacey exclaimed, her hands tightening into fists. "You know it's not okay! Your music is so loud it's rattling the walls. It's going to make my china fall off the shelf!"

The two swan-necked women looked over, frowning at the sound of Lacey's raised voice. Of course, Taryn was making *her* look like the crazy one.

"Oh, I didn't realize it was so loud," Taryn said, feigning innocence. "Would you like me to turn it down?"

Lacey ground her teeth as Taryn went over and turned the volume down.

"Thank you," Lacey said through her gritted teeth. "And stop putting your sandwich board over my door!" she added, as she marched back out, ignoring the tutting coming from Taryn's giraffe customers.

Lacey's pulse rate started to lessen as she headed back into her own store. But once inside, she realized Iris Archer had gone.

She stomped her foot with frustration. The woman had known her father! She'd wanted to ask her how, to learn everything she could from this person who would so brazenly utter aloud the name that had been banned in her own household.

But not all hope was lost. Because Lacey was meeting Iris Archer at seven tomorrow morning, at Penrose Estate. She'd just have to be patient. In the meantime, she held out hope that once they met, this strange aristocratic woman might just give Lacey all the answers she craved.

CHAPTER ELEVEN

Lacey flopped into her bed, exhausted.

She'd had to put in an extra-long shift at the store today but she didn't resent it, like she had before when working for Saskia. Now, whatever she put into the store, it would reward in dividends her later. It was thrilling to be so in control of her own destiny like that. It was almost intoxicating.

But it wasn't the store that was exhausting her, though. It was her chance meeting with Iris, and all the emotions hearing her father's name had stirred within her. That, more than any hour worked at the store, was zapping her energy.

Chester curled up at her feet, and Lacey fell quickly into a deep sleep.

Ever since she'd started putting all her time into the store, Lacey had stopped dreaming. But tonight was different. Tonight, Lacey found herself walking down the cobbled high street of Wilfordshire that she now knew so well. But rather than wearing her work suit and brogues, she was wearing shiny black patent-leather T-bar shoes and little white socks. She was a child again, a child of seven, and her hand was wrapped in her father's.

Her heart started to pound as she looked up at him, the rays of the sun behind his head obscuring his features. But it was still unmistakably her father. The feel of his rough skin against hers was so familiar she'd know it anywhere.

"Well, if it isn't Francis Doyle," a woman's voice said then.

Lacey looked back ahead. There was a woman approaching, her appearance also obscured by the bright sunburst.

Lacey recognized her only by her shapely figure. It was the store clerk from the antiques store where Naomi had cut her finger.

Lacey woke up with a start, sitting bolt upright in bed. Chester quirked his head up to look at her, his eyes roving across her face as if with concern.

"I'm okay, boy," Lacey assured him, though her heart was hammering and she could feel sweat running down the back of her neck.

Chester let his head sink back down onto his front paws.

Lacey lay back against the pillows, her mind racing. The dream had felt so real, more like a memory than a dream. And it was another one that featured the same woman, the clerk from the antiques store. Had her father been a philanderer? Lacey wondered. Was that why her parents' marriage had ended so abruptly, after a seemingly idyllic summer vacation in Wilfordshire? Or was her dream just a fabrication? Something she'd invented?

Obviously, something about seeing Iris Archer today, someone who'd actually known her father, had prompted Lacey's mind to return back to her childhood. The elderly woman had said she trusted Lacey's father ... What could that mean?

Lacey guessed she'd just have to wait until morning and her breakfast meeting with Iris Archer. Perhaps then, she might get the answers she so desperately craved.

The next morning, Lacey awoke at the crack of dawn, feeling groggy from such a poor quality night's sleep. She downed a coffee—she couldn't function without some caffeine in her blood, especially not at this time of day—then loaded Chester into the back of her champagne-colored stick shift. Gina had agreed to open up the store at nine for her, and without her usual sidekick, Lacey decided Chester ought to come along instead.

She drove through the beautiful countryside, following the same route Tom had taken her on their day trip, turning at the road that led into the valley where Penrose Estate was nestled.

The estate was even larger than it looked from afar, the enormous castle-like stone structure covered in dark green ivy.

Lacey parked and hopped out, with Chester at her heel. She was excited to find out more about what the woman knew about her dad, and was also reveling in the excitement of valuing her antiques. It would be her first time doing it for herself, and she was eager to try out her fledgling skills.

The path was lined with rose bushes filled with blood red roses, and the smell was intoxicating. She reached the large oak door and knocked. As she waited, she gave Chester a little pat behind the ears. The dog whined sweetly.

There was no answer, and no sound coming from the other side, so Lacey tried again. This time she knocked a little louder, and to her surprise found the door inched open with a creak under her knuckles.

She looked at Chester. "It's open?" she said, perplexed.

Lacey pushed on the door. It creaked open farther, showing a dark corridor with a gray slate tiled floor.

"Hello?" Lacey called into the darkness.

There was no response.

Lacey felt the hairs on her arm begin to lift. Something didn't feel right.

She checked her watch. It was seven a.m. on the dot, the exact time she'd promised to be here so as not to miss the breakfast delivery. Perhaps the older woman routinely left the door open for the deliverers. Perhaps she'd left it open specifically because she knew Lacey was coming.

Either way, it felt very rude just to walk inside, and Lacey hesitated on the doorstep, torn.

Just then, Chester burst into the house and went skittering off into the darkness.

Well, that's one way to solve the dilemma, Lacey thought.

She hurried down the hall after her English Shepherd. As she went, Lacey couldn't help but notice all the awesome artwork on the walls, and the amazing architecture of Penrose Estate beneath.

The house itself was something of an antique. She wondered about its history.

Just then, coming from somewhere in the distance, Lacey heard the sound of Chester barking. She'd never heard him bark in such a way. To her ears, it sounded insistent, like he was calling for her to come to him.

Lacey quickened her pace, racing toward the sound.

She whirled in through a door—recognizing it to be a library within a split second—before her gaze fell to a large lump of something on the floor. Lacey gasped and reeled backward.

There, sprawled on the floorboards, her skin pale, her lips rimmed with purple, her eyes open, glazed and unseeing, lay Iris Archer.

She was dead.

Chapter Twelve

Lacey stood outside the cottage shaking, her arms wrapped about her middle. Chester sat obediently and reassuringly at her feet, but she couldn't get the image of the dead woman sprawled on her floor out of her mind. She was shaken to the core.

After what felt like forever, she finally saw the police cruiser crawling up the drive toward her. They parked and an officer stepped out. He was a portly man, and he moved slowly like he was in zero hurry at all, which seemed a bit odd to Lacey considering her panicked phone call explaining there was a *dead body!*

"Superintendent Karl Turner," he announced, holding his hand for Lacey to shake.

She shook it, a little confused as to why they'd sent out someone as high ranking as a superintendent to a simple death scene, before deciding it must be a British thing, something to do with the fact the deceased was a wealthy aristocrat.

"This is DCI Beth Lewis," he added, pointing toward a woman getting out of the vehicle. "You're the one who called it in, correct?"

"Yes," Lacey said, looking around for a vehicle that might be a hearse but seeing none.

"And you are?" the superintendent added.

"Lacey Doyle. I'm an antiques valuer," Lacey explained, taking a business card out of her pocket and handing it to him as if it were a receipt for her claim. "I'd come over here to value some antiques."

"In the morning?"

Lacey nodded. "Iris wanted us to talk over breakfast, which she said would be delivered at seven a.m. When I got here, the door was open. I assumed she'd left it unlocked for me, since our meeting was scheduled, but when I went in, I found her lying there ..." Her voice cracked. "Dead." Tears at the memory started to flood her eyes.

"Huh," the superintendent grunted, his tone suggesting that everything Lacey had just told him was a fabrication.

She felt herself bristle. Sure, there was doing a job, and then there was just acting like an ass to someone who was clearly in a traumatized state. Maybe PC Plod saw dead bodies every day, but this was Lacey's first—and last, she hoped—and so it was all rather shocking to her.

The superintendent turned to DCI Lewis. "You get details off Mrs. Doyle here—"

"Ms.," Lacey corrected him, firmly. "I'm not married."

Supt. Turner looked at her and grunted like he couldn't care less, or like he wasn't surprised Lacey was single. He turned back to his partner. "Get some details off *Ms.* Doyle while I take a look at the scene."

He went off inside the house.

DCI Lewis looked at Lacey. She held herself with the same stoic stiffness as Supt. Turner, but there was an element of warmth to her, too.

"Bit of a shock, huh?" she asked Lacey in a kind manner. "Not what you want to see over breakfast."

Lacey nodded, not really knowing what else to say.

DCI Lewis asked her some questions, jotting down information about how Lacey had first met Iris Archer, and how she'd come to be outside of her house on this particular morning. But then Lacey noticed Superintendent Turner waltzing out the front door and thundering toward them.

"Beth!" he barked to the officer in front of Lacey. "Get CSI on the scene. Stat. We're dealing with a homicide here."

Lacey gasped, her hand flying to her mouth. *Homicide?* That meant Iris Archer had been *murdered!*

Oh, that poor woman! Lacey thought, her mind suddenly racing at a mile a minute. *She must've been so scared.*

While DCI Lewis began talking into the walkie-talkie at her shoulder, Lacey noticed Superintendent Turner watching her closely. His face was a blank mask, revealing nothing at all, but she'd seen enough detective shows in her time to know what he was thinking: she was his prime suspect. Before, she hadn't even considered that Iris was the victim of foul play—the woman was elderly, she'd assumed her time had simply come—but now that Lacey knew she'd been murdered, she realized just how odd her presence there must look. Just how suspicious. She felt her heart leap in her chest as she realized that as the person to have called in the death, she'd put herself right in the frame.

She took a step back toward her vehicle, suddenly desperate to get out of there and hide under her duvet.

"Ms. Doyle?" she heard the superintendent call as she fumbled with her car keys in shaky hands.

"I'm going home," Lacey stammered. "I've answered all your questions, so I'm free to go, aren't I?"

"Of course," Superintendent Turner said, his face remaining completely blank and unreadable. "I just wanted to ask you not to leave town. We'll likely have a few more questions for you in the future."

He'd said it plainly enough, but the subtext was obvious for Lacey. They'd have more questions for her once they'd gathered evidence. His words may have been said dispassionately, but they were very much a threat.

Lacey got in her car and sped away.

CHAPTER THIRTEEN

Lacey couldn't bring herself to return to the store that day. Luckily Gina was happy to take up the shift, after Lacey had told her she was feeling under the weather.

When evening rolled in, Lacey heard her neighbor knocking on the door to return the keys—and on getting no response, sticking them through the letterbox. Lacey felt guilty about not answering the door, but she just couldn't face her. She was too rattled to face anyone. All she wanted to do was sleep that nightmare scenario away.

Sadly, sleep didn't come easily. Even with Chester at the foot of the bed, keeping her toes warm, acting as guard dog, she couldn't relax. She kept thinking about a murderer being out on the loose, and how terrified the old woman must have been in her final moments.

In the morning, she awoke feeling even more drained and exhausted than the day before. Two nights of poor quality sleep following so many long hours at the store left her feeling like a zombie. She'd just about managed to operate the coffee machine to make herself a steaming black Americano, when she heard her phone pinging with messages. She suddenly recalled how she'd deliriously tapped out a message on the *Doyle Girlz* thread about the murder, and instantly regretted it now that she realized it must be her family responding.

She checked her phone to see that Mom had sent her some supportive words of encouragement. Naomi, for once, hadn't replied with sarcasm or derision, but the hugging person emoji. But it only made Lacey feel worse—if Naomi could see the gravity of the situation then it must be really bad!

She devoured a cereal bar while Chester munched down his doggy chow, then collected the store keys from the welcome mat where they'd fallen after being posted through the door by Gina.

When she opened her front door, Lacey discovered a casserole dish sitting on the step, wrapped in aluminum foil. An attached note, in Gina's distinctive, scrawling handwriting, read: *Homemade shepherd's pie to help you feel better soon!*

Touched by her neighbor's sweet gesture, Lacey picked up the dish and looked inside. A layer of creamy mashed potatoes lay on top of a layer of what she assumed from the name of the dish was minced lamb in a tomato sauce.

It must've been sitting there all night, and Lacey was surprised that the foxes hadn't gotten it. At least it had been a particularly cool night and morning so it wouldn't have spoiled at all.

Lacey carried the dish inside and put it in her fridge, then left Crag Cottage, Chester by her side, and drove to the store.

As she turned the key in the lock, she realized she was still shaking. Not as much as when she'd discovered Iris dead but there was an unmistakable tremor in her hand.

"Everything okay?" came the voice of Tom from behind her.

Lacey jumped a mile and spun around to face him. His friendly, suntanned face was a welcome sight for sore eyes.

"Yes. I'm fine. My mind was in the clouds."

"I'm not surprised," Tom commented. "I heard what happened. You must be shaken to the core."

Lacey's eyebrows shot up. "You heard? But how? It only happened yesterday morning."

"Small town," Tom said with a shrug. "News travels fast."

Then, to Lacey's surprise, he pulled her into an embrace.

Nothing had ever felt so right to Lacey as that moment, standing in Tom's warm, strong, reassuring arms. The support she'd gotten from David had always felt stilted. Sometimes stifling. But with Tom it was as if she was being hugged for the first time since she'd been a child. It held the same comfort as her mother's hug after falling down.

The whole experience was disarming, and Lacey felt herself sag a little from the expulsion of previously held in emotion.

"How are you doing?" Tom asked, as he released her. "Really."

Lacey shook her head. "I honestly don't know. It was a shock."

"I bet it was."

She opened the door, making the bell tinkle in a way that felt strangely incongruous to her now.

As the door swung open, Chester trotted right in, as he was becoming accustomed to do. Lacey went to follow after him and heard the store phone ringing. She hurried in and grabbed it.

"Murderer!" came a voice she didn't recognize, before the call cut out.

Lacey slammed the phone down and staggered back.

Tom was immediately there, with his reassuring expression and kind voice. "What is it? What happened?"

"Someone called me a murderer," Lacey stammered.

She noticed then the light blinking on the answering machine. The phone started to ring again.

"Don't answer it," Tom said, gently resting his hand on hers. He tugged the cord from the wall.

Lacey felt bewildered. "How does everyone know already? And why on earth are they blaming me?"

But she knew why. She was the outsider here. The new person in town. Everyone else knew each other, and if one of their own had been murdered then who else was there to point the finger of blame at?

Through the window, Lacey noticed people standing outside Tom's locked store.

"You have customers," she told him.

"I can stay here if you need me," he said.

Lacey shook her head. "I'm fine. You can't let your business suffer because of me."

"I'll call Paul to cover me," Tom said, reaching for his pocket where the outline of his cell phone bulged through the fabric. "He's my trainee."

As touched as she was by the offer, Lacey really didn't want Tom to go to any special trouble for her.

"Honestly," she said, more firmly. "I'm okay. I have Chester for protection."

At the mention of his name, the dog raised his head and let out his characteristic whining noise.

Tom withdrew his hand from his pocket, leaving the cell phone behind. "If you insist," he said, relenting. "But why don't we do dinner tonight…"

"Oh!" Lacey exclaimed, taken aback that he'd used the moment to suggest a date. Tom hadn't seemed like the type to her.

Tom immediately looked flustered. "Sorry, no, what I meant was I could deliver some pastries to you after work." He spoke very quickly as if in an attempt to clarify his earlier comment. "Because it's so hard to keep on track with things when you're emotionally bogged down. And because it might be hard for you to take your mind off things without some company to distract you." He rubbed his neck, which was going pink. "Only now you obviously think I'm a creep who preys on vulnerability…" he added with a mumble.

His awkwardness made Lacey immediately relax. If Tom had the wherewithal to see how his offer might have been misconstrued, then he already had more emotional intelligence than half the men she knew. She'd been right to think Tom was one of the good guys.

"Pastries would be great," she told him with a smile.

"Really?" he said, letting out a relieved sigh.

"Yes. But not tonight. My neighbor made me a shepherd's pie. Besides, I don't think I'd be particularly good company. Tomorrow?"

With the misinterpretation cleared up, Tom returned to his usual cheery self. "Sounds perfect."

He hopped up and gave Lacey's hand a squeeze.

The contact made her tingle all over. And with his hand lying gently over hers like that, the temptation to blurt out, *"Actually, let's make it an official date!"* almost overwhelmed her. But somehow, she held her ground and stayed strong, as Tom gave her a final parting look of reassurance and exited through the door.

Lacey watched him cross the street, feeling like her breath had gotten stuck in her lungs, mulling over her reaction to his suggestion of dinner. It hadn't been about feeling like her vulnerability was being exploited at all. It was something about the thought of getting close to Tom, of moving on from David.

With her gaze out the window, her mind sifting through the myriad of emotions her meeting with Tom had stirred in her, Lacey was interrupted by the sight of some people strolling down the cobblestones, whispering. They paused, one of them pointing at her store, then all hurried onward.

Lacey felt a pit of trepidation open up in her stomach. News of Iris's murder was spreading like wildfire, and people seemed to think *she* had something to do with it! This wasn't how she thought her life in Wilfordshire was going to go at all, and as the hours ticked by without a single person coming into the shop, Lacey felt worse and worse. Every time she peered through the window toward the patisserie, she saw Tom with his usual busy trade. Yet not a single person decided to venture into her store.

Her gaze went to the man sitting on the bench beside the red mailbox. Despite the cool, early spring temperature, he'd been there for at least an hour now, engrossed by his phone, earbuds in. Either he was totally addicted to his apps, or something more sinister was afoot. That's when Lacey noticed something peculiar—he wasn't wearing standard cell phone headphones. The earpiece was made of thin plastic that looped around his ear. The wire was thin, snaking in through the collar of his bomber jacket. It wasn't even connected to the phone at all.

Lacey gasped as she realized she was looking at a plainclothes police officer.

Superintendent Turner was keeping tabs on her! If the police thought she might have something to do with killing Iris, what chance did she have with the locals?

CHAPTER FOURTEEN

Back at home, Lacey was just in the middle of heating up her shepherd's pie in the microwave when she heard the sound of a dog barking coming from outside. Her immediate fear was that Chester had somehow gotten out of the house, and so she bolted for the front door. But as she pulled it open, revealing a clear evening sky blanketed by twinkling stars, she realized it was Boudicca who was barking. Coming up the path behind the Border Collie was Gina.

"Cooey! Lacey!" the woman called, waving an arm over her head in a big arch, as if Lacey were a mile away rather than a matter of feet.

Chester appeared by Lacey's legs, sniffing the evening air and, presumably, the scent of another dog.

"Is everything okay, Gina?" Lacey asked.

Gina reached the porch step. She was panting, as if she'd hurried here.

"I heard what happened," she said, puffing her cheeks and grabbing the wooden post for support. "You should've come to me right away!"

"You mean about Iris Archer?" Lacey asked, her stomach swirling anew with that now familiar sense of apprehension. "Honestly, I didn't realize it would be such hot gossip." She slumped her shoulder against the doorjamb. "Besides, I didn't want to burden you."

"This is a small town," Gina said. "New spreads fast. Especially when you have awful women like Taryn around, who like nothing more than to gossip and spread rumors!"

Lacey started. *"Taryn?"* she exclaimed. "What on earth has *she* got to do with it?"

Gina explained. "I overheard her in the Coach House telling Brenda the barmaid that you killed Iris and stole her antiques."

Lacey felt her legs weaken—and suddenly, the doorjamb she'd wedged her shoulder against was the only thing keeping her from falling to the floor.

She knew Taryn hated her, but this was going way too far. This wasn't just some loud music making her walls vibrate, or a purposefully disruptively placed sandwich board—this was someone actively trying to ruin her. To tarnish her reputation, which would in turn ruin her business, her livelihood, and ultimately the new life she was beginning to build for herself here.

"Why would she do that?" Lacey stammered, completely taken aback by the level of vitriol that must be required in order to behave in such a manner.

Gina tutted and shook her head. "Who knows what makes people tick. I'm an old lady and I still haven't figured out the mystery of humankind."

Lacey shook her head. This wasn't okay. This was so far from okay. And she wouldn't stand for it. For years she'd had David standing in the way of her true happiness, and Saskia, and even Naomi and her mom. Now it was time for her to do things her way. No one would stop her.

She looked up at Gina with resolution. "Come in. We're having shepherd's pie."

The next morning, Lacey was a different woman. She and Gina had spent the evening strategizing, and today her trusty neighbor would be taking over shop duty so that Lacey could play sleuth and clear her name.

Lacey sipped her coffee, feeling focused, determined, and filled with drive. Pen in hand, notebook open on the table, she went online to the local Wilfordshire news site. The murder of a local elderly aristocrat was obviously the main story, with numerous spin-off articles also devoted to it. She read each one with a meticulous eye for detail, combing for anything that may be a clue, and wrote each one neatly down in her pad in a bullet point list. As she scanned through, two things on her list leapt up at her:

- No forced entry
- No defensive wounds

So this was evidently done by someone Iris knew, Lacey thought, tapping her pen on the notepad. *Probably even someone she trusted. That poor woman.*

Lacey had seen enough cop shows in her thirty-nine years to know that the main suspect in most homicides was the person closest to the victim, and so she jotted down the names of the deceased woman's family members—a younger half-sister whose Alzheimer's had seen her committed to a care home for the last three years; a son, Benjamin, a successful businessman residing in South Africa with his wife and children; and a daughter, Clarissa, whom one paper scathingly referred to as "the spinster CEO of a bankrupt fashion brand."

The papers also told Lacey that the estate, Penrose Manor, had once been owned by the aristocracy, and passed down the generations through the male heir line through the system of primogeniture. So, presumably, her son was set to inherit the estate. Perhaps he'd flown over to settle the will. Maybe he was at the house right now!

Lacey leapt up, her chair scraping against the kitchen tiles. "Come on, Chester, it's time to solve this crime."

Her trusty companion trotted beside her as she left Crag Cottage—cautious to deadbolt the door with the Rapunzel key, her paranoia spiking thanks to the threats of yesterday—and headed into the car.

On the one hand, Lacey knew how suspicious it would make her look to drive back to the scene of the crime, but the other part of her knew she was going to have to take risks if she stood any chance of clearing her name. And so that's exactly what Lacey decided to do.

When she reached Penrose Estate, she saw the remains of the police cordon tied to the trunk of a tree, flapping in the breeze, the only evidence of the gruesome crime that had been committed within its walls.

With her heart slamming into her rib cage, Lacey went up to the door and knocked. Her hunch that someone would be home was correct; the door was opened by a man with a grief-stricken face. He looked to be around fifty. He'd certainly be around the right age to be Iris's son.

"I'm sorry to disturb you," Lacey said. "I'm Lacey Doyle. I was—"

"I know who you are," the man snapped back.

Lacey noted his accent—it was regional, not South African and not plummy like Iris's, either. This wasn't Iris Archer's son at all, but someone else entirely. Someone unrelated.

"The police told me," the man continued in his same abrupt, angry manner. "You were coming over here to value her antiques. If I hadn't been out collecting her prescription you'd never have had a chance to hurt her!"

"I didn't do anything to her," Lacey refuted. "I didn't take a single one of her antiques. They're all there. I'd be a pretty bad burglar if I killed the homeowner without taking all their stuff, wouldn't I?"

The man paused.

"Who are you?" Lacey asked. "You're not her son."

He shook his head. "Not by blood, no, though I've shown her more care than either of her awful children ever did. I'm Nigel, her valet. *Was* her valet, I should say. We were very close. I live here." He began to weep. "Now I don't know what's going to happen! She left me the responsibility of settling the estate and I've no idea how to do anything like that!"

Lacey found that curious. Iris had children. A son, who should automatically inherit the estate. "Why aren't her kids figuring all that out? Surely the estate should go to them in her will?"

Nigel paused and stared at Lacey. He went to close the door. "What am I doing talking to *you*?" he said, as if musing aloud. "You're the police's main suspect!"

"I told you, I did nothing to hurt her. And by the sounds of things you were the last person to see her alive. So you'll be a suspect as well, even if the police haven't told you as much."

"I have an alibi," he said haughtily. "Which is more than can be said for you. Now get off my porch. Go on, go away!"

He slammed the door in Lacey's face.

She took a step back.

Nigel the valet was certainly suspicious. He ran errands for Iris—getting her prescriptions, for one—but it had been Iris herself who'd come to see Lacey in person. Perhaps she didn't trust Nigel when it came to her antiques. Could he have killed Iris purposefully when he knew she had an appointment so that someone else other than him would find the body?

Whatever was going on, Lacey thought it was all very strange, and she was determined to get to the bottom of it. For her reputation. Her store. And for Iris.

CHAPTER FIFTEEN

Lacey got into her car and took out her cell phone. She found the little business card she'd been given by DCI Beth Lewis during her questioning and dialed the number. She wanted to know what was going on with the investigation—if Taryn was spreading malicious and unfounded rumors about her involvement, she had a right to know what the police were doing about it.

But as she listened to the ringing through the speaker, Lacey realized that she wasn't going to get anywhere with them. The cops were suspicious of her too—the plainclothes officer outside her store yesterday was all the evidence she needed of that.

On the spur of the moment, Lacey decided that the only way she'd get any info out of the police would be if she pretended to be someone related to Iris Archer. She made a snap decision to pretend to be a daughter, and put on her best British accent.

The call connected.

"Hello," Lacey said, pronouncing the word as if it were spelt with three o's. "I'm calling to speak to Superintendent Turner regarding Iris Archer from Penrose Estate."

"Who's calling?"

"This is her daughter." Lacey paused, wracking her mind for the name of the daughter that she'd read in her research. "Clarissa," she blurted the second she recalled it. But her surname escaped her.

Luckily, the receptionist didn't seem to need a full name.

"Transferring," she said.

There was a pause. Lacey could feel her heart thrumming while she waited to be connected to Superintendent Turner. She may have

95

fooled the receptionist, but it would be a different matter entirely fooling a police detective. They were trained to smell BS, after all, even if it was coming through a telephone handset.

"Superintendent Turner," the familiar gruff voice came on the other end, giving Lacey an immediate mental image of the man who'd been so rude to her that dreadful morning a few days ago.

"Hello, it's Clarissa, Iris Archer's daughter. I wanted an update on my mother's case."

There was a long pause.

"And you're Clarissa Archer?" Superintendent Turner said finally.

Archer, Lacey thought, recalling how the papers had described her as unmarried.

"That's right," she said aloud.

There was an agonizingly long pause. Superintendent Turner seemed very fond of them, Lacey thought.

"Really?" he said finally, in a slow, drawn-out manner.

Uh-oh. He was on to her.

"Yes," she tried, in her poor attempt at a well-to-do British accent.

In the seat beside her, Chester gave her a look of derision. Even he wasn't falling for it.

"Let's stop playing games," Superintendent Turner said in her ear. "I think you're Lacey Doyle, putting on a fake English accent. A very *bad* fake English accent, I might add."

Damn. She'd been caught.

"I don't understand what you're saying," she said, grimacing, her voice about ten octaves higher now than when she'd started. "This is Clarissa Archer. Iris Archer's daughter."

"No it's not," Superintendent Turner barked. He'd clearly reached the end of his rope and had snapped. "I know it's not because Clarissa Archer is sitting at the station as we speak!"

Lacey gasped. Clarissa was there? If she could speak to her, perhaps she'd be able to get some useful information on the case.

"I mean…" the Superintendent began to say, clearly in an attempt to backpedal from the confidential information he'd just blurted in a moment of frustration.

But there was no backing out of this one. What had been said had been said.

Lacey hung up and punched the air.

"Come on, Chester, let's go speak to daughter dearest."

She turned the ignition of her car and drove away at speed.

Lacey parked around the corner of the station. Her champagne-colored rust bucket of a car was hardly inconspicuous, so it was better for her to keep it out of sight.

"Chester, you can come with me," she told the dog. "But you must be completely quiet, okay?"

Chester raised his head and regarded her with his intelligent eyes. It really looked as if he understood the instruction, and since he didn't whine like he normally did when she spoke to him, Lacey decided that must mean he'd understood every word she'd said.

They walked around the corner together. It was an overcast day, dark enough to activate the automatic streetlights. Each time Lacey passed beneath one, it felt like a spotlight being shone on her.

The police station was sleek looking, with bright yellow light streaming from its large glass front onto the paving slab steps leading up to it. Lacey and Chester shuffled into the hedges to obscure themselves from sight and watched silently, with bated breath.

Before long, the glass door was pushed open and a woman exited the police station, trotting down the steps with a handkerchief up to her eyes. She was dressed quite glamorously, and Lacey recalled that she'd once run—then run into the ground—her own fashion brand.

"That must be her," Lacey whispered down to Chester. "Clarissa. Come on, let's go and see what she's up to."

Chester gave her a silent look of understanding and followed Lacey as Lacey, in turn, followed the woman.

The three moved along the street, Lacey and Chester staying close to the protection of the straggly hedgerows, the daughter rummaging in her purse for something. Just then, Lacey heard the tinkle of keys and deduced that the woman must be heading for the single car parked against the sidewalk.

"Quick," Lacey said to Chester. "We'd better talk to her before she drives away."

Lacey was more than acutely aware of the fact that approaching a lone woman on an empty street was far from polite, but with her reputation on the line, she had no choice but to do it. She hoped Clarissa Archer didn't carry pepper spray.

"Excuse me," Lacey said, hoping that an overly formal greeting would ease any terror her sudden appearance might spark in the woman.

Clarissa swirled, startled. "What? Who are you? What do you want?"

She didn't seem to be reaching for pepper spray, and so Lacey relaxed and took another step forward. Clarissa had her mother's eyes—dark brown, sparking with astuteness—but unlike the kindness Lacey had seen in Iris Archer's eyes, her daughter's were filled with suspicion.

"I'm sorry, I didn't mean to startle you," Lacey began. "My name is Lacey Doyle. I'm an antiques dealer and I had a meeting with your mother—"

"The day she died," Clarissa interrupted. With a cold tone, she added, "I know who you are. What do you want?"

"I wanted to ask you about Nigel," Lacey said. "Your mom's valet. Did you know him well?"

Clarissa shook her head. "No. But Mother adored him. She never stopped talking about him." She dabbed at her eyes with the kerchief. "Why are you asking me that?"

"He told me that he's the one settling the estate," Lacey explained. "That your mother left it to him in her will. But I thought there were all kinds of laws around estates, about them staying within the family and passing down the firstborn male's line."

Clarissa sighed loudly, as if she thought Lacey was a moron. "Like most English estates, Penrose Manor had that law written out about a hundred years ago. My mother inherited it from her father, after all, and she's not the firstborn male, is she?"

Her condescending manner made Lacey bristle. It reminded her of the way Saskia would speak down to her. Lacey drew on all her years of experience of handling Saskia to remain cordial in the face of this rude woman. The important thing was to keep Clarissa speaking, even if the woman couldn't help herself from schooling an ignorant yank.

"So yes, before my mother the estate passed down the male bloodline, but it's changed now and she has the liberty to leave it to whomever she wanted." She punctuated her words with gesticulations, several rings adorning her fingers, and bangles around both wrists. "She could've left it all to her cat, Albert, if she'd taken the fancy."

Lacey let what she'd heard sink in. "So, if there hadn't been a change in the law, your mother wouldn't have inherited the estate in the first place?"

"My goodness, there is a brain in there!" Clarissa said snootily. "My mother was the oldest of two girls. Her sister had a son first, so if the old laws were in place, it would have been he who inherited the manner."

"And that son would be your cousin?" Lacey clarified. "The son of your aunt, who has Alzheimer's?"

The woman's brown eyes narrowed, becoming even colder. "You seem to know a lot about my family."

"Only what's been printed in the papers."

Clarissa scoffed. "Yes, and we all know we can trust what we read in the papers!"

Her sarcasm was obvious to Lacey. Being referred to as "the spinster CEO of a failed fashion brand" had obviously gotten under her skin.

Clarissa folded her arms, her metal bracelets jangling. "Why are you so interested in what the papers have to say about my family anyway?"

Lacey didn't think it was a good idea to reveal that she was a suspect. "Your mother knew my father. I haven't seen him since I was seven. I thought she might be able to help me answer some questions about him."

Clarissa arched a single eyebrow, clearly unmoved by Lacey's plight. "Well, I'm afraid there's nothing to be done about that now. Once Mother's buried, I'm going back to London to put this rotten business out of my mind. Now if you'll excuse me."

She unlocked her car, slid into the driver's seat, and slammed the door shut in Lacey's face.

Lacey hopped back onto the sidewalk as the car kicked into life and Clarissa sped away into the gloom, her brake lights quickly becoming two floating red dots as the car was swallowed by the mist rolling in from the ocean.

Lacey shivered beneath the darkening clouds. Clarissa's irritation was evident. But it felt to Lacey like its cause was much, much more than just the incessant questioning of a meddling stranger. There was definitely a strange family dynamic going on in the Archer family, one that Lacey suspected had something to do with the history of Penrose Estate, who had inherited it, when, and from whom. Clarissa Archer seemed bitter about something, and Lacey was going to find out what.

CHAPTER SIXTEEN

The fog had thickened considerably as Lacey drove toward Crag Cottage. Her headlights barely illuminated the rocks and shrubbery that lined the narrow cliff-side road.

I guess this is a typical British springtime, Lacey thought with a smirk.

As she turned into her driveway, pebbles crunching beneath her tires, the beams caught something in them—a silhouette of a shape that was distinctly human.

Lacey's heart began to race. Was there a shadowy figure lurking on her front lawn?

She squinted through the windshield. But the mist was too dense for her gaze to penetrate.

She looked over at Chester in the passenger seat. He whined. Her guard dog and protector was as sharp as a tack. If he wasn't barking, then surely everything was safe. That flash of a figure must've been a figment of her anxious imagination, a ghoul born out of stress.

She got out of the car.

"Aha!" a voice exclaimed.

Startled, Lacey swirled on the spot. A person was emerging through the mist like an apparition. Her legs began to shake.

That was, until Lacey saw their features. Sharp jawline. Handsome eyes.

"Tom?" Lacey exclaimed, the terror leaving her body in one sudden whoosh. "What are you doing here? Why aren't you at your store?"

"Paul took over my shift so I could knock off earlier and make something special for our dinner," Tom said conversationally, clearly oblivious to how much he'd startled Lacey. "I went into your store to see if you ate fish and met Gina, who told me you'd taken the day off. So I figured if you were home, I may as well come right over"—he held up his trusty basket—"and do the cooking here."

The plan they'd formulated yesterday morning suddenly slammed back into Lacey's mind. She'd been so wrapped up in her detective work, she'd forgotten all about their date. Or not-date. Whatever it was.

Feeling terrible for having forgotten about him, Lacey quickly fumbled in her purse for the Rapunzel key.

"Have you been waiting long?" she asked, as her fingers anxiously combed through her overstuffed purse.

"Not really," Tom said with a breezy shrug. "Only half an hour. Give or take five minutes. Well, give ten minutes."

"You were waiting *forty* minutes?" Lacey exclaimed, her still empty hand withdrawing from the purse as her gaze automatically went up to the gray clouds.

"It was a nice day when I got here!" Tom justified. He could probably tell how eager it appeared for him to have been waiting around in misty conditions for the last forty minutes. "I just sat on the cliffs and read a book. Besides, I had plenty of company."

He gestured to the right, where Lacey saw a group of Gina's sheep had munched their way around to the front lawn.

"Those belong to Gina," Lacey said, plunging her hand back into her purse in an even more frantic effort to find that blasted key.

"Gina from the store?" Tom asked.

"Yes, that's right. She's my neighbor. Her sheep come over here to dine."

"Free gardening service," Tom joked. "Maybe I should get some sheep too."

Finally, Lacey found the key. It had fallen right to the bottom of her purse, of course. She unlocked the front door and pushed it open.

"Come on, let's get inside before it starts to rain," she said.

Chester muscled his way in first. Lacey wondered why he hadn't barked at Tom emerging from the mist. Evidently, the dog was a very good judge of character and could sense Tom was a friend even before he'd gotten a good visual on him. He probably recognized his smell.

Tom stepped over the threshold into Crag Cottage and Lacey tugged him by the arm down the corridor toward the kitchen as if in an attempt to make up for lost time. The basket swung between them.

"There's not a teapot in there?" she asked, recalling the hilarious moment Tom had produced one from his basket at lunch. If he'd pulled the same stunt again this time, it would surely be cold.

Tom laughed. "No. Just the ingredients to make salmon coulibiac."

They entered the kitchen. Tom whistled as he looked around. His eyes practically bulged at the sight of the original Arga.

"Salmon coulibiac?" Lacey asked, slinging her bag into a chair. "I've never heard of that."

"It's a Russian dish," Tom explained. He placed his basket on the counter. "Pastry-wrapped spicy salmon." He turned to face her. "You do eat fish?"

"Yes. I love it."

Lacey went over to the cupboard where she stored the wine, very much wanting a glass. Her day had been particularly trying, and she was flustered by Tom's sudden appearance. She hadn't mentally prepared herself for seeing him. When was the last time she'd touched up her makeup? She buried her face in the cupboard and called out, "What wine should we have to complement the dish?"

"A Viongnier or white Rioja would be perfect if you have either," she heard Tom say. "Failing that, a Pinot Grigio will do."

"Pinot Grigio it is," Lacey said, a little embarrassed by her unsophisticated wine collection.

She transferred the bottle from the wine rack to the fridge to cool; she had enough worldly knowledge to know white wine was supposed to be served chilled, at least.

Tom had already begun unloading the ingredients from his basket onto the counter. He'd brought a huge blob of pastry—presumably made up during his day at the patisserie—and it was wrapped up in a muslin cloth like it was some kind of precious gem. Then he removed the huge salmon fillet, the sight of which made Lacey's mouth begin watering with anticipation. She realized that she'd been so caught up in the whole murder mystery, she hadn't eaten anything since her cereal bar, and before that, the closest she'd come to a "proper meal" had been Gina's reheated shepherd's pie (not that that could be classed as "proper" food; for all Gina's awesomeness, she was a terrible cook).

Lacey took a stool at the island as she watched Tom scour her kitchen for just the right pots and pans, weighing each one in his hand before turning it over and knocking the undersides. Once he had everything he needed within hand's reach, he got to work on the salmon coulibiac.

Lacey rested her chin on her fist. "So where did you learn to cook a Russian coob-ee-ak?" she asked.

Tom chuckled at her mispronunciation. "Coulibiac," he said. "And I learned it in Moscow."

Lacey's mouth dropped open. "No way! You've been to *Russia*?"

"I've been to a lot of different countries," Tom said. "If you want to learn to cook a dish properly, you're best off doing it in its country of origin. I make a mean curry thanks to a week training in Delhi, and to die for jerk chicken thanks to Jamaica. But you can probably guess that as a pastry chef, I spent the longest time training in Austria and France."

"Hence the infamous macarons," Lacey replied in an almost dreamlike voice.

She was awed by Tom's life experiences. Especially considering she herself had rarely left the States, and even then it was mainly for work trips, where she'd be shunted straight from the airport to auction house or display room or conference, without the chance to experience any of the culture.

"Exactly. We're having kouign amann for pudding, which originates from Breton."

He pronounced the name of the French region with a perfect accent that made Lacey swoon.

"I've never heard of it," she said. "Queen-armarn, I mean, not Breton. I've heard of that."

But only because France was the country she and David had spent their honeymoon in, she reminded herself.

Still, Lacey didn't feel the usual sense of intimidation she normally did when dealing with people more knowledgeable than herself. The annual work parties David had dragged her to were always mortifying experiences for Lacey; conversations flew over her head, David's boss had it stuck in his mind she was an "upholsterer's assistant," and someone, without fail, would ask her if her dress was by a certain designer she'd never heard of, prompting her to reveal that it was actually off the rack. Speaking to Tom was a breath of fresh air. Even if he'd done more and knew more about the world than she did, he didn't gloat about it. He didn't talk arrogantly. There wasn't even the smallest hint of showboating in his personality. It made Lacey feel able to let down her guard in a way she rarely did.

"Kouign amann is basically a croissant," Tom replied with a laugh. "The big difference being it's folded up like a little origami square, and slow baked so all the layers puff up perfectly."

His passion for cooking glinted in his eyes, making Lacey smile.

"I can't wait," she replied, feeling a bit like she was slipping into a dream.

Tom had even brought all his spices, and Lacey watched as he put cardamom, cloves, and chili into the pan. He did everything with the same theatrical gestures as he did when frosting his cakes or preparing cream tea and scones. She loved watching him. Whenever she cooked—which was rarely—she'd try to get everything done as quickly as possible. But Tom took care with every step of the process, from cutting the fish to the way he gently pressed the pastry into the dish.

"Oh, the wine is probably cold now," she said, hopping up and taking it from the fridge.

She poured them both a glass.

"Cheers," Tom said, holding his up to her. She clinked hers against his, remembering the joke he'd made with the quarters of scone when they'd first met. It already felt like a lifetime ago.

"So, what did you get up to on your day off?" Tom asked, as he set his wine glass down on the counter and returned to his task. "Anything fun? Or did you just need some space away from the local gossipers?"

Lacey hesitated. She wasn't sure whether she should divulge anything to Tom about what she'd really been doing. Surely it would make her seem like a bit of an oddball. But then she remembered how Tom had seemed very interested in the mystery of Chester's deceased owners. Maybe he would be interested in this mystery as well.

She decided to bite the bullet and go for it.

"I was talking to Clarissa Archer. Iris's daughter."

Tom stopped mid-chop, the knife hovering in the air as he glanced over his shoulder at her. *"Really?"*

Lacey couldn't fully decipher what his expression and surprised tone were conveying. Either he thought she was a complete lunatic, or he was genuinely curious about what she'd learned. She proceeded with caution, assuming the former was more likely than the latter.

"Superintendent Turner accidentally let slip that she was at the station, so I went down there to speak to her. I'm hoping to find some information that might help me to clear my name."

"You're playing amateur detective?"

Tom laid the knife down and picked up his wine glass, turning so his rear end was resting against the counter. The casual posture suggested to Lacey that he was actually on the side of intrigued, and she felt a surge of confidence.

"Yes, I am. I'm not going to stand around and let my reputation turn to filth."

"Good for you!" Tom exclaimed. "Tell me everything. What did you find out?"

He flashed her an encouraging smile. Finally accepting that he wasn't judging her, Lacey decided to open up to him about everything.

"I found out that Iris left her estate to her valet rather than her kids."

"Oh yes, I read something in an article about that once. She always said that her responsibility as a mother was to provide her children with all the tools they needed to succeed in the world, not give them handouts." He shrugged. "Seems a bit rich coming from a woman who lived off of handouts."

"I think that's why," Lacey explained. "Iris wasn't happy about inheriting the estate. Her daughter said she was the first person to benefit from the law change regarding male heirs and it caused a rift in her family, between her and her sister, and her nephew who would have been the next in line if the law hadn't changed. I can only guess she wanted to prevent the same thing from happening with her own kids."

"That's a good point," Tom said. "I hadn't thought of that. But leaving the estate to her valet? That's surely going to stir up some bad blood."

"When I spoke to him, he said that she treated him like family. It was weird."

"You spoke to him too?" Tom exclaimed.

Lacey realized then that Tom was more than just interested, he was fascinated. And there seemed to be an air of admiration in his tone.

"I did," she said, her cheeks warming with pride instead of embarrassment for once.

Tom suddenly seemed to remember his coulibiac sitting on the counter, and turned around.

"I'm really impressed by your fortitude, Lacey," he said, as he carried the dish over to the Arga and placed it inside. Then he collected his glass of wine and sat on the stool opposite her at the butcher's block table. "Do you think she was killed for her money?"

He gazed into her eyes with deep contemplation and curiosity.

Lacey wasn't used to someone being so attentive to her. David certainly hadn't been, at least not after those first few months of newly wedded bliss had worn off. With Naomi she couldn't get through a sentence without being interrupted, and her mom was prone to emotional breakdowns when anything more taxing than the weather was discussed. And then of course there was Saskia, who could go an entire day barking orders at her without once making eye contact. Over the years of interacting with them, she must've unwittingly absorbed the belief that nothing she said was of any worth, and so to now have someone looking deeply into her eyes—someone stunningly *gorgeous,* no less—well, it made her feel a whole host of new sensations.

She drummed her fingers on the countertop. "I mean, that would be the most obvious explanation. But the valet did seem genuinely torn up. He'd have to be a really good actor to fake that kind of grief."

"So one of the kids?" Tom suggested.

Lacey shook her head. "You said it was public knowledge that Iris wasn't leaving them anything in her will. They'd be set to gain nothing from her death."

"She might have had a good life insurance policy though. A wealthy rich woman like that?"

"Maybe," Lacey said, considering his point.

"Or maybe someone was trying to coerce her into changing her will," Tom added. "You hear about that all the time. Someone who makes friends with the elderly just to get them to leave all their money to them."

"That's awful," Lacey said.

"Some people are evil," Tom said.

Lacey pondered his words. Could someone have gone to Iris's house that morning to get her to change her will? Or to steal from her? Maybe Lacey had interrupted them mid-burglary. There had to be more to the story.

With their theories exhausted, Tom retrieved the spiced salmon coulibiac from the Arga—putting the dessert inside to cook while they ate—and placed it on the table in front of them.

All conversation about Iris Archer ceased as Lacey tucked into the pastry-wrapped fish and rice, spiced with cardamom, cloves, and chili. It tasted divine. The salmon was baked to perfection, its subtle flavor perfectly complemented by the unusual combination of spices. The pastry was similar to the rich, buttery one Tom made his scones with, but a savory version. The whole meal was rounded off with the perfect amount of chili to make her mouth tingle but not make her eyes or nose water.

Once they'd consumed the main course, Tom retrieved the kouign amann from the Arga and presented the little steaming parcels of flaky excellence to the table. The pastry had puffed up into layers. Lacey's taste buds tingled with anticipation. Even Chester raised his head at the smell.

"These look awesome," Lacey said.

She took one and bit into it, the layers of pastry crackling beneath her teeth.

The taste of caramelized sugar flooded Lacey's mouth and Lacey realized instantly that she'd tasted it before. She was hit by a memory. Not of her father, for once, but one from much more recently in her life: her honeymoon with David fourteen years earlier. They'd spent two weeks in France, during a glorious heat wave whereby a single cloud hadn't blemished the sky. They must have tried the dessert at some point during that wonderful fortnight of wedded bliss.

Lacey suddenly became overwhelmed with emotion.

"Are you okay?" Tom asked, concerned.

She put the pastry back down onto the plate, feeling foolish. "I'm sorry, I had a memory. Of my ..." She paused, uncertain she wanted to go into her ex with her new romantic interest. But this was *Tom*. He seemed interested in everything she had to say. He didn't have a single judgmental bone in his body. "My ex-husband," she finished.

Tom nodded slowly, sipping his wine as if to bide time. "I was wondering how you were single."

Lacey blushed and shrugged. "Now you know."

"Well. I'm divorced as well."

"When did you divorce?" Lacey asked. "If you don't mind me asking."

"Not at all. Last year. And you?"

Lacey counted back in her mind. "Two weeks tomorrow."

Tom almost spit out his wine. "Two *weeks*? How are you functioning? I was a shell of a person for at least the first month."

"Maybe because separating from David was exactly what I didn't realize I needed to do."

She was shocked by the certainty with which she said it. All along, she'd been thinking the divorce had been foisted upon her and this whole trip to England was her making do with a bad situation. Now she realized it was a blessing. She'd never have gone if she'd not been shoved, and yet look at the life she'd already built up around her!

So Naomi had been right. It hadn't been the ultimatum that had ended things with her and David... it really had been a choice Lacey herself had made.

Tom raised his glass to Lacey's. "Amen. Let's drink to that."

Lacey clinked the rim against his and smiled, the feelings that had been evoked by the intrusive honeymoon memory already gone. Now she felt like there wasn't anything in the world she couldn't face.

Even if it was a murder mystery she'd found herself in the center of.

Chapter Seventeen

Lacey decided to walk into work the next morning, taking the beach path she'd discovered on her first day at Crag Cottage. She needed to clear her head, and a long stroll with Chester was just the way to do it.

Because the path took her a different direction than her car route, Lacey passed the coffee shop where she'd gotten her first Americano. She decided for nostalgia's sake to buy one from there.

The same barista who'd served her the first day was behind the counter. As she joined the short queue, Lacey flashed her a friendly smile. The woman narrowed her eyes.

She must not remember me, Lacey reasoned.

But when it was her turn to order, she was shocked by the words that left the woman's lips.

"What are *you* doing here?"

She said it with such hostility, Lacey was taken aback.

"I just wanted to get a coffee," Lacey said.

The woman shook her head. "I'm not serving you."

"I'm sorry, what?" Lacey stammered, completely shocked.

"I heard what you did," the woman added, her voice now a hiss. "You killed Iris Archer." Her eyes fell to Chester then. "*And* you stole the dog from the home and garden store!"

Lacey was stunned by what she'd heard, and what she'd been accused of. But it seemed extremely unwise to correct the woman by explaining Chester's owners were deceased, because she'd probably find a way to blame Lacey for that as well!

111

"You're not welcome here anymore," the woman finished. "So go away."

Lacey staggered back out of the store. Her heart was racing. How terrible. How could these people really be accusing her of such a dreadful crime? It was so awful.

Feeling low, Lacey scurried out of the store, Chester in tow. As she hurried along the cobblestones toward the safety of her store, she felt like every pair of eyes was on her.

By the time she reached her store, her heart was beating wildly. She let herself in, shutting the door securely behind her.

Once inside, she felt a little calmer, but she was in no hurry to open the shutters or turn the *closed* sign to *open*. Instead, she peered out through one of the gaps in the metal sheeting, surveying the street to see if Superintendent Turner had sent any more plainclothes police officers to keep tabs on her. She couldn't see anyone suspicious.

With her heart rate now back to normal, Lacey decided it was time to open up fully, and so she raised the shutters and wedged open the door with a heavy metal paperweight. Chester, evidently satisfied that it was business as usual, took his spot beside the counter.

Lacey stayed by the door, watching the streets. The morning tourists were milling around, as well as many of the locals. A lot of folks seemed to be turning their heads and whispering to one another as they passed her store.

In the patisserie opposite, Tom's store was filled with customers as per usual, and there was an average amount of footfall going into Taryn's boutique next door. It was only Lacey's store that everyone ignored.

With a horrible crushing sensation, Lacey realized just how damaging the rumors were going to be to her business. This wasn't just Taryn whispering to a few people in the Coach House, this was a whole town of folk who no longer trusted the outsider. People genuinely thought she was a murderer! How long before they got their pitchforks and ran her out of town? She was going to have to ramp up her investigation if she stood any chance of not only keeping her business afloat but perhaps even keeping it from an arson attack.

Feeling panic begin to rumble through her body, Lacey heard her cell ringing. She took it from her pocket and saw an unfamiliar number on the screen.

The sight of an unrecognized number made her panic even further. What if the same person who'd bombarded her landline with accusations of murder had gotten hold of her cell number as well? She was already rattled, the last thing she needed was another accusation thrown at her.

Cautiously, Lacey hit the green button and answered the call, her breath stalling in her lungs.

"Lacey?" came a man's voice.

The accent was familiar to Lacey, but she couldn't quite place it. Where had she heard that voice before?

She frowned, panic giving way to curiosity. "Yes. Who am I speaking to?"

"It's Nigel. Nigel King."

Lacey gasped. Iris's valet? The man currently claiming bronze-medal position on her list of suspects? What was he doing calling her?

But before she had a chance to ask her question aloud, Nigel answered it.

"Can you come to the estate? I think we need to talk."

Lacey couldn't work out if she was crazy or desperate, but she found herself agreeing to meet Nigel that evening at Penrose Manor.

Ending the call, she looked over at Chester. He gave her an alert look of contemplation.

"What do you think, boy?" she asked. "Am I crazy or desperate?"

He tipped his head to the side, raised an eyebrow and whined.

"That's what I thought, too," Lacey replied.

At the end of a customer-less day, Lacey locked up the store, collected her car from Crag Cottage, and drove to Penrose Estate. It was the third time she'd visited the manor house, and far from the awe it had inspired in her on first sight, the place now looked foreboding and unfriendly. Lacey shivered.

"Come on, Chester," she said, getting out of the car.

The English Shepherd hopped out after her and walked in perfect synchronicity beside her up the rosebush-lined path to the front door. Last time she'd been here, Nigel had accused her of killing Iris Archer herself. Returning felt extremely unwise, but with her whole life in England on the line, what other choice did Lacey really have?

Squaring her shoulders, Lacey raised her fist to knock on the door. To her surprise, it swung open. She staggered forward and slammed right into someone. Nigel.

"Oh!" she exclaimed.

"Sorry," he said, catching her by the elbows. "I heard your car coming up the drive."

Lacey looked over her shoulder at the old Volvo.

"I guess its engine is pretty loud," she conceded, brushing herself down.

Nigel moved back from the door, gesturing for her to enter.

Swallowing her nerves, Lacey went inside.

They walked together into a drawing room.

"Please sit," Nigel said.

Lacey did, perching awkwardly on the edge of the elegant couch. She felt extremely uncomfortable to be sitting on a dead woman's furniture to have a chat with someone who might be said woman's killer.

"Why did you call me?" Lacey asked, jumping into the deep end with both feet, in an attempt to get this over with as soon as possible.

"I realized what you said was true," Nigel told her. "The collection of items Iris wanted to appraise was right where she left them. If you'd killed her in an attempt to steal her expensive collectibles, well then you'd done a terrible job of it because you'd left every single one of them behind."

"Thank you," Lacey said, relieved. At least someone was seeing sense at last!

"I can only apologize," Nigel continued. "For being so suspicious of you. I guess I fell for all the rumors."

Lacey squirmed. She was suspicious of Nigel, after all. She'd pegged him as a suspect.

"Will you come and look at the items?" Nigel asked. "Iris wanted them appraised by you. In a way, it was her last living wish. I feel we ought to honor that."

Despite her wariness, Lacey felt humbled. And curious. "Of course."

Nigel led her up the vast, sweeping staircase into a room at the front of the house. It was a very regal study—a big desk with a banker's lamp took up one corner, a stack of papers and letters on it. There was a large bookshelf filled with crimson leather-bound books, beside an archway that presumably led into a separate, more private, offshoot of the room. Beneath the large windows was a chaise lounge with a small table beside it. Lacey could imagine Iris sitting there, reading the morning paper as daylight streamed through the windows.

"Here," Nigel said, opening a drawer in a matching dresser that sat behind the desk. "I stored them all away for safekeeping, but these were all the items she had laid out ready to show you."

Lacey gasped as its contents twinkled under the lights. It looked like there was a *lot* of stuff in the drawer, and a lot of sparkly treasures too.

Nigel began to carefully remove each boxed item, laying them on the desk side by side. There were watches, rings, and necklaces— a lot of things Lacey had no real understanding of, her experience being in furniture and ornaments. She didn't have any real working knowledge of how to appraise jewelry.

"I can't value these," Lacey confessed, her stomach dropping at the realization she was woefully underqualified for the task that had been presented to her. "I don't know if Iris realized, but I value ornaments rather than jewelry."

"I'm sure she knew," Nigel assured her. "She wanted you to do it. She was insistent about it. She didn't even want me to go to your store and speak to you, she wanted to do it herself. To see you with her own eyes. Iris was a strong believer in intuition, you see, and she trusted you to do the job. I don't want to go against her last wishes and find someone else. Please. It has to be you."

Lacey recalled the way Iris had stood in her shop and told her she reminded her of her father. She felt a lump form in her throat. Though she didn't understand, a feeling of resolve overcame Lacey. She could do this. For her father. For Iris.

"Well?" Nigel asked. "Will you do it?"

Lacey nodded. "I will."

Nigel visibly sagged with relief.

"But it will take me a while," Lacey qualified, thinking of all the antique dealer contacts she'd have to hassle. "I'm going to have to make a lot of phone calls."

"In which case, I'll fetch you some refreshments," Nigel said, his mood instantly lightened. "Tea? Coffee? Cakes? Or some fresh-pressed apple juice from the estate's orchard?"

"How about all of the above?" Lacey said with a grin. "Like I said, this will take some time."

"Take as long as you need," Nigel told her. "I'll be back shortly."

He left the room, and Lacey flopped into the desk chair, losing herself in the welcome distraction of work.

❧ ❧ ❧

The voice of Percy Johnson, Lacey's Mayfair contact, crackled through the earpiece.

"Ten. Possibly eleven if the right auction house sold it. Thousand pounds, I mean, of course."

Lacey's grip on the telephone handset tightened, and her mouth dropped open as she penciled the price of the ring onto her list of items.

Unsurprisingly, Iris Archer's items had turned out to be extremely valuable. Amongst the treasures, Lacey had found artisan crystal and Swiss pocket watches, the types of things that fetched tens of thousands of dollars in New York auction rooms, the types of things that even an untrained eye would know were very valuable. None had been taken by the murderer—the itemized ledger she was working from listed them all—despite them being laid out and in plain sight. And since none of them were particularly rare, traceable only by a serial codes that could easily be filed off by your average dodgy pawn-store clerk, then money couldn't have been the motive. It was all very strange.

"Tell me, Lacey," Percy said in his doddering manner, his accent about as close to an English king as Lacey could imagine, "Where did you come across this hoard?"

"It's a long story," Lacey replied. She rubbed the furrow between her brows. "And a little too complicated to get into right now."

"Fair enough," Percy replied kindly. "But if you're planning on auctioneering it, I'd be very interested in buying some of the pieces. Some of them are very easy sales that fetch a lot indeed!"

"Oh, no, I won't be auctioning them," Lacey explained. "I'm just valuing. But I can let you know what auction house it does eventually go to, once it's decided."

"Thank you, my dear. That's most kind and attentive. I shall await your correspondence with bated breath."

Lacey responded to Percy's extreme Britishness with her own Americanness. "You bet!"

She put down the phone and uncurled herself from the desk chair. Every bit of her ached from the hour she'd spent hunched over, totally absorbed in the valuations. In fact, it had been so enjoyable, Lacey hadn't even noticed the time passing. She'd been "in the flow," that creative Zen-like state where time lost all meaning. Maybe she really did have a natural flair for valuations. Maybe it ran in the blood, passed down to her through her father. The thought comforted her.

In desperate need of a stretch, she stood and cricked her back. No use. It still ached. She'd have to pull out the big guns—yoga poses. Naomi had taught her yoga after a "transformative" trip to India. Well, taught might not be the right term for it. *Forced* was more apt. Every morning for a month she'd dragged Lacey to the park for sun salutations and positive affirmations, only to give up on the whole spiritual thing after a particularly gin-soaked work event reminded her how much she loved liquor. But Lacey had secretly gotten a lot out of their sessions, and often found herself returning to the practice in order to calm her frantic mind.

She went through some of the postures, mirroring her breath to her movements in that way that was so calming. As she maneuvered herself into downward dog, her gaze went through the gap in her legs and to the archway in the wall. Her curiosity about what was on the other side was piqued, and so she straightened up to standing and paced over, peering inside.

The small room on the other side was in darkness, the window covered by a red velvet curtain so thick its effect was like a blackout blind. There was a couch and armchair, positioned in such a manner as to remind Lacey of a therapist's office, the coffee table, plants, and vases making it even more so. A large fireplace took up one wall and, looking rather out of place in the otherwise serenely decorated room, was a large grandfather clock made from walnut wood.

Lacey was immediately drawn to the clock. Her father had loved clocks, and she paced over to get a better look.

It was beautiful. It had clearly been hand-crafted, a pattern of twisting roses etched into the dark mahogany wood by an artistic and skilled carpenter. The pendulum was bronze and it hung motionless behind the glass door.

The sound of the study door opening made Lacey turn. She headed back through the archway into the main part of the study to see Nigel holding yet another cup of steaming coffee for her, and a pouch of kibble for Chester tucked under his arm.

"There you are," he said, handing her the mug.

"Thank you," she said, gratefully. "I was just stretching my legs. The grandfather clock in there is stunning."

"It's beautiful, isn't it?" Nigel agreed, straightening up from where he'd been filling Chester's bowl. "I can't remember the full story but it's a one of a kind. It doesn't work anymore, sadly. No one can fix it because the cabinet is locked and the key lost. Iris got a locksmith to look at it once, one who was experienced in antiques, and he explained that if he picked the lock, it would scratch the piece and devalue it by a few thousand pounds. Iris decided it would be better to have an unticking clock than a damaged one."

"That was a smart call," Lacey said, thinking how her father would have done the exact same thing if presented with the same dilemma. Altering an antique was basically sacrilege as far as he was concerned. "Besides, it functions just as well as an objet d'art."

Nigel looked over to the desk, at all the acrylic boxes containing the treasures Lacey had been appraising. "How are you getting on here?"

"At the moment, we've topped over a hundred thousand pounds' worth. And I'm barely a quarter of the way through. Is it true that she's leaving everything to charity?"

"Yes, that's correct," Nigel explained. "She vowed to pass all her wealth to charity. She had an extremely strong moral compass, and thought the laws of inheritance were deplorable. She didn't want her children doing nothing with their lives, resting on their laurels while they received monthly allowances. She had nephews and cousins who lived like that, throwing money away on gambling. Some of them ruined their lives over it. There's quite an addictive streak in the family for gambling and she didn't want to enable that behavior in her own children. So, no allowances and no inheritance. The children knew there'd be nothing for them in her will once she died. If they wanted to become a neurosurgeon or an astronaut or anything their passions desired, then she'd pay for them to go to the top university to train. She'd pay for all the tutors and the equipment. Everything. Even if they changed their mind, she never complained. Clarissa spent years being schooled in piano by one of the finest teachers money could buy, only to decide she was done with music and wanted to be a sculptor! More courses and training from the best of the best, and what does she decide to do at university? Business!" He sighed. "But Iris never ever complained. As long as her children could show her they had passion, drive, and a strong work ethic, she'd do everything she could to support them. But handouts? Absolutely not. She was a very principled woman." His voice cracked with grief.

Lacey felt for him. "What did her children make of that?"

"I honestly don't think they really believed her. Benjamin especially seemed convinced the law would protect his male heir rights. I'm sure he's shocked now he's seen the will for himself and knows how precisely it was worded, in order to prevent it being twisted in any way."

"Do you know them?" Lacey asked. "The children?"

Nigel shook his head. "Not well. The daughter, Clarissa, lives in London, so I've met her a few times when she came over to see Iris. Can't say I cared for her much. It seemed like every visit ended the same way—her getting furious that her mother wouldn't buy shares in her failing business or help her out of debt. The sons, I've never met. They both live abroad."

"Sons? Plural? You mean to say Iris had three children?" Lacey was surprised. All the research she'd done in the papers had only ever spoken of two. One son, one daughter.

"Yes, that's right. The eldest son runs a business in South Africa. He's a bigshot CEO with a model wife and three perfect model children and couldn't care less about his family back in the UK. All he cares about is money and beautiful women. The youngest lives in Australia, and as far as I understand, he inherited the gambler's gene. Iris doesn't invite him over to the house because of his temper. He once clocked the chef square in the face for spilling soup in his lap."

Lacey listened attentively. "Why don't the papers ever mention the third child?"

"Ah," Nigel said, with a knowing nod. "There's a bit of a story behind that. You see, there's quite a gap between Clarissa and the youngest. Eight years, I believe. By the time he came along, Iris had gotten injunctions against the press reporting on the kids because of this terrible scandal with Benjamin being awarded inflated grades by the headmaster—to make sure those expensive school fees kept coming in, you see—and some awful business over the paparazzi stalking Clarissa. Iris became especially protective over Henry. His birth was never announced, or printed, and his name never publicly made known. He went to a different school to his siblings. As far as I understand, his famous connection was never actually discovered."

Lacey was becoming more intrigued by the third mysterious son by the second. "And how did Henry feel about all that?"

Nigel let out a rueful laugh. "Well, let's just say there's a reason he chose to move to the opposite side of the world." He sighed. "Poor Iris. What a waste of energy. She was trying to do the best by them but the three turned out bitter. And the boys were terrible to their sister, too, because she was 'only a girl.' Ben must've spotted the devious streak in Henry off the bat, because he used him like his gofer. Henry would do *anything* Ben asked of him; trash Clarissa's stuff, spread rumors about her, all kinds of nasty things. She became quite troubled over it all, and still has therapy for anxiety to this day. Whether it was nurture or nature with Henry, I'll never know, but he never grew out of that mean spirit. At least he channeled it into his work eventually. He wasted his twenties partying, but he settled eventually, and I believe his chain of surfing stores are quite profitable now."

"Do you think the sons will come to the funeral?" Lacey asked Nigel. "Flights from Australia and South Africa to the UK must take ages and cost a ton. Based on what you've told me, it sounds like neither of them liked their mother enough to visit her while she was still alive, let alone for her funeral."

"Coincidentally, all three were in England at the time," Nigel replied.

Lacey paused. Slowly, she raised her eyebrows. Well, now *that* was suspicious! The three children of a dead wealthy heiress just happened to be in the country she lived the day she died?

Nigel must've read her expression, because he started to shake his head. "It's not them. I thought the same, believe me. But no. Henry was in London, a two-hour drive away, visiting Clarissa at the time the coroner's report says Iris died. Benjamin was in Devon for a business conference. Clarissa begrudgingly gave Henry an alibi— although I suspect she was tempted not to, just to see him stew in jail—and Benjamin's key card shows he was inside his hotel room at the time of the murder."

"So all three have alibis," Lacey said. "And the police have checked they hold up?"

"I assume so," Nigel replied with a small shrug. "Really, they may be awful people, but I can't see any of them purposefully harming their mother. Clarissa's so mentally fragile she needed grief counselling for a year after the family dog was put to sleep. She faints at the sight of blood. She closes her eyes if there's so much as a dead body on television! I doubt she'd be able to see one in the flesh, much less cause someone's death. And Benjamin wouldn't hurt his mother, either. He's more of the manipulative type. He's a 'don't get mad, get even' type. If he had a reason to harm his mother, he'd do it through lawsuits and cruel words rather than physical harm. And Henry…" He paused. "Well, from what Iris has told me, Henry *has* been violent in the past. But she wrote most of that off as stress from his gambling addiction. Since he found his wife and settled down and started his surfing business, he's been much calmer. If Henry was angry with his mother, he'd be more likely to just distance himself from her. Indeed, as he has done." He shrugged again. "The children aren't suspects. If only because they had nothing to gain from their mother's death."

Lacey let his words sink in, absorbing all the tidbits he'd given her and padding out the picture the papers had formed. Along with Nigel and herself, the three children would definitely be high on the police's suspect list, and by the sound of things they'd already found enough evidence to exonerate them all.

Just then, Lacey heard the sound of car tires coming from the gravel drive outside. She looked to Nigel and frowned.

"Sounds like we have guests," he said, curiously, pacing over to the window to peer out. Then he gasped and glanced back at Lacey. "You'll never believe it. It's them! The children!"

Lacey hurried to the window and glanced out as two vehicles parked in the drive. Out emerged the three children of the late Iris Archer.

Well, well, well, Lacey thought. *Things are about to get very interesting.*

CHAPTER EIGHTEEN

The siblings were already hammering on the door by the time Lacey and Nigel hurried down into the corridor. The valet opened the door to them. The three were clearly in a foul mood, with matching scowls plastered across their features.

They barged inside, overpowering Nigel, not waiting to be invited.

Lacey hung back, Chester at her ankles emitting a low growl, but Clarissa noticed her.

"What is *she* doing here?" she demanded.

The sons turned their attention to Lacey as well.

"Who is she?" the youngest asked. His skin was bronze, evidence of how he'd only recently come over to England from Australia.

"The antiques dealer!" Clarissa exclaimed indignantly. "The one the police think killed Mother!"

Lacey balked. But Nigel stepped up as if to protect her.

"The police are following a number of leads," he explained calmly. "Your mother personally hired Lacey. She trusted her and so do I."

The kids glared at her. It was all very tense, and Lacey felt like she'd prefer to be anywhere in the world right now rather than here.

"Please," Nigel stammered. "You know you're no longer allowed to be here. This isn't your home, it's my private property and you're trespassing."

"Not yet," Ben said, waving some papers in Nigel's face. "You obviously didn't read the will closely. There's a clause right here!

We're allowed anything that belonged to us when we were children, and we have the right to enter the house in order to do so. You can't block us access from the things that are rightfully ours."

Lacey wondered about the character of these three people, that they'd barge in here and demand some old toys. They didn't seem to be sentimental types, and she wondered why they were so adamant about getting their hands on their old stuff. Sure, there was a chance that *some* of the items were valuable—like the vintage annuals Lacey had enjoyed reading in her father's old store—but even they didn't fetch much. Were they so determined to profit from their dead mother's estate that they'd settle for *anything* over nothing?

Nigel flashed Lacey a look that told her he'd been very aware of the clause in the will, and let out a weary sigh. "You've read the will very diligently," he said through pursed lips. "So I presume you're aware that there's also an itemized ledger, and that there must be lawyers present to prepare documents indicating who is taking what from the property."

Lacey thought of the neat ledger she'd been working from.

Ben brought his face up close to Nigel's. Chester began to growl.

"Then we'll just look," Ben said through clenched teeth.

Despite his threatening demeanor, Nigel stood his ground. "By all means," he replied.

With a harrumph, the three Archer children marched past him and thundered up the staircase.

Lacey caught Nigel's eye, then they both followed after them.

"Keep an eye on them," Nigel whispered out the side of his mouth as they ascended the staircase. "We must make sure they don't sneak anything out they're not supposed to. Knowing them, they'll take something then sue me for theft."

Lacey nodded.

They went into the playroom. The children were already waltzing around, examining things.

"Where is the grandfather clock?" Ben demanded. "It used to be right here!"

He gestured to a patch on the floor where the wooden boards were a different color, the perfect size and shape of the base of the clock Lacey had just minutes earlier been admiring.

So that's what they were really here for! The unique clock was surely worth a fortune, even in its unworking state. One of them must've realized it was their best bet at getting some money out of their mother.

"Iris had it moved to her study," Nigel explained calmly. "It was amongst the items she wanted Lacey to value and sell."

His words sent a bolt of confusion through Lacey. She was under the impression that Iris had hired her to value a drawer full of jewelry and nothing more, certainly not a rare grandfather clock. Had Iris actually intended for her to undertake significantly more work than Nigel had led her to believe?

She held her tongue, not wanting to fan the flames by admitting to her cluelessness, instead choosing to put on a united front with Nigel in the face of these angry individuals.

"Show me where it is," Benjamin demanded. "It's ours."

He seemed quite agitated. Lacey wondered why the clock was so important to him, beyond the fact that it was evidently more valuable than any of the other items in the playroom.

He's money hungry, Lacey noted. *Addicted to getting it, as much as Henry once was to gambling it away.*

Nigel remained stoic in the face of Benjamin's mounting fury. "You cannot take the clock," he said.

"Why not?" Henry interjected.

It was the first time he'd spoken, Lacey noted. Unlike his siblings, he appeared quite calm on the surface. There were no hints of the past streak of anger Nigel had mentioned—indeed, if she'd had to guess which of the brothers had a troubled past, she would've picked Benjamin, who had anger etched into every furrow on his brow. Henry, on the other hand, just seemed exhausted. During the tense altercation inside the manor house, his golden skin had turned pale, giving him an unwell appearance. Of the three, he looked like the only one who was actually grieving.

Lacey tuned back into the conversation.

"The wording of the will was very precise," Nigel was saying to Benjamin. "You are entitled to *anything inside* the playroom."

"That's wrong," Ben spat. "We're entitled to anything that belonged to us when we were children."

The standoff was extremely uncomfortable.

"Iris had the clause reworded," Nigel finished.

Silence swelled like a balloon.

"What?" Clarissa asked, her voice meek in comparison to her overbearing brother.

She seemed like a shell of the woman Lacey had met in the alleyway. She was pale, like Henry, her anguish expressed in her face in exactly the same way as his. Henry was reserved, showing few signs of the angry streak he'd apparently once possessed. In stark difference, their bulldozer of an older brother showed no outward signs of grief at all. Lacey filed all her thoughts and suspicions away in the back of her mind.

"The wording was changed?" Henry asked, as if he had not fully comprehended what that would mean.

Nigel nodded. "Yes. Her lawyer came the day before she died. The clause was rewritten in a manner that ensured it could not be misinterpreted in any way."

Misinterpreted? Lacey thought ruefully. *More like deliberately twisted...*

The three children were stunned into silence.

"She really had such low opinions of us," Clarissa finally said. She folded her arms with a bitter look on her face.

Justifiably so, Lacey thought wryly, *considering how you're now acting...*

"I don't believe you," Ben accused Nigel. "I bet Mother changed the will and then you moved the clock yourself, so it wasn't inside and could be amongst the items you sold for profit."

Nigel shook his head. "I can assure you I do not set to profit from the sale of any of Iris's items. The money will all go to charity. Every last penny."

Lacey didn't know what to believe. The grandfather clock was very large in the small study offshoot, not to mention the fact it didn't even tell the time. Whether Iris had moved it there, or Nigel had after her death, there was evidently only one reason for it—to prevent her children from getting their hands on it.

But why? Why had the woman gone to such great lengths to stop her children profiting after her death? Because she was afraid they may harm her for her money? Or because she was attempting to prevent the same squabbling and drama that had torn her own childhood family apart?

Whatever Iris's intentions had been, Lacey felt suddenly relieved that she came from a humble background; the only things she and Naomi would have to squabble about in the event of their mom's death was her flat-screen TV and a double-sided refrigerator.

Clarissa and Henry's gazes went to their feet, but Benjamin kept his chin up and glared squarely at Nigel.

"We'll be back," he finally said. "And we'll be bringing our lawyer."

"I think that's for the best," Nigel replied.

The three marched out of the room and Nigel and Lacey followed them as they thundered back down the stairs and out the door, slamming it shut behind them.

The whole thing left Lacey stunned. She felt like she was standing in the aftermath of a hurricane.

"What *delightful* people," she said.

Nigel turned to her. "I'm so sorry about all that, Lacey. You shouldn't have had to bear witness to that kind of behavior. I'm sorry you were dragged into it."

Lacey folded her arms. "You mean about valuing the grandfather clock?"

He nodded. "It was me who moved it, on Iris's instructions, I must add. And not a moment too late, evidently." He shook his head. "I should have been honest from the outset about what Iris wanted you to do here. She wants *everything* in the house valued, then auctioned so the profits can go to charity. The jewelry was meant to be a trial run, you see, to gauge whether you were indeed the right person for the job. But I can tell she absolutely would have gone on to hire you for the rest of it. So, what do you say? Will you appraise the rest of the furniture?"

"Well," Lacey said, thinking about all the doors she'd seen, each one containing a room that must be filled to the brim with treasures. "That will be a lot of work to do alongside my store."

"Please," he added. "You saw what the children are like. They're vultures. I've no doubt they'll try to find loopholes to claim things that weren't really their childhood items. You saw what they were like with the clock, for goodness' sake! I thought Iris was overreacting when she instructed me to move it to the study. But now I can see where she was coming from."

Lacey was filled with empathy for Nigel. His grief was real, more so than that of Benjamin and Clarissa, Iris's own children, who seemed to be dealing with the death with anger and hostility.

"Yes, okay, I'll do it," she told him.

Nigel sagged with visible relief. "And you'll auction everything too?"

"Auction it?" Lacey repeated.

She opened her mouth, then closed it again, almost too stunned to speak. She'd been dreaming of holding an auction and now suddenly the opportunity was here!

"Me?" she asked, timidly, feeling suddenly intimidated.

"You," Nigel said, nodding with affirmation. "There's no time to waste. The children are probably calling their lawyers as we speak, searching for a loophole that will let them bleed the estate dry against Iris's express wishes. I have the estate's lawyer on speed dial. Let me call and see if he'll oversee the handover."

"Now?" Lacey squeaked.

This was all going so fast. On the one hand, Lacey was facing the most exciting opportunity of her new career. But the circumstances surrounding it were gruesome at best, and the suddenness of it all was intimidating her.

"Maybe I should take a day to think about it," she said. "The manor has a security system, doesn't it? You can keep the children out one night."

Nigel shook his head and spoke firmly. "All it would take for them to get inside is a call to a locksmith. There's not a single person in Wilfordshire who'd question whether the children should have access to the estate or not. And even if they did, who in their right mind would be able to stand up to Benjamin? You saw him." He looked frantic. "Lacey, we *must* take everything to your store for safekeeping. Nothing is safe here."

Lacey had to admit he was right. She had specialist insurance to store antique items. And she was also itching to appraise everything, like Golem with his precious ring. But would Lacey be putting a target on her back if she transported Iris's items to her store? Nigel seemed to think the children were capable of theft, and at the moment none of them knew where she worked. How quickly would that change?

But the look of anguish on Nigel's face made Lacey's mind up for her.

"Okay. I'll store them. And I'll learn everything I can about how to hold an auction."

Nigel grabbed her hand and shook it with gratitude. "Thank you, Lacey. I'm eternally grateful."

Lacey took his gratitude gracefully, though she felt less than comfortable about her part in the plan.

CHAPTER NINETEEN

That evening, Lacey sat cross-legged on the floor of her store's large back room. It was no longer empty, now stuffed to bursting with some of the more treasured items from Penrose Manor.

It had all happened so fast—Nigel calling the lawyer, arranging the specialist deliverers, the paperwork being signed, following the large removal van from the manor to her store. Lacey felt like she'd blinked and her back room was suddenly full.

It was only once the flurry of activity had died down that Lacey was able to take stock. Some of Iris's items weren't covered by her specialist antiques insurance. The gold Grecian harp, for example. She knew from her rare instrument contact in Suffolk that there were only a handful of specialist companies who would insure such a rare and magnificent item.

And then there was the unique, handcrafted, one-of-a kind grandfather clock. Lacey didn't even know where to begin with regards to insuring that.

She sat staring at all the acrylic boxes filled with jewels and looked over at Chester lying beside her, his flank butted up to her left knee so she could feel his steady, rhythmic breathing. He was a very patient companion, Lacey thought, considering how her schedule seemed to be all over the place at the moment.

She gazed back at the gems laid out before her, her mind going to the woman they'd previously belonged to. Iris Archer. She wondered if there had been motive after all for the children. Even if it was public knowledge they were set to inherit nothing, Nigel had said Benjamin was convinced the law would favor him as the male heir. At the very least he *thought* he could gain from Iris's death, and he'd seemed like the instigator of the playroom raid as well. But if he had murdered his mother for her wealth, was an itemized ledger really enough to stop him from taking Iris's treasure? He'd had to have been pretty confident the law would fall in his favor to risk leaving everything behind. Wouldn't it be easier to steal the items and amend the ledger than leave them all behind on the presumption the clause in the will could be twisted?

And besides, was a few thousand pounds really worth murdering your own *mother* for? Benjamin was a successful businessman in his own right. He probably worked with six figures on a daily basis. While she understood the power of addiction—the one Nigel said ran in the Archer family's genes—something didn't quite add up.

"I guess staring at them all night won't get me any answers," Lacey said with a sigh as her eyes roved over all the precious gems.

She'd called Percy Johnson, her Mayfair dealer, regarding auctioning them, and he'd agreed to help her properly appraise all the items through a video call. She was so excited about it all, she wished the call was happening tonight, but she couldn't exactly demand time from an elderly man, so she'd have to be patient.

Chester whined in response to her words. She looked over at him and patted his head. "You just want your walkies, huh?"

His eyes sparked with understanding and he began to wag his tail eagerly. Lacey couldn't help but chuckle.

"All right, all right. I'll stop staring at it all and lock this stuff away."

She collected all the boxes and placed them in the safe. Then she checked the back door was securely locked, and headed back out through the front store onto the street, closing and shuttering everything up behind her.

The lights were still on in Taryn's boutique, but Tom's patisserie was in darkness. Lacey had a vague recollection about him playing badminton on Thursdays.

She headed toward her car. But then she heard Chester growl.

She turned back. He was standing by the store where she'd been a moment earlier, looking at the shutters and growling.

With a frown, Lacey hurried back to him.

"What's wrong, Chester?" she asked.

He barked, loudly, insistently. Lacey heard a sound coming from inside the store. A loud crash. The sound of breaking glass.

"If that's Taryn kicking over my trash cans again ..." Lacey said aloud, her eyes flicking over to the brightly lit boutique, "then she's messed with me one time too many."

She fumbled to unlock the shutters and heaved them up. Then she unlocked the door and hurried inside, Chester racing past her barking all the while.

As she hurried into the auction room, Lacey felt sharp wind blow into her face. Glass littered the floor, catching on the moonlight.

She gasped as she saw the back door standing several inches open, the wood splintered as if someone had used a crowbar to force it open. This wasn't Taryn ... surely not!

Suddenly, there was movement. A masked figure sprung up from behind the safe and went streaking across the room toward the back door. It was like something from a horror movie and Lacey felt herself freeze on the spot. But Chester leapt into action. He moved in a blur, charging at the figure.

"Careful!" Lacey cried.

The stranger might be armed. The last thing she wanted was her dog getting hurt.

But Chester ignored her cries.

He leapt, jaws exposed, and latched onto their ankle. Lacey heard the assailant cry out, their deep voice indicating they were most definitely male.

He began to shake his leg, trying to get Chester off. Lacey saw something long and metal flash in the moonlight. A crowbar. He was going to strike her dog!

"Chester!" Lacey bellowed, her voice no longer frantic but commanding.

This time, the dog obeyed. He released the man's leg from his jaws.

The man staggered back, the arm holding the crowbar flopping to his side. Then he scurried out through the broken door.

"Stay!" Lacey commanded Chester, since the dog looked like he was about to take chase. "It's not worth it. Just let them go."

Lacey felt her chest sink. So the hounding had begun. Only the mob wasn't carrying pitchforks, they were armed with crowbars.

Lacey saw the flashing blue lights from all the way at the other end of the long high street. The harsh, bright lights looked so wrong on the quaint historic street, beneath the pretty gingham bunting. This witch hunt against her was certainly ruining any sense of idyll.

As the police car approached, Lacey waved her arms over her head to flag it down, and it pulled to a halt against the curb. The driver's door opened and DCI Beth Lewis emerged from the vehicle. From the passenger door, rising up slowly and nonchalantly like nothing ever roused him, was the bulky frame of Superintendent Turner.

He turned and fixed his gaze on Lacey. Her chest sank.

She'd called the police to report the break-in—first incorrectly dialing 911 in her confused, panicked state, before remembering it was 999 in the UK—and had been expecting them to send over their usual on-the-clock staff. Instead, the two detectives had come themselves. Way to make it obvious they suspected Lacey was fabricating the whole thing. They already thought she was a murderer so faking a burglary at her own store wouldn't take too much of a leap of imagination.

"Miss Doyle," Superintendent Turner said flatly, bobbing his head once down then back up.

"Good evening," Lacey said, rubbing her forearms from the chill of the evening and the superintendent's frosty tone.

"You called about a break-in?" he asked, with about as much emotion as someone reading the TV listings.

She nodded.

"What's been stolen?" Superintendent Turner asked.

"Nothing," Lacey told him. "I was working late. I'd literally just locked up when I heard them breaking in through the back door.

They must've been waiting for me to leave. I hurried back in and interrupted them before they were able to take anything. *If* that was why they were breaking in in the first place. A lot of people around here are out for me since they incorrectly think I'm a criminal now, thanks to you guys."

The superintendent ignored her jab. His eyes were roving from the metal shutters Lacey had now fully raised up, to the double glazed storefront windows and door.

"You were able to hear a break-in at the back of the store through double glazing and thick metal?" Superintendent Turner stated flatly.

Lacey's jaw tightened. "*Chester* heard it." She gestured down to her trusty companion sitting obediently at her feet. "He started barking and alerted me."

Superintendent Turner's expressionless gaze fell to Chester. "The dog?" He sounded nonplussed. "The dog saved the day?"

"Yes. The dog," Lacey replied tersely. "He's very smart."

"And do you think Lassie would be able to identify the perp out of a lineup?" Superintendent Turner returned in a dry, sarcastic manner. He didn't even smile at his own joke.

Lacey's arms tightened even more against her chest. She chose not to rise to him. "Would you like to come in?"

DCI Lewis answered, her eyes darting from the superintendent to Lacey as if a little uncomfortable with the atmosphere. "Yes, we'd better. Can you show us where they gained entry?"

She was the more diplomatic of the two. Lacey wouldn't go as far as to say she liked the woman, but she liked her a whole lot more than Superintendent Turner.

Lacey led the two detectives through the main store and into the auction room where the wind was making the back door bang against the frame, its lock having been broken by the crowbar. Shards of glass from the window littered the floor.

"So the door was jimmied open," Superintendent Turner said, looking at the splintered wooden frame. "But they also broke the window?"

"I assume the window broke from the force of the door swinging open and hitting against the wall," Lacey countered.

"Oh, you assume that, do you?" Superintendent Turner said, dispassionately.

DCI Lewis interjected. "You said you interrupted the assailant. Did you get a visual on them?"

"Just his silhouette. He was hiding behind the safe." She gestured toward it.

"He?" DCI Lewis said.

Lacey nodded. "Chester bit him. He shouted out. It was definitely a man."

"I'll call the hospital to see if anyone's admitted themselves with a dog bite," DCI Lewis said.

Superintendent Turner nodded in affirmation.

"You're lucky you're in the UK," the man told Lacey. "You'd get sued for the medical costs if your dog bit someone in the US, wouldn't you? Litigation Nation and all that."

He was trying to rattle her. Lacey wasn't going to let him.

"So he sprung up from behind here," Superintendent Turner said, knocking his knuckles against the top of the steel safe. "Was he targeting it?"

"Maybe," Lacey said. "He was holding a crowbar so there's a chance he was going to try and get inside."

"What's kept in here?"

"Jewelry," Lacey said.

"Is that typical in an antiques store? To keep jewelry in a safe?"

"It's standard practice in any store to keep small valuables in a safe."

"Right. But what I'm getting at is that this was targeted. For some reason, your store was chosen. Maybe what's inside this safe is the reason."

Lacey really didn't want to divulge the truth. Surely it would make her look super suspicious. But holding back information from the police was the worst of two bad options.

"They're Iris Archer's jewels," Lacey said tensely. "Her valet has tasked me with valuing them and auctioning them."

"Is that so?" the superintendent said, his tone staying as flat as always.

DCI Beth Lewis stepped back over to them. "I've put an alert out to the hospitals to ring us if anyone admits themselves to A&E with a dog bite. What have we found here?"

"Ms. Doyle was just informing me that she has a safe stuffed full of a murdered woman's jewelry."

DCI Lewis's eyes darted to Lacey.

"I was explaining that I'm auctioning them," Lacey said, knowing she must look extremely suspicious right about now. "The valet inherited the estate in Iris's will but her children are trying to get their hands on anything of value. He asked me to take them for safekeeping until they can be auctioned and the money given to charity as per Iris's wishes. I have the legal paperwork to prove it, signed off by a lawyer."

"As the auctioneer you get commission, right?" DCI Lewis asked, completely ignoring the comment about the paperwork. "A percentage from the sale?"

She was correct—not that Nigel and she had discussed the exact fee yet—and Lacey was aware of how black and white it must seem to them—she may not have stolen the jewels from Iris's estate, but she was going to be profiting off them anyway.

"The valet knows they're here," Superintendent Turner said. "Maybe he was the one who broke in."

Lacey shook her head. "Nigel? No way. If it was anyone linked to the estate it would've been one of her kids. Well, sons, since the burglar was a male."

"You sound pretty chummy with the valet if you're on first-name terms with him. Maybe you two cooked this whole thing up together. Commission from the jewels. Extra money from an insurance scam. The lawyer could be in on it as well. It won't be the first time we've dealt with a crooked lawyer, believe you me."

Lacey frowned, growing more furious by the second. "Maybe you should check his leg for teeth marks? Check the sons' legs too, while you're at it."

"Oh, don't worry, we will," Superintendent Turner said. "Any more suggestions for how I should do my job?"

Even DCI Lewis bristled at the comment. "I think we have enough information now to be getting on with," she said, shutting her notepad in a gesture of finality. She handed a card to Lacey. "This is the number of the service we recommend for securing properties after break-ins. They're pretty quick."

"Thank you," Lacey said, grateful that at least one of the detectives didn't have it in for her.

They headed back into the main store.

"A bit of advice," Superintendent Turner said to Lacey as he strode toward the exit. "Don't sell the jewels anytime soon. They might well be evidence, in the break-in, and in Iris's murder."

"If they might be evidence, you should probably get a warrant to take them in for safekeeping," Lacey replied. She was suddenly worried about the fact her fingerprints were all over the plastic cases containing the gems, and that they were probably perfectly preserved thanks to the acrylic surface.

"Look," the man said, gruffly, reminding Lacey of the way he'd snapped at her over the phone. "You don't need me to tell you how bad it would look if you hold an auction right now. In the eyes of the public, I mean."

"You mean the public you're allowing to believe I may be a criminal?"

He stepped closer, in a threatening manner that took Lacey by surprise. Chester growled.

"I'll get a court injunction to stop you," he said between his teeth.

"That won't be necessary."

He backed away. "I'm glad to hear it."

They left the store, DCI Lewis flashing Lacey an apologetic expression. Superintendent Turner didn't look back.

CHAPTER TWENTY

"**K**nock knock."

Lacey glanced up from the store counter to see Tom standing in the doorway, holding his wicker basket. The smell of fresh croissants wafted into the store, making Lacey's salivary glands react immediately, which was a relief; the stress of everything had massively impacted on her appetite.

"What are you doing here?" she asked Tom, her mood automatically lifting at the sight of him. She was having another customerless day. Not even the Chester-petters were coming in anymore.

"I wanted to see how you were," Tom said, coming over and placing his basket on the counter. "After the break-in."

Lacey sighed. "Does *nothing* stay private in this town?"

"I'm afraid not," Tom said. He bit his lip and handed Lacey a piece of paper about the size of the page of a novel. "This had been posted through the patisserie's letterbox when I opened up this morning. Every store on the high street will have had one delivered, too."

Frowning with curiosity, Lacey turned her gaze down to the flier he'd handed her. The local Wilfordshire police crest was printed in the top righthand corner, dark blue against the glossy white paper. There was a yellow-and-black-striped banner with the words WARNING printed in bold red.

Lacey's stomach dropped.

"*There has been a BURGLARY in your area,*" she read aloud. "*PLEASE be vigilant. PROTECT your property by following these simple steps.*" Lacey crumpled the paper up without even reading the bullet point list that followed and snapped her gaze back up to meet Tom's. "What the heck? This is practically advertising me as a troublemaker! How can the police do this?"

Tom gave her a sympathetic look. "It's standard practice over here. Obviously, the victim is supposed to remain anonymous but it took me about five seconds to figure out it was your store that was targeted. I'm sorry. Hopefully this will help a bit."

He produced a teapot from the basket and set it down in front of her. Steam coiled from its spout.

Despite her morose mood, Lacey couldn't help but chuckle at the sight of it.

"Does it have liquor in?" she quipped.

Tom produced two porcelain mugs from his basket and began to pour. "No, it's your classic English Breakfast, but I promise you it'll relax you just as well as alcohol. Better even. No hangover."

He smirked playfully, then reached back into his basket. Out next came a large plate piled with all manner of croissants and Danishes, the whole thing wrapped in plastic wrap—or *cling film,* as Lacey had discovered it was called over here—like some kind of Christmas parcel. Tom unwrapped the mini-mountain of pastries, placed one on a delicate china plate, and slid it across the counter to Lacey. The comfortingly familiar smell of Tom's special pastry wafted into her nostrils.

"You're right," she said. "This is exactly what I need." She'd only managed to force down a banana that morning, which could hardly count as breakfast.

But Tom wasn't done yet. From the basket he began to produce miniature glass jar after miniature glass jar of homemade preserves: strawberry jam, apricot jam, blackberry jam, cherry jam, gooseberry jam…

"I wasn't sure what flavor jam you like best," Tom explained, after noticing Lacey's amused expression. "So I brought one of everything."

"I'm not sure either," Lacey said with a chuckle, selecting the apricot because she liked its vibrant orange color the best.

"So what happened?" Tom asked as he slathered a croissant with strawberry jam. "Last night?"

Lacey shook her head, feeling exhausted and overwhelmed by everything that had been going on. She didn't really want to go into it. But then she reminded herself it was Tom sitting in front of her, and not her mother. He handled difficult situations with calm reassurance, rather than panicked outbursts.

"I'd just closed up for the evening," Lacey explained. "Chester heard something, so I turned back and heard the glass smash. Someone had bashed in the back door with a crowbar. Chester bit them as they tried to run."

"That's terrifying," Tom said sympathetically. "Do you think it was the same person who left you threatening voicemails?"

Lacey paused. She had indeed been thinking someone was out to get her—no one knew what items specifically were in her storeroom. But on second thought, the van Nigel had delivered the jewels in had been far from inconspicuous, especially when one of the items they'd wheeled out had been a six-foot tall, 180-pound antique gold harp, when there'd been a lawyer present. Far from a local thief witnessing the delivery and deciding to try their luck, the break-in could've been for Iris's belongings.

She repeated the moment in her mind when she'd disturbed the intruder. They'd leapt up from behind the safe, which was the opposite end of the room from the back door through which they'd entered. That meant they'd crossed the entire room, passing other obviously valuable items, to go straight for the safe.

"They were looking for something," Lacey said as it dawned on her. "Something specific. If it was a random thief, they would've taken the items closer to the door. And if the attack was against me, they would've damaged something. They had a crowbar, after all, and there were plenty of fragile things around to break. I think it was someone who knew that it was *Iris's* items."

"Who?"

"One of her sons."

Tom's eyes widened with intrigue. "One of her *sons?*"

Lacey nodded. "They barged into Penrose Estate yesterday because the will says they're entitled to take anything from their childhood playroom. But then there's this whole complicated business about Iris having the wording of her will changed to make sure they couldn't exploit a loophole and take a grandfather clock. Nigel was terrified they'd come back with a locksmith in the night and steal it anyway, so he begged me to store some things here for safekeeping."

"Huh," Tom said, contemplatively. "So he might well have been right about the children breaking in. Only he offloaded the danger onto your shoulders."

"He was desperate," Lacey explained, hearing the accusation in Tom's words. "We didn't think the children knew where my store was located, but I guess it's easy to get hold of any information these days online."

Tom was silent for a moment, in quiet consideration. "If the sons were the ones to break in, and they did pass loads of other valuable items, what do you think they were trying to get hold of specifically?"

"They jumped out from behind the safe, so maybe the jewels..." Her voice trailed away as she was hit suddenly by a thought. "Which was next to the grandfather clock! The much disputed clock. *That's* what they wanted. It was all they cared about back at the manor, and obviously the thing they honed in on here."

"I can't imagine it would be easy for one person to steal a grandfather clock on their own," Tom mused aloud.

Lacey paused. "You're right. It would be impossible to move on your own."

"The brothers were working together?"

Lacey shook her head. "There was just one burglar. A lone wolf."

She'd hit a wall. Drawn a blank. She couldn't help but sigh with frustration.

Tom reached across the counter and patted her hand. "It'll be okay, Lace. I know this is stressful right now but it will all blow over."

Lacey froze beneath his touch. *Lace.* David had been the only person to call her Lace in her entire lifetime. She wasn't sure how she felt about hearing the pet name come from Tom's lips.

He must've noticed her tense because he removed his hand from hers.

Just then, the door swung open. Lacey flinched with shock—she'd gotten so used to having no customers it was a surprise to hear the bell tinkle again. She looked up to see Taryn waltzing in.

At the sound of her stilettos clacking loudly on the floorboards, Chester raised his head and grumbled. Like Lacey, he was *not* a fan of the boutique owner next door. In fact, Lacey would quite like to growl at her as well, but social convention meant she'd have to make do with glaring.

Taryn marched toward the counter and slapped the police warning notice down in front of Lacey.

"This is your doing," she said. "Attracting burglars to the area. We were a quiet town before you came along. Now it's all murder and break-ins! If you're not directly responsible for it, you sure are good at attracting criminals."

Tom frowned. "Taryn, have you forgotten about your break-in a few years back? None of us stormed your store and blamed you for it. If I recall, we rallied around to help you. Perhaps you might want to extend the same courtesy to Lacey?"

Taryn looked at him coldly. "Well, Thomas, I think you'll agree that things change."

Lacey picked up on the veiled tone, Taryn's passive-aggressive suggestion that things between her and *Tom* had changed. Did the two have history? Lacey wondered.

Tom, on the other hand, seemed oblivious.

"And when it affects *my* business, I have every right to get involved," Taryn finished.

She spun on the spot and marched away, Chester growling until she was out of sight.

Lacey picked up her teacup and looked over the lip at Tom.

"It'll all blow over?" she said ruefully, then took a sip.

❧ ❧ ❧

After Tom left, everything at the store became very quiet. Lacey busied herself by doing valuation research online and speaking to her antiques contacts in London for their expert advice, a task that absorbed her almost entirely. Though not enough to distract her from the sound of hammering coming from next door.

"You've got to be kidding me," Lacey muttered, looking over at her adjoining wall with Taryn, from which the hammering noise was coming. "DIY? Really?"

She was about to go next door and find out what was going on when she was interrupted by her cell ringing.

She looked down at the flashing screen. Her first surprise was to see that it was her mom calling her. Her mom hated phone calls. She said they frayed her nerves. She only ever joined in on them when Naomi insisted. The second surprise was the fact that—she made the calculation on her fingers—it was only 6 a.m. in New York!

Filled with panic that there was some kind of emergency, Lacey quickly answered the call.

"Mom? Is everyone okay? What's wrong?"

"Wrong?" her mom squeaked. "What's wrong is my daughter is the victim of crime in a foreign country! I'm going out of my mind with worry!"

"Oh. That." Lacey's chest sank. She always regretted keeping her family up to date on her life events. They weren't very good at being supportive. It almost always ended up with Lacey having to reassure them, something she suspected would happen this time, too.

"Yes, that!" her mom exclaimed. "What on earth made you think you can just send me a couple of lines on an *app* about something like that? *'Got burgled. Everything's fine.'*"

Lacey cringed as she heard her mom read her own words back at her, adopting a nonchalant voice that made Lacey sound like a beach bum, and couldn't be further from reality.

"Everything *is* fine," Lacey said.

"No, it's not! England is dangerous!" her mom wailed.

Lacey looked out at the cobblestones and the gingham bunting and Tom's pastel-colored macaron display. *So* dangerous...

"I've just had some bad luck," Lacey said.

"Bad luck? A murder? A break-in? That's not bad luck, Lacey, that's a sign from God or the Universe or whatever it is you believe in these days! It's time to stop this silly fantasy now. You had a good life here! A good job. A nice husband."

Lacey could endure much of her mother's ramblings. But claiming David was a *nice* husband? No way, that was where she drew the line.

"Nice husbands don't use ultimatums to pressure their wives into having children when they're not ready. David left me, remember? Not the other way around."

"David loves you and wants a family with you. What's so bad about that? All you have to do is say you'll have a baby one day and he'll forget all about the divorce debacle in an instant."

Lacey ground her teeth. How had a conversation about the burglary descended into an argument about David?

"He said forty was too old," she said, bitterly, David's harsh words ringing in her ears, the taste of that Merlot echoing on her tongue.

"You're thirty-nine."

"Not for long."

"I don't know what on earth makes you so opposed to it!"

Lacey raised her eyebrows. Beyond her mom's neurotic parenting style? Beyond the fact Dad walking out had emotionally scarred her for life?

"If you don't come back he'll marry that awful Edda woman," her mom continued. "I should say girl really, she's barely legal."

Lacey frowned with confusion. "What are you talking about?"

There was a pause on the other end of the line. It was practically the first time her mother had drawn breath this entire conversation.

"You didn't hear?" she said, finally. "David's seeing someone new. The daughter of a nail salon empire, or something silly like that. They're engaged."

Engaged. The word hit Lacey like a punch in the stomach. Even her jaw dropped like she'd been winded by a blow.

But before she had a chance to say anything in response, the bell above the door tinkled. Lacey looked up to see Superintendent Turner and DCI Lewis coming into the store.

Great, that's just what I need, she thought, her stomach tensing.

Still reeling from the news of David's engagement, Lacey quickly spoke into the cell phone. "I'm sorry, Mom, I have to go."

"Lacey, don't hang up on your mother just because you don't like hearing hard truths—"

"Love you. Bye." Lacey ended the call and looked up at the two detectives striding toward her. "Can I help—"

But rather than stop at the counter, Superintendent Turner marched straight past it. "I need to take another look at the crime scene," he said as he disappeared through the back door.

"—you?" Lacey finished pointlessly, addressing the empty space he'd once occupied.

DCI Lewis reached the counter. "Sorry about him," she said. "He's a good detective, but his bedside manner leaves a lot to be desired."

Lacey shrugged. She'd taken too many blows now to feel anything but numb. "I've got nothing to hide," she murmured.

"Did you get the back door secured?" DCI Lewis asked, propping her elbows onto the counter. She gave Lacey a small, sheepish smile of concern.

Lacey nodded. "Yes, the contact you gave me was very fast. They were here within the hour with plyboards to board it up. Glass repairs are coming tomorrow. Thanks for the recommendation."

"No problem. Happy to help."

It occurred to Lacey then that DCI Lewis was actually attempting to be personable. Lacey wondered whether this might be an opportunity to get some information out of the officer, without her dragon of a partner breathing down her neck, and while she was in a pleasant enough mood.

She quirked her head to the side. "Did you follow up on the brothers?"

DCI Lewis nodded. "Yeah. Henry and Benjamin were in the Coach House last night at the time of the break-in. Brenda the barmaid provided a witness statement."

"They were *here*? On the high street?" Lacey gasped. She'd tuned out the bit about the witness—people were notoriously wrong about times, after all—and honed in instead on the fact they'd been placed barely a hundred feet away from the location of the break-in.

"Yes, but—"

"What about dog bites?" Lacey interrupted. "Did you check their legs?"

Beth's lips turned into a straight line. "They have an *alibi*, Lacey. We have zero grounds on which to conduct a body search."

"But how can you be so certain Brenda's statement was accurate?"

"*Because*," the detective said, her voice sounding weary, "the pub was showing the footie match. Arsenal versus Wolverhampton. The brothers were seen there from kickoff to final whistle. We have a witness statement and the superintendent has been working on all the alibis personally. I'm sorry, Lacey, but your hunch was wrong. The Archer brothers had nothing to do with the break-in."

Lacey felt at a total loss. How could she be wrong? Who else would have broken into her store if not one of the brothers?

Maybe she'd been barking up the wrong tree by thinking the intruder had been heading for the grandfather clock after all. Maybe it really was just a local trying to drive her out of business. Targeting *her*, specifically, to run her out of town.

She sagged. Her mom was right, after all. Perhaps the time had come to admit her dream of living an idyllic seaside life was over.

CHAPTER TWENTY ONE

Lacey maneuvered her laptop so the webcam was pointing at the footstool, oblong with rounded corners covered in golden paisley fabric. On the screen, beamed in live from Mayfair, London, was Percy Johnson, Lacey's favorite bumbling valuer. He squinted through his thick-rimmed glasses, the lag in the connection making him judder.

"Ah, yes," he said in his plummy accent. "That's a lovely piece indeed. So, what is your assessment?"

"Well, it's an ottoman, with a lifting lid. I'd say with that fabric we're talking Victorian. And the feet are mahogany." She paused. "The other Victorian ottomans we've seen were worth about a thousand pounds."

"Yes," Percy said, drawing out the word as if to indicate she was only half correct. "Your average Victorian ottoman fetches around a grand at auction. But the one you have there is certainly rarer. I've seen ones like that sell for twice that, if they're in good condition."

Lacey whistled and jotted down the information. Then she tapped into her calculator to convert the figure into dollars—her mind could more easily comprehend worth in her familiar currency—and saw $3,100.

"Wow," Lacey said. "Okay. And there are at least five of them here."

"That estate is a treasure trove of delights."

"You can say that again."

Lacey was at Penrose Manor, in one of the myriad guest bedrooms at the top of the house. With the auction on hold for the

148

foreseeable future, she'd decided to keep busy valuing the rest of the items Nigel wanted appraised, and Percy was providing her with invaluable support and guidance. Lacey was proud of how quickly she was absorbing everything he taught her. Her eye for Victorian furniture in particular was getting sharper and sharper, thanks to the abundance of pieces the manor contained.

Her plan was to go from room to room—skipping over the contentious playroom, of course, the door of which had remained securely locked ever since the three little piggies had left—working methodically through each one. It was a long task and Lacey was loving every second of it. It really helped her take her mind off her troubles with the police and the store, which was ironic considering she was in the house of the dead woman who'd started this whole thing in the first place.

"Lacey, dear, I must end the call now. Karen is calling me to tea. She's a little exasperated by the amount of time I'm devoting to this. I don't think she's coping well with my hobby taking longer than hers for once."

He said it in good faith, but Lacey still felt guilty. She hadn't even noticed the sky turn dark during their call.

"Oh, I'm sorry," Lacey exclaimed. "Thanks for all your help. Please apologize to your wife. I won't take up any more of your time."

Percy chuckled. "Not at all. I've lost two hours a night for the last thirty years to her French horn practice. It's about time she learned what it feels like when the shoe is on the other foot."

He laughed and they bade one another farewell before exiting the video chat.

Lacey turned to Chester. "Just you and me now, boy. Shall we see if there's anything interesting in the drawers?"

She went over to a dresser, but before she had a chance to pull open a drawer, something peculiar caught her eye. The bottom drawer was partially open, as if someone had pushed it shut in a hurry. In any usual room, that wouldn't pique Lacey's curiosity, but in the pristine guest room, where everything else was meticulously organized, it certainly did.

She sat down cross-legged and tugged open the bottom drawer.

Inside, it was mostly empty. A small hand towel was folded up in one corner. Lying in the middle was a copy of the Bible, a beautiful copy with a red leather cover. She took it out, wondering if, like everything else Iris Archer owned, it was some ancient relic that would be cherished by the right owner if they could find them.

She'd just opened up the cover and began to leaf through the tissue paper–thin pages when something fell from inside and clattered to the ground.

Lacey frowned and picked up what looked like a ring fashioned out of copper wire.

She turned her attention back to the Bible, flipping the pages again until she saw that the ones in the midsection had been cut, as if with a scalpel, to create a small rectangular space. Inside appeared to be an array of handmade jewelry—a necklace made of dried macaroni, woven friendship bracelets made of colorful yarn, and earrings made from milk bottle tops. Clearly the handiwork of a child.

Then Lacey frowned as she saw something wedged at the back of the cut space, like some kind of decorative backing. Was it a photograph?

She turned through the neatly cut pages and the picture that had been inside became dislodged. It fluttered to the floor, landing face down beside her right knee.

Chester made his whining noise.

"I know," Lacey told him, as she reached for it. "How curious."

She flipped the paper and saw it was indeed a photograph. The grainy quality of the image made Lacey think it was taken in the 1990s.

"Oh, look, it's Iris!" Lacey told Chester, recognizing the woman instantly from her distinctive eyes. That sparkle of mischief and intelligence was unmistakable, even in eyes that were twenty-five years younger.

Iris was sitting in an armchair like it was a throne, a martini glass in one hand, a delighted smile on her face. The photographer had caught her in a candid moment of genuine laughter. She was wearing a simple black satin dress, but she'd accessorized it with some distinct gold pieces, including a pair of studded earrings in each lobe, and a delicate chain around her neck with a key pendant that hung just past her exposed clavicle. Her hair—brown, but with streaks of gray—had been twirled into a sophisticated updo, and she was wearing heels that made her crossed legs look long and shapely.

"Wow," Lacey said aloud. "Iris really took the phrase 'aging gracefully' to its glamourous extreme!"

If Lacey herself had the energy to be even half as put together as Iris looked at that age, she'd be thrilled. But she knew in her heart she was more likely to go the way of her mother by reaching for a comfortable chunky knit cardigan and giving up the battle with gray hair before it had even begun.

Lacey's eyes roved over to the other two people in the photograph, two men standing either side of Iris's shoulders.

She gasped and almost dropped the photograph. One of the men looked very familiar indeed. Curly dark hair. Dimples. He looked just like Lacey's father.

CHAPTER TWENTY TWO

"Nigel!" Lacey cried, bolting out of the guest bedroom, the photograph clutched tightly in her hand as if it were a life raft and she were adrift in the ocean. "Nigel?"

She thundered down the first staircase, almost stumbling in her haste to locate the valet and ask him if he had ever met her father, or if he knew anything about how Iris and Frank were connected, to be posing in a photograph like old chums.

Beside her, Chester seemed to have picked up on the urgency in her tone and movement, because he kept flashing her anxious looks, and kept right beside her as if to protect her. But little did Chester know, he couldn't protect Lacey from emotional pain. There was no perp to bite in this scenario.

She reached the landing and peeled along the hall for the main staircase that led down to the foyer. As she went, she slammed right into Nigel coming out of one of the bedrooms. Nigel staggered back several steps, his back hitting the wall with an audible *thud*.

"Oof!" Lacey grunted.

"Are you okay?" Nigel asked, grasping her by the elbow to stop her from falling. "I heard you calling me."

Lacey righted herself. "Yes, I was ..." She paused, seeing Nigel's expression for the first time. His cheeks were stained with tears. All thoughts of the photograph left her mind. "Oh, Nigel. What's wrong?"

"I just realized something *is* missing. Something *has* been taken."

Lacey gasped. "Really? What?"

Nigel showed Lacey into the room. It was a bedroom, bigger than Lacey's old apartment had been, with a space to do makeup and dress, an en suite bathroom, a walk-in closet, and a fireplace with a couch beside it. The wall opposite the couch was filled with hundreds of small framed artworks—mainly depicting women in different outfits throughout the ages, a sort of visual love letter to the evolving art of fashion.

"There," Nigel said, gesturing to a patch where the colors of the wallpaper were more vibrant.

It was a small square, an inversion formed by years of sun bleaching the paper around it. There had been a picture there before, another amongst the myriad hanging on the wall, and it had been removed.

"Wow, how did you even spot that?" Lacey asked. Amongst the sea of paintings, it would take the keenest of eyes to even notice one had gone.

"Because it was a valuable one. A rare original by Lady Isabelle Wiccomb Defante. She was an ancestor of Iris's. She painted women in a variety of natural poses—cradling their infants, brushing their hair, that sort of thing—and it was considered extremely daring at the time. Some claimed it was almost pornographic. So her husband put a stop to her painting. She secretly began to paint miniatures. But when her husband found out, he had them all burned. Lady Isabelle supposedly went mad after that. There was a rumor that one miniature survived the blaze."

He pointed at the small space on the wall.

Lacey, enthralled by the tale of the rebellious Lady Isabelle, widened her eyes. "Iris had the miniature all along?"

Nigel smiled as if reminiscing about his former mistress's devious streak. "She did. Lady Isabelle was her heroine. She wanted to honor her by displaying it. But she didn't want to draw too much attention to the fact she was in possession of such a rare piece of work. It's not in the ledger. She hid it in plain sight, amongst her wall dedicated to fashion."

Lacey shook her head with awe. "She obviously inherited Isabelle's rebelliousness."

"Yes. And her stubbornness." His smile faded as grief took over. "Isabelle Wiccomb is considered a master now, a pioneer amongst female artists. The discovery of her lost miniature would rock the art world, I can assure you."

"Did anyone else know about it?" Lacey asked.

Nigel shrugged. "Honestly, I've no idea. She may have told the children but whether they were interested enough to retain it is another thing. They never paid any attention to Iris's love of fashion so I doubt they cared about art, either. Her sister might well have known. But, as you know, she's unwell with Alzheimer's now. She may have told her husband as well, but he is now sadly deceased. Once I saw the painting was no longer there, I checked to see if she'd moved it to her safe. She'd moved other things before her death as well, as you know. But no. It's gone. Someone must've realized what it was … and … Oh, Lacey, do you think she was murdered for a *painting*?"

Nigel sank onto the couch and broke down in tears.

The sight made Lacey's heart ache. She reached for him and rubbed his back for comfort.

As he wept, she ran through everything in her mind. The person who took the painting must have known the story behind it, or else they wouldn't have singled it out. And they must have known it was there, on the wall.

She looked at the space the rare piece had once occupied. Something about the sun-bleached paper around it struck her.

"Hiding in plain sight!" she blurted. "Whoever took it did so because it was virtually untraceable. The painting was only rumored to still exist. It was hidden amongst all these other works and its removal wouldn't immediately be obvious to the police when they searched the house for signs of theft after the murder. She didn't even have it listed on the estate's ledger, she wanted to protect it so much. All the thief needed to do was wait long enough for the sun to bleach out the wallpaper and no one would be able to claim the painting was ever there in the first place. Whoever took it is literally sitting on a gold mine!"

Despite her excitement at finding a clue, Lacey was more than acutely aware of the reality behind it. An old woman was dead. Possibly over a painting. Her life had been brutally taken from her. It was too horrible to bear thinking. The deviousness needed to plan such a deed left Lacey cold.

Nigel looked up then, his weeping fit having subsided.

"You were calling for me," he said.

Lacey jolted, suddenly remembering the photograph, still clutched in her hand. She'd been so wrapped up in the story of Lady Isabelle and the clue with the stolen painting, she'd completely forgotten all about it.

She held it out to Nigel and he took it with a frown of curiosity. "What's this?"

"I found it inside a copy of the Bible. Someone had cut the pages to make a sort of compartment, and it was wedged inside."

Nigel looked bemused. "What room was it in?" He took the photo from her.

"One of the guest rooms on the third floor. There were some bits of jewelry in there as well, that looked like they'd been handcrafted."

"That sounds like Clarissa. From what Iris told me about her, Clarissa always admired her jewelry and tried to make her own as a child, but the boys used to wreck her creations so she took to hiding them. You must've stumbled across one of her old hiding places."

Lacey frowned. Hiding her creations from her monstrous brothers certainly made sense, but why would Clarissa also put a photograph in there? A photograph of a man who looked like her father!

"Do you know either of the men in the photo?" Lacey asked, purposefully keeping her question vague so as not to accidentally implant any information into Nigel's mind that might lead to a false memory.

Nigel studied the picture for a while, then shrugged. "No, sorry, I don't. This looks like it was taken twenty or thirty years ago. Long before my time at Penrose Manor. Why do you ask?" He handed it back to her.

Lacey felt disappointment settle in her chest. "I just thought it might be a clue. I guess not. Anyway, the missing painting is quite enough of a lead to be getting on with."

Nigel nodded. The discussion of the theft seemed to have turned his mood morose. Lacey decided she'd better give him some privacy with his grief.

"Chester and I ought to leave now," she said.

"I'll show you out," the valet replied.

Ever since the three wicked kids had barged into the house, Nigel had taken to deadbolting all the doors. The only way for Lacey to get out was with his accompaniment.

Nigel stood, his knees cricking loudly, and, ever the polite valet, gestured for Lacey to exit Iris's bedroom first. He followed after her.

As they began to descend the staircase, Lacey heard Nigel wince.

"Are your knees giving you problems?" she asked, looking over his shoulder.

"Not at all," Nigel replied, dismissing her concern. He kept his eyes averted, but the wince was evident on his face.

"Oh no," Lacey said. "It was me, wasn't it? I hurt you when I bumped into you in the hallway. I'm so sorry."

It was just like the polite valet not to make a fuss; he was practically the human personification of a Stiff Upper Lip.

"No, no, no," Nigel said, looking increasingly awkward. "It's nothing."

Lacey wanted to comfort him, but he was clearly uncomfortable with her bringing attention to it. But he was evidently in quite a bit of pain, and they had collided quite hard on the landing. Lacey couldn't help but feel responsible and, in turn, want to fix the problem in some way.

She was about to ask him if he'd allow her to fetch him some painkillers at the very least, when a new thought suddenly struck her. Nigel's wince was in time with his steps. He was limping, as if the pain was from putting weight down on his leg rather than a bump or swelling that was causing him issues.

With a sudden dawning, Lacey felt a horrible swaying, swirling in her head. She grasped the banister tightly, it suddenly feeling like the only thing stopping her from collapsing down the staircase.

Was Nigel in pain because of ... a dog bite?

CHAPTER TWENTY THREE

Lacey's hands shook as she clutched the steering wheel and plowed the Volvo down the winding country streets. In the passenger seat beside her, Chester sat alert. The window was open a crack and wind whipped in, ruffling his fur.

"Sorry," she said, leaning across him and winding it up with the hand crank.

Chester whined.

"What do you think about all this?" she asked him. "I mean, we know Nigel. We know him well. He wouldn't do anything to hurt Iris, would he?"

As much as she didn't want to even entertain the thought that Nigel might somehow be involved, Lacey found herself running through all the evidence she'd gathered so far to see if any of it might fit with a theory of Nigel being the culprit.

"Let's start with the burglary at my store and work backwards," she said to Chester, turning off the main street onto a darker side alley that was lit by a few sporadic lampposts. "Let's assume the person who tried to rob me was specifically after Iris's belongings. Who knew they were there? Nigel, of course, because he arranged for the delivery. The lawyer. The delivery firm. Oh, and the specialist music insurers, because I had to get them to insure the Grecian harp. Well, we can count them out right away. They'd run their business into bankruptcy if they went around stealing the very harps they insured! And the same can be said for the deliverers. They were specialists. Companies like that only survive through having a stellar reputation. If there was even a whiff of a scandal going on there, they'd fold right away. I mean, look at my store as a prime example of that."

She scoffed. Then she paused. She was talking to her dog. Not just a couple of sentences here and there that Chester may comprehend, but she was monologuing at him and theorizing as if he were her actual sleuthing partner. The thought was so absurd, she managed a laugh, despite the heaviness of the situation.

But though Lacey wasn't crazy enough to think Chester could understand her more complex thoughts, speaking them aloud was actually really helpful. And so she continued.

"That leads us back to Nigel. He was the only other person who knew for certain that Iris's items were at my store."

Her stomach swirled as she gave Nigel his first strike.

"But that's only assuming the break-in *was* targeted. Tom thought it might have been a local trying to scare me, like the person who'd left me threatening messages."

But then she remembered that they'd come to the realization—during their chat over jam-filled croissants—that the perp had been targeting the grandfather clock specifically.

That's when the *aha!* moment hit Lacey. And it was nothing like she imagined. She felt no relief, but instead a horrible, dull, aching thud in her chest. It did not feel good. It felt downright awful. The answer wasn't one she wanted, even if it was right. The pieces of a puzzle were falling into place in her mind, building up a picture she just didn't want to believe. But seeing, as they say, is believing, and the picture forming in her mind was as clear as day.

Heart heavy with realization, Lacey said aloud; "They weren't trying to move the grandfather clock. They were trying to get inside it. Inside its locked cabinet. The one with a missing key. The one small enough to hide a miniature painting in. The thief was wielding a crowbar, not to break into the safe—that would be impossible—but to break into the clock to retrieve something hidden inside."

She made the final turning into Crag Cottage and parked outside the house, killing the engine. Her shoulders slumped. In the silence, she spoke.

"Benjamin accused Nigel of moving the grandfather clock out of the playroom in order to exploit the wording of the will, the wording that Iris had had changed just before her murder, a change that only Nigel knew about."

Moonlight streamed in through the windshield. Lacey looked over at Chester. He regarded her with the same attentiveness as always.

"Why would he do it?" she asked the dog. "Why?"

Nigel knew he would inherit the estate in Iris's will—and soon, since the woman was old and ailing. But none of the money from the sale of her items would go to him at all. That was all going to charity. How was he supposed to pay all the expenses having such an enormous estate would entail? Essentially, the house would become an albatross to him, if he didn't have some kind of income. A rich woman like Iris probably didn't realize how impossible it would be for a normal guy like Nigel to pay for upkeep. She was essentially leaving him a multimillion-pound rot bucket.

"He could have refused the estate!" Lacey exclaimed aloud, thumping her fists on the steering wheel as fury raced through her. "But he must have succumbed to greed. Turning down the gift of a famous, multimillion-pound manor would take willpower of steel. Knowing all the money you needed to upkeep it could be earned through the sale of just one painting ... one that no one even knew about, that was rumored to have been destroyed." She sighed. "Of all the people in Iris's life she'd told about the rare, rumored artwork, it was *Nigel*. And that one small, hideable item alone would pay all the bills and taxes and maintenance on the manor for years to come."

She got out of the car, Chester hopping down to walk beside her, and headed inside the cottage. Her mind seemed to be ticking at a million miles a second. She went straight to the kitchen, filled Chester's bowl with kibble, and poured herself a glass of wine. Then she sat on the stool at the butcher's block table where her notebook was still lying open to all the notes she'd made from the news reports about Iris's murder. There, her list of suspects stared up at her.

Benjamin.

Henry.

With a sad sigh, she picked up her pen and circled the last name on her list.

Nigel.

From his name she drew an arrow and added the word *greed.*

"Nigel got greedy," Lacey said. "Iris told him he was going to inherit the estate but none of the money for its upkeep, and he figured out there was a way to pay for it. To sell the painting. He couldn't take it while Iris was alive, because she'd notice its disappearance immediately. She'd have to be dead for him to take it. But why not just wait until Iris died a natural death, then take the painting? Why kill her? There must've been some urgency. Perhaps he had some kind of ticking clock. Bills mounting for whatever reason. Something that forced his hand."

She added a word beside *greed. Urgency.* And then another word: *Hide?*

Because why would Nigel need to hide the painting inside the clock? Why not just remove it from the house? He could've put it in his car, perhaps, during the so-called prescription pill run. Because he was worried his car might also be searched by the police? Or possibly because the painting was so delicate and precious he didn't want to risk it being damaged?

"Yes, that's it!" Lacey said, writing down *insurance* to her list of words.

Nigel knew there were special insurers involved for antique items because they'd discussed it! He'd known full well that everything inside Iris's house was protected, and that everything inside Lacey's store was as well. If the painting was *anywhere else* but the manor or store, then any damage it incurred would render it worthless. Since he was worried the children might break into the house, the only place the painting was truly safe was Lacey's store.

"That's why he was so desperate," Lacey said, her guts swirling. "He used me. Pretended I was an ally. Brought me in on the scheme under the guise of being a friend. Laid all that stuff on my shoulders about Iris wanting me to value her items as her dying wish. He chummied up with me so I wouldn't suspect him. To deflect attention. He was … hiding in plain sight."

She put down her pen and sank her head into her hands.

This whole elaborate scheme had been so well planned it left her feeling cold. Nigel had had the clock moved from the children's bedroom so he could use it to hide the painting inside, claimed the key was missing so no one would check, then had the clock delivered to Lacey—an amateur who knew no better—for safekeeping. He must've known that it wouldn't take long for the sun to bleach the wallpaper and hide his crime forever.

Of course, he wouldn't have been able to sell it outright because of the obvious link between him and Iris's estate. There must be a middleman, some kind of backstreet dealer who'd be the one to take all the fame and glory of finding the infamous lost miniature of Lady Isabelle Wiccomb Defante.

Lacey had heard of them—there was a whole black market of people who traded in stolen Nazi artwork, after all, despite how thoroughly illegal and reprehensible such an act was.

Obviously Nigel didn't have much patience. Whatever urgency had led to him killing Iris then led to him breaking in to try and steal the painting back.

"Oh, Chester." She looked at the dog. "Was it Nigel you bit that night? Did Nigel do it all?"

Chester seemed to be a good judge of character for the most part. But then, she always thought she was as well, and yet had she been duped by Nigel? Had they both been? Did it only take some homemade apple juice and doggy kibble to manipulate the pair of them?

Lacey felt awful. She desperately didn't want Nigel to be the culprit.

She stared at her paper, at the words she'd drawn and connected with arrows, the ones she'd circled and underlined, pleading them to tell her something different. She urged her mind to fit the formula together in a different way, to do a 180-degree turn and counteract her theory.

That's when her gaze fell to the word *crowbar.*

"The crowbar! That's it! For Nigel to lock the painting away, he'd need the key. If he had the key, he wouldn't need to use a crowbar to break into the clock!"

But almost as soon as she'd hit on the possible revelation, she shook her head as a counterpoint popped into her mind.

"Except we don't know the crowbar was for the clock at all. The crowbar may just have been used to force open the back door. He may well have had the key in his pocket the whole time."

So that didn't exonerate Nigel at all.

She shook her head sadly, morosely, as it appeared to her that Nigel may well have been playing her all along. Hiding in plain sight. Letting her play detective to think she was an ally, all along using her.

But to truly be certain, Lacey had to put her theory to the test. And there was only one way to do that.

She was going to break open the clock.

It was midnight, but the clock in front of Lacey had stopped at four thirty. How many years had the grandfather clock not ticked for? How long had that ancient pendulum not swung?

Her hands tightened on the crowbar. The metal was heavy, weighty in her hands. Its destructive force was palpable. She heaved it over her head.

Then froze.

Lacey simply couldn't do it. If her father could see her now, about to smash an antique clock! No, she couldn't. It was unique. One of a kind. More valuable than its worth because of the intricacy and care that had gone into its construction.

Sighing, she crouched down so she was face to face with Chester—who'd been sitting patiently by her legs—and put his face in her hands.

"There has to be another way," she said, ruffling his fur. "Well, I suppose there *is* one other option ... If I put the grandfather clock up for auction, the killer will try to buy it, so as to get their hands on the painting inside."

Chester barked, as if agreeing with her.

"But it's not quite that easy," Lacey told him. "Superintendent Turner made it perfectly clear if I held the auction, he'd take me to court."

This time, Chester's response was to growl.

Lacey gazed into his alert eyes and the dog quirked his head to the side, blinking attentively.

"You're right," Lacey said, suddenly, feeling a wave of determination ripple through her. "We can't let that bully Superintendent Turner tell us what to do!" She ruffled Chester again. "We have to do it. We have to hold the auction, threat or not. Because if Nigel *is* the killer, he'll have no choice but to come and bid on the clock. It's a trap. One the killer will be forced to walk right into."

Chester began to bark.

CHAPTER TWENTY FOUR

Ivan Parry placed his black marker down on Lacey's kitchen table, beside the pile of handmade posters for her auction.

"That's it," he said. "I'm spent."

Gina looked up from the handmade poster she was working on. She had pen marks on her face. "I've got five years on you and I'm still going strong. Come on, Parry, put your back into it!"

Tom wiggled his eyebrows at Ivan mischievously. "That sounds like a challenge."

Ivan picked up the discarded pen. "Challenge accepted. A few more won't hurt."

Lacey looked over the lid of her laptop at the rag-tag team, a smile on her lips. "I really appreciate you guys doing this," she said, with sincere gratitude.

"You and I both," came Percy Johnson's voice through the webcam.

They'd been organizing the auction all morning. Ivan had come over to Crag Cottage before breakfast to shave down a swollen door that wouldn't shut properly, while Lacey had been right in the middle of an emergency morning call with Percy regarding arranging a snap auction. Ivan had been so intrigued by the sale of Iris Archer's goods that he wanted to help right away.

Then Gina had popped over to see if Chester wanted to join her and Boudicca on a beach walk—the two dogs got along famously these days—and had immediately thrown herself into the fray. "Superintendent Turner forbade it?" she'd exclaimed, rubbing her hands together with glee. "Then I'm definitely on board!"

Then Tom had arrived at the cottage to see if Lacey wanted to share yesterday's batch of unsold croissants with him before work, and had been surprised to discover a sort of grassroots town rebellion taking place in her kitchen. But he'd taken it all with good humor and joined in with the arrangements, sharing his pastries with the hungry troops.

Between the four of them, they'd arranged for an advertisement to appear on the council's website and had created a bunch of posters to put up in the high street stores. The fliers had been inspired by the police notice that had been posted in every mailbox after the burglary. Lacey was particularly proud of herself for using it as creative inspiration. When life gives you lemons, as they say...

After an hour, Tom checked his watch. "We'd better go. If I'm not open by eight thirty, I'll have a whole queue of hangry folk to deal with!"

Gina collected the stacks of fliers and rolled up posters. "I'll do the first half of the high street."

Ivan stood. "I'll give you a lift to town. Get a head start."

Gina nodded and she and Boudicca followed Ivan out the cottage.

Lacey looked over at Tom. "I guess I'm really doing this," she said.

He gave her an encouraging smile. "Wilfordshire's very own Nancy Drew. How do you feel?"

Lacey chewed her lip with trepidation. "Like I'm about to catch a killer."

At the store, Lacey hung her poster in pride of place in the window. It was almost parallel to the one Tom had put up in his. They smiled at one another through the glass from their respective stores, and Lacey felt a tingle in her stomach.

But the smile was wiped off her face the moment she saw Superintendent Turner's cruiser pull up outside of her store.

He was evidently furious. His face was red as he came marching toward the store. He shoved the door open so roughly the bell flew off its hinges and slammed into the ground, rousing Chester, who flew to Lacey's side with a low growl, taking up a protective stance.

"I told you not to hold the auction," Superintendent Turner barked. "That I'd get a court order to stop you if I had to."

"Then get the order," Lacey replied, coolly.

Superintendent Turner elbowed his way past her.

"Hey!" Lacey exclaimed as she staggered back, shocked by his roughness.

Chester snapped his jaws but Lacey hushed him. The last thing she needed was a dog bite to add to her woes.

The superintendent ripped the poster off the window.

"Hey!" Lacey exclaimed. "What are you doing?"

He scrunched it into a ball and threw it to the floor. "I'm just playing fetch with Fido," he said with feigned innocence, pointing at Chester.

Lacey folded her arms and shook her head. "What do you want? Don't you have better things to do with your time then stop an innocent antiques valuer from holding an auction? Like, I don't know, catching a killer?"

Superintendent Turner clearly had zero patience for Lacey's sass today. He sneered nastily. "There you go again, telling me how to do my job. If you're such a great detective, why don't *you* catch the killer?"

"That's exactly what I'm trying to do. I'm quite certain the killer will come to my auction. I'm trying to lure them in."

"Ludicrous," the officer scoffed.

Just then, Tom entered the store. He must've seen the altercation unfolding from the patisserie window and wasn't impressed with the show.

"What's gotten into you?" he said, marching up to the detective.

Karl Turner stared Tom down. "Fly-posting! Without a permit! From one end of the high street to the other. I could issue her a

Fixed Penalty Notice for eighty pounds per poster, if I wanted." He motioned as if to reach for his ticket book.

"Karl, that's a load of bunk and we both know it," Tom snapped. "Even if my mom wasn't a lawyer, I'd know that a poster can be displayed in the window of private property without a license. This is hardly fly-posting! You have absolutely no right to come in here and tear her picture down."

The detective held his ground for a moment, his cheeks puffed with air. But the red of fury that had colored them before started to fade. Slowly, he withdrew his hand from his pocket, where he'd been about to produce a ticket book, and seemed to come back to his senses.

But clearly needing to save face, he held a finger up at Lacey like she was a naughty school child. "I'm watching you," he warned.

Then he marched away.

As soon as he was gone, Tom turned to Lacey with worried eyes. She'd never seen him look so serious, or tense.

"Are you okay?" he asked with tender concern.

"Just a little shaken," she told him, as she scooped up the broken bell from the floor. "I've never seen Superintendent Turner behave like that. I'm used to him being like a Vulcan, so his temper took me by surprise."

A flicker of a smile crossed Tom's face in response to her Star Trek quip, but it faded quickly and his look of concern returned.

"Yes, well, he definitely stepped over the line if you ask me," he said thinly. "But in my experience, Karl Turner is all talk and no trousers."

Lacey raised her eyebrows, amused by the unfamiliar idiom. "He's what now?"

"All talk and no trousers," Tom repeated with the same level of seriousness.

Lacey started to giggle. "And what does that mean exactly?"

"Oh!" Tom said, chuckling as he finally realized. "You don't say that over the pond, do you? It means he talks about doing things but never takes action. And I hear how silly it sounds *now*," he confessed.

The tension was broken and the frown lines on his forehead smoothed out. Trust Tom to come over and not only diffuse the situation, but inject some much needed humor into it. He really had a knack for cheering Lacey up.

Lacey retrieved the screwed up ball of poster and unscrunched it. She began to smooth it out on the countertop.

"So you don't think he'll get a court order to block the auction?" she asked Tom.

"No. If Iris's stuff had any evidential value, they would have seized it already. But I can call my mom and get some legal advice if you want extra reassurance. I didn't make up that thing about her being a lawyer just to scare Superintendent Turner away."

"Don't you think it's a bit early to meet the parents?" Lacey joked, already in a significantly lighter mood thanks to Tom.

"You'll have to meet her soon enough," Tom replied. "We are married after all."

Lacey laughed. But her laugh was drowned out by the sound of banging coming from the wall she shared with the boutique next door.

"What the heck is that?" Tom asked.

Lacey rolled her eyes. It was one thing after another today! "Taryn. She's been 'renovating' all week." She used air quotes around the word. "I threatened her with a noise order for always playing music against our joined wall. Well, that did the trick. The music stopped. But almost immediately the hammering began." She let out a wry laugh. "Conveniently, you can't get a noise complaint against DIY."

Tom tutted. "Wow, she really does play dirty. Have you said anything to her since?"

"Not this time. The handyman she has over there looks like he's just come out of prison. I was hoping she'd eventually get a migraine and call it off, but she obviously has access to some hardcore painkillers."

Tom took Lacey's hand, interrupting her sarcastic commentary. "Let me have a word with her," he said.

Lacey looked down at her hand grasped in his. It felt so right, so comforting, Lacey didn't want any reason to let it go.

She hesitated. "I really don't think we should. I wasn't joking when I said her handyman looks like an ex-con."

Tom smirked. "Didn't you just see me back there with the police officer? I can handle it."

Despite her better judgment, Lacey found herself nodding. Tom gave her hand a little tug, and they crossed the store floor to the exit, Chester's nails clicking on the floorboards as he followed behind them.

As he pulled open the door, Tom finally let go of Lacey's hand.

Probably for the best, Lacey thought, despite her disappointment. *Taryn might burst a blood vessel if she sees us hand in hand.*

They headed inside the boutique. Sure enough, Taryn's hired hand was aimlessly hammering nails into the adjoining wall between their two shops. There were about a hundred nails now marring the otherwise pristine white wall. Either Taryn was going to hang her stock of absurdly expensive, delicate, one-of-a-kind necklaces off of *nails* or she was going to hang up a hundred tiny works of art side by side. *Or* she was literally damaging her own wall just to piss Lacey off. Clearly, there was no low too low for Taryn to stoop.

The woman herself was standing at the counter, her head slumped in her hands. So the noise *was* getting to her, Lacey realized, but she was so petulant she'd keep it going anyway.

Chester began to emit a low growl, as he did whenever he saw the shrew of a woman. Taryn was like his very own Cruella de Vil.

At the sound, Taryn's head snapped up, an angry scowl in her eyes. But when she noticed Tom was there, she straightened up like a dart and smoothed down her hair. Which she'd recently had cut, Lacey noted with a grimace, in the exact same style as hers ...

"Tom Forrester," Taryn said, smiling sweetly, ruffling her new short do in order to draw even more attention to it. "Pastry chef extraordinaire. To what do I owe the pleasure?"

She completely ignored Lacey. Clearly she was unworthy of a greeting in Taryn's eyes.

The handyman stopped hammering and glared over his shoulder. His eyes flicked from Tom to Lacey with an expression that seemed to switch from hatred to jealousy in turn. Great, another local who had it in for her.

"Lace and I thought we'd come and see how the renovations were going," Tom said innocently enough. "They seem to be taking quite a while." He glanced over at the nail-pocked wall. "With not much improvement."

The handyman's glower deepened. The hammer in his hand suddenly looked like a weapon.

"You what?" he said gruffly.

Lacey shrank back. This was a bad idea. And now Tom was caught in the crossfire.

"It's almost done," Taryn said brightly, as if in an attempt to paper over the evident threatening atmosphere. "Isn't it, Keith? One more day, you said?" The tone in her voice made it obvious this was all a ruse—that she'd hired the man to make a ton of noise and then leave once she was challenged over it.

Keith the handyman paused. He let the arm holding the hammer flop down to his side. "Yeah. I'll be done by the end of the day."

"See," Taryn said breezily, her fake friendly eyes fixed on Lacey. "It will be nice and quiet again soon. And I'm *so* sorry if it inconvenienced you. But that's how it goes, doesn't it? You renovate your store for a week and make a racket, then I renovate mine." She let out a forced cackle, the one she did whenever she'd said something icy and was trying to play it off as banter between friends.

Lacey rolled her eyes, and then she and Tom headed back to her store.

Gina was there, in a brown knitted cardigan that perfectly complemented the Nordic Corner of the store. She had a tote bag slung over her shoulder, with last night's handmade posters poking out the top. Boudicca was sniffing the place beside the till where

Chester usually slept, wagging her tail with excitement at the scent of her best doggie friend.

Gina turned to the door as Lacey entered. When she noticed Tom at her side, her eyes sparked with mischief.

"Lacey!" she exclaimed in her usual ebullient way. "I've finished postering the first half of the high street. I wondered whether you'd like to do the next half? I could cover the store for an hour or so? I'm sure Chester would like his walkies."

Chester's tail began to wag at the mention of his favorite thing.

But Lacey shook her head. "You know that's not a good idea. We chose you to do it because of your magic silver tongue and persuasive technique. I'm the town pariah. If people see it's me delivering the posters, they'll refuse to put them up outright."

It was the same reason they'd omitted Lacey's name from the poster, choosing instead to advertise the auction under Percy Johnson's name, with the tagline *Mayfair's Finest Antiques Dealer Coming to Your Town!*

"The least involvement that seems to be coming from me the better," Lacey finished.

"Take Tom," Gina said, completely unsubtly. "He has a lot of clout in the town, too. More than me, really, since he's so handsome."

Lacey blushed. Gina was making it very obvious she was attempting to get the two of them together. Lacey felt like a teenager being match-made by an aunt or something.

"Tom's way too busy," Lacey said.

"Paul's in today," Tom said quickly, pointing through the window at the young trainee chef he occasionally gave work to. "He can cover the shift."

Lacey knew very well that Tom only ever drafted Paul in when he was planning on redoing the window display. Obviously helping her was more important to him than his infamous macaron sculptures. The thought warmed her.

"Besides, I've hurt my ankle," Gina continued, fake-wincing while rubbing her leg.

"Okay, okay!" Lacey said, caving. She'd had more than enough of Gina's cajoling and bad acting.

She did want to spend time with Tom. But she didn't really feel like getting abuse from the townsfolk today. The interaction with Taryn and Keith the handyman had left a sour taste in her mouth and she wasn't sure how much more bitterness she could stomach.

She took the tote bag of posters from Gina, flashing her a discreet *I-know-what-you're-doing* look as she did—to which Gina grinned widely in response—then she and Tom went up the high street.

They only went inside the stores that hadn't been outwardly hostile to Lacey, and Lacey was surprised that people were still showing interest in the auction despite her obvious involvement. *Tom has a soothing effect on everyone he meets,* Lacey thought.

They went into the children's toy store. The woman behind the counter—a portly thirty-something who gave off jolly-teacher vibes—had been nice enough to Lacey when she first arrived in Wilfordshire, though their paths hadn't crossed since Iris's death. But as she noticed Lacey, her encouraging smile turned into an anxious grimace.

"Oh," she said, before shaking herself. "I mean, hello!"

Lacey felt her stomach clench. The woman wasn't being hostile toward her, she was *scared* of her. The feeling was awful. Lacey actually preferred the aggressiveness of the coffee store clerk to this trembling. She could cope with schoolyard bullies, but she couldn't cope with being perceived as one.

Tom handed the clerk a poster, his smile bright. "Hi, Jane. Would you be able to put this poster up in your window? It's for Wilfordshire's very first antiques auction, and everyone's invited."

Jane looked at Lacey with a timid expression. "You're hosting it?"

"It will be in my store, yes," Lacey said, a little evasively. Percy, Mayfair's Finest, was going to be present at the auction, but she was the one conducting it.

"I'll think about it," Jane replied, taking the poster.

"Everyone else has put them up," Tom added. "It won't hurt."

Jane looked even more tense. "I don't usually put anything in the windows..."

That was a lie. When Lacey arrived in town she'd noticed a poster for last summer's fairground was still in the window.

Tom was about to say something, but Lacey rested a hand on his arm and spoke out the side of her mouth. "Come on, let's go."

He obliged. Lacey glanced back briefly as they left, just in time to see Jane throw the poster in the bin.

"This was a bad idea," she said, her stomach swirling with disappointment.

"Not at all," Tom told her. "We've put loads up. Are you worried about Jane?"

"She was *frightened*," Lacey sighed. "Of *me*. It's a horrible feeling."

Tom paused and took her by the shoulders, the weight and warmth coming from his palms grounding her. "Jane's scared of everything. Spiders. Moths. Fireworks. Open-toed sandals..."

Lacey laughed.

"You think I'm joking?" Tom said, grinning. "I promise you. I went in there once with my toes on display and she nearly fainted. The point is, the way other people perceive you really has nothing to do with you and everything to do with themselves. Some people see the world through very skewed lenses." He shrugged.

"Huh," Lacey said. "That's pretty good advice. Although open-toed sandals *are* a fashion crime for men. You do know that, right?"

Tom laughed.

Buoyed by the pep talk, Lacey felt a renewed sense of purpose, and she held her head high as they continued along the high street distributing their posters. Some people were receptive, others weren't, but Lacey didn't let their opinions get to her. It was as if Tom had handed her a bulletproof jacket and she could deflect any blows thrown at her. Besides, she was about to realize a dream—to hold her very own auction! And it wasn't just *her* dream, it was her father's dream too! She was about to achieve something for the both of them, despite the difficulties and hurdles she'd faced on the way. That was something to be extremely proud of.

They reached the Coach House Inn at the end of the high street and went inside. It was very quiet. Brenda the baby-faced barmaid looked bored out of her mind to be working the dead early shift, with no one but her usual drunk snoozing at the bar to keep her company.

"Morning," Lacey said, approaching the bar.

Brenda flashed her a skeptical look. But then again, she always looked wary. Working in a bar had probably made her cautious of everyone.

"Yeah?"

Lacey rummaged for a poster. "We were wondering if we could display this?" she asked, unfurling it to show Brenda.

The girl shrugged nonchalantly, not even looking at what it said. She gestured to a wall that was crammed with posters.

"Help yourself," she said blandly, her lips smacking loudly from the gum she was chewing. "You can take down anything that's out of date."

Lacey and Tom exchanged a glance of amusement, then went over to the wall of crowded posters. Hers would surely get lost in the fray.

As Lacey searched for old notices she could discard, one caught her eye. The words *ARSENAL v WOLVERHAMPTON* had been crossed out with a big black marker pen. Underneath, someone had scrawled: *Not showing! Pub closed! Sorry for the inconvenience!*

"Tom!" Lacey exclaimed, yanking it off the wall and shoving it at him. "Look at this!"

Her heart was starting to race as she watched Tom's eyes scan the notice. When he connected the dots, he looked up at her, eyes wide. "I don't believe it. The pub was closed—"

"—at the time my store was robbed." She nodded vigorously.

"But Brenda was the witness that gave an alibi to—"

"—Ben and Henry! Exactly!"

They stared at one another, searching each other's eyes as they attempted to calibrate the new piece of information. If Ben and Henry weren't in the pub, witnessed by Brenda, on the evening the store got robbed, then they were back on her suspects list and there was a glimmer of hope that Nigel wasn't her guy after all!

"Let's ask Brenda," Tom said. "And see what this is all about."

He seemed energized by the clue, and hurried to the bar. Brenda was now lazily flicking crumbs off the tables with a dry dish cloth.

"Brenda, what's this notice about the pub closing for the day?" Lacey asked, showing her the poster.

"That was last week," the barmaid said with an air of irritation. "You can throw it away."

"But what happened?" Lacey pressed. "Why was the pub closed? Why didn't you show the match?"

Brenda frowned. "A faulty beer pump flooded the basement and it was all hands on deck to sort it out." She sounded defensive, like she was being accused of something. "So?"

"So Superintendent Turner said you gave a witness statement for two men on that day," Tom said.

"Huh? I haven't even seen Superintendent Turner. He's not even allowed in here."

Lacey's eyes widened. "I'm sorry, what? Why?"

"He got signed off. A perp broke both his knees and then he turned into one of those." She pointed at the drunk sleeping at the bar. "But he cleaned himself up and got therapy for his PTSD and now he's back. Top of his game."

Top of his game seemed a bit rich, but Lacey was glad to hear the man had confronted his demons. She felt a bit more sympathy for him now that she understood some of what he'd been through. It didn't excuse him breaking her bell and screwing up her poster, but it did explain why he was so quick to temper.

You really never know what a person's been through, Lacey reminded herself.

"So no one came in and took a statement from you about two men being in the bar on that day?" Tom asked.

Brenda tugged at the big bun of blond hair piled onto her head, in an attempt to make it look even *more* messy than it already did, a style that was, inexplicably to Lacey, very popular amongst British youths. "Like I said. Pub was closed. I think the match was shown at Carol's as well, so maybe that's where they were seen. But it definitely wasn't by me. I was on my knees in the basement getting soaked in beer."

Tom and Lacey exchanged a look. Their suspicion was confirmed, straight from the horse's mouth. Benjamin and Henry had no alibi for the robbery. Either one of them could have been the one who broke into the store. The brothers were back in the frame.

They left the pub, stunned by what they'd learned.

"Superintendent Turner lied to me," Lacey said once they were back on the cobblestone sidewalk outside the inn. The sea was very gray today, the weather having taken a chilly turn over lunch.

Tom didn't look concerned by Lacey's accusation. "He was using deception to try and provoke a spontaneous confession from you."

Lacey raised an eyebrow. "That sounds like lawyer speak."

Tom smiled sheepishly. "I guess I'm a mommy's boy."

But Lacey was suddenly lost in thought. Had the detective lied to her, or had he been duped by the brothers? Had he been given an alibi that he'd then failed to check up on; perhaps out of shame, as he wasn't allowed into the Coach House to follow it up?

"What is it?" Tom asked, presumably in response to Lacey's sudden silence.

She held up a finger to pause him. Mind racing, Lacey searched her memories, trying to recall what DCI Lewis had told her about Brenda's supposed statement, the one she now knew to be false.

"The brothers were seen there from kickoff to final whistle. We have a witness statement. The superintendent has been working on all the alibis personally."

"That's it!" she exclaimed, snapping her fingers.

Tom frowned, looking perplexed. "Want to let me in on your lightbulb moment?"

"Superintendent Turner has been *personally* taking charge of *all* the alibi statements," Lacey explained, echoing what she'd heard from DCI Lewis. "Not just for the break-in, but for the ones related to the murder as well."

"And?"

"He wasn't using deception to provoke a spontaneous confession. He dropped the ball!"

Tom looked more even more confused. "I'm lost. What are you getting t?"

"I'm saying we shouldn't take *any* of the alibi statements as truth. Superintendent Turner's been doing some sloppy work." She lowered her voice, aware she was in a public place slandering a generally well-respected police officer. "Think about it. Clarissa was Henry's alibi during the murder. And he hers. Well, what if they were lying? Covering for one another? And Superintendent Turner for whatever reason failed to properly corroborate their statements. What if they weren't scrutinized properly?"

"Then they'd be back in the suspect pool." Tom paused, as if contemplating the ramifications of her words. "Wait. Why were Henry and Clarissa one another's alibis in the first place? I thought they hated one another."

Lacey recalled what Nigel had told her about the relationship between the three Archer children. Henry and Ben were the tag team, *not* Henry and Clarissa. He'd even said she'd given the alibi for him begrudgingly.

"You're right. And yet, they were supposedly together at Clarissa's house in London at the time of the murder. Clarissa couldn't have hated Henry that much if she let him into her home."

"Perhaps they were finally old enough to let bygones be bygones," Tom suggested. "People change. Rifts heal."

Lacey considered his words. Maybe she was barking up the wrong tree. But it was certainly odd. And whatever the truth of the matter was, the revelation of Brenda's statement being uncorroborated by Superintendent Turner had blown her suspect pool wide open again. Nigel may not be her perp after all. And the Archer children were back in the frame. That little glimmer of hope buoyed Lacey.

Anything that hinted Nigel might not be her guy was a relief to her. She missed him and wanted her old friend back.

"We have to get the children to come to the auction," Lacey said. "That's the only way we'll be able to see whether one of the brothers has a dog bite."

They'd been keeping the fact the furniture of the auction belonged to Iris out of public knowledge—nothing made Lacey look more guilty than to be selling the valuables of the woman everyone thought she'd murdered, after all—but now she realized if they didn't make it obvious then Iris's children would never come.

She got out her cell phone.

"Who are you calling?" Tom asked.

"Nigel," Lacey replied. "I'm going to ask him to tell the kids about the auction."

She felt herself tremble with nerves as the call connected to her former friend turned suspect turned, well, who even knew anymore? All Lacey could cling to was that there was hope for him after all. But hope for Nigel meant the pendulum had swung back toward an even crueler reality; that Iris Archer was murdered by one of her own children.

CHAPTER TWENTY FIVE

A black taxicab pulled up outside Lacey's store, and from the back seat emerged a familiar face. Lacey hurried from behind her counter—Chester leaping up, mirroring her excitement—and ran to the door.

She heaved it open and waved eagerly at Percy Johnson. The old man was looking exceptionally professorial today, in a smart brown tweed jacket and gray trilby hat, which he tipped to Lacey as a way of greeting. He paid the cabby through the window, tucked his folded newspaper under his armpit, then doddered across the uneven cobblestones toward her.

Lacey felt giddy with excitement. She'd spent so much time on video calls with Percy—him imparting his vast knowledge to her in the soothing voice of a BBC presenter—they'd formed something of an almost familial bond. He'd become so much more than just her Mayfair contact during this whole debacle over Iris's furniture, he'd become a mentor and confidant to Lacey. Seeing him again in the flesh rather than over a fuzzy, lagging webcam was like being reunited with a friendly grandfather.

She hugged him.

"Hello, dear," he said, patting her back, his plummy voice croaking. "How are you?"

She pulled away. "Relieved to have you here. I'm a bag of nerves."

"First auction," he said with a nod. "I'm not surprised."

Lacey smiled in response to his warm encouragement. "Come inside. Tom's made a Victoria sponge."

"My favorite!" the old man replied.

"I know," Lacey said, grinning.

They headed back into the store, where Lacey had laid out a spread of Tom's most delicious pastries. He'd also loaned her some of his finest English Blue China crockery for the occasion, and the Victoria sponge was on a beautiful display dish that wouldn't look out of place on Lacey's shelves. She was extremely grateful for all the help Tom had given her; his continued involvement in everything happening in her life made it very clear where he'd like to stand with her, but he was gentleman enough to leave the ball in Lacey's court when it came to crossing over the line into romance. It only made her like him more, but with the divorce so fresh in the back of her mind, a relationship seemed incomprehensible right now. Not to mention the fact she was trying her best to solve a murder at the moment. To say she was distracted was an understatement.

Percy whistled as he glanced around at the store. "Very nice. It all looks quite professional indeed."

Chester trotted up to the man, who reached down and petted him like they were already firm friends.

Lacey poured Percy a cup of tea—something she was still no expert at but had certainly gotten the hang of—placed a slice of cake onto a pretty floral plate with a silver fork, then led him into the auction space.

Getting the room ready had been a challenge, but she'd enjoyed it. It reminded her a lot of the work she'd done with Saskia—of how best to organize a room for maximum usefulness without compromising on aesthetic value. She was proud of what she'd done, of the red velvet chairs she'd rented from the town hall, and how she'd utilized Iris's Japanese shōji screens, made of bamboo lattice, to hide all the various items to be sold behind. The room was a combination of modern and vintage, just like Lacey liked, and she was pleased to have injected some of her own personality into it, rather than just going along with what was considered standard in the world of auctioneering.

"Oh, I like this a lot," Percy said with a tone of pride and admiration. "You must be expecting a lot of attendees?"

181

Lacey looked at the row of chairs. She'd borrowed fifty from the town hall—the stock was usually used in their civil service ceremonies—but she had no idea whether she'd overdone it. Percy must've thought so, and she chewed her lip with uncertainty.

"I'm not sure. We flyered almost every store on the high street, and put posters up all around the town. But everyone knows it's Iris Archer's stuff I'm selling, and since most people in town think I killed her for her riches, well, I have a feeling it will put a few people off." Her voice trailed away as the heaviness of that reality settled on her shoulders once more.

"So the ruse is up?" Percy asked. He'd been privy to all the goings-on in Lacey's complicated life and was well aware of the cover-up mission.

Lacey sighed. "Yeah. We had to make it obvious we were selling Iris Archer's belongings in order to lure her sons and the valet here." She shrugged. "If it's only the three of them, it's worth it to clear my name. I'm certain one of the three of them is the murderer."

Percy wiped the cake crumbs from the corners of his lips. "What makes you think they'll reveal themselves?"

"I have a theory. Well, a few actually."

"I have time," Percy chuckled, holding up his half full teacup.

"Okay," Lacey said. "Theory one. It was common knowledge the children weren't set to inherit anything after Iris's death. The sons always thought they'd be able to circumvent it because of some old law about being male heirs, but they weren't. The only thing Iris left to them in the will was the contents of their childhood playroom. One of those things was the grandfather clock. My theory is that one of them murdered Iris, and hid a valuable painting of hers inside the clock. But the clock had been moved out of their playroom into the study, which meant it wasn't amongst the items they could claim. I think they panicked and broke into my store to try and steal the painting back, getting bitten by Chester in the process."

"Sounds perfectly plausible to me," Percy said. "Our history is filled with stories of wealthy heirs doing away with their parents for the inheritance. And yet you have another theory?"

Lacey nodded. "Iris left Penrose Manor to her valet, Nigel."

"Her valet?" the old man repeated with bemusement. "That's ... unusual to say the least. What are you thinking, an illicit affair turned crime of passion? A secret child to whom she felt obligated to support in her death? A charlatan who wormed his way into her life?"

Lacey's stomach squirmed at the thought that Nigel could indeed be any one of those, and that his likelihood of being involved was just as strong as the sons'.

"I think it might be a little less salacious than that," Lacey countered. "The valet was left the estate by Iris in the will, but all her money and any profit from the sale of her belongings was going to charity. He had nothing to upkeep it with."

"I see," Percy said, nodding with understanding. "I've heard of this before, heirs sitting in rotting manor houses because they can't afford the upkeep of such protected historic buildings. And gosh, the taxes! Those alone could ruin him!"

"Exactly," Lacey replied. "Nigel was the only one who knew Iris had sought additional legal protections against the loophole in the will being exploited upon her death. He was the one who moved the grandfather clock out of the playroom to stop the children taking it. He was the one who knew that Iris owned an exceptionally rare and expensive painting, the sale of which alone would make him a millionaire."

"You have quite a case against this man," Percy noted.

"Yes," Lacey said with a sigh. "And then there's the limp ..." She felt her shoulders slump again at all the signs that pointed to Nigel.

"The limp?" Percy asked inquisitively, the cake crumbs stuck to each corner of his lips making him look like an absentminded old professor.

"Remember when my store was broken into?" Lacey reminded him, and he nodded with affirmation. "I think the person who did it knew I had Iris's things. They were looking for something. Perhaps something hidden in the clock. Chester bit the perp on the leg."

Percy nodded with understanding. "The sale of the clock will lure the killer here. A dog bite will confirm a robber. Buying the grandfather clock will confirm a killer."

"And I suspect the same person is behind both."

Silence fell. Percy appeared to be lost in deep contemplation. Lacey felt heavy from the burden of what she was about to do.

"What a tangled mess," Percy said finally. "I hope you get your answers, Lacey."

Their conversation was interrupted by the sound of the bell above the door tinkling. Ivan had fixed it for Lacey, reasoning he was her handyman for everything at the cottage, so why not the store as well?

"Could that be your first patron?" Percy asked.

"Maybe," Lacey replied, standing. "Excuse me."

She left Percy to finish slurping up the last dregs of his tea, and exited the auction room. Her stomach swirled with anguish. She may very well have just had a murderer walk into her store.

But when she made it back into the main store and saw who was examining the furniture in the "Nordic Corner," her mouth dropped open, and she wondered whether having a murderer there might've been better.

"SASKIA?" Lacey cried.

Her former boss swirled around to face her. She widened her arms—not in an embracing gesture but in an *I-have-arrived* one.

"Did you think I'd miss this?" Saskia said.

Just the sound of her voice sent a bolt of familiar anguish through Lacey, as if she was about to be told off for something she'd failed to do perfectly. It left Lacey completely tongue-tied.

"What are you doing here?" Lacey finally managed.

Things hadn't exactly ended well between the two of them, not that they'd ever been good to begin with.

Saskia flapped a hand dismissively. "Water under the bridge, Lacey darling. We're business associates now. You're not a subordinate anymore, you're a potential colleague."

So now I'm worthy of your respect? Lacey thought, wryly.

Saskia's eyes flicked over Lacey's shoulder. Lacey turned to see Percy emerging from the auction room into the main store.

"Ah," Saskia said with barely veiled irritation. "I heard on the grapevine that Mayfair's finest was helping you on your little venture. I suppose that explains why we've not had much in the way of correspondence these last weeks?" She held her bony hand out to Percy. "Mr. Johnson."

Percy looked flustered as he took it and shook. "Business is business, Saskia. You know that as well as I do."

"Of course," she replied through pursed lips.

This was all getting too tense for Lacey.

"Cake!" she exclaimed, clapping her hands. "Saskia, please, help yourself." She gestured to the display of pastries.

Saskia raised an eyebrow. "You have *food* at an auction?"

Typical Saskia, trying to make Lacey feel inferior for her choices. But Lacey found the hold her old boss's opinion had once had over her seemed to have dissipated.

"Call it the Doyle touch," Lacey replied jovially, wiggling her eyebrows with confidence.

Out of the corner of her eye, she saw Percy smirk.

"Looks like you're catering for an army," Saskia added, looking over at the display. "I'm surprised you're expecting that many people since it's the day before Easter. I mean, in *my* experience, not many people like to attend events like this before a public holiday."

"I don't know how many people to expect," Lacey said with a breezy shrug. "I'm just thrilled to be realizing yet another one of my dreams."

She smiled at Saskia in a way that showed her boss she couldn't bring her down anymore. Saskia's top lip twitched, but she failed to smile in return.

Just then, the door flew open, the bell letting out an urgent-sounding jingle, and in waltzed a group of smartly dressed people Lacey had never seen before. They weren't locals to Wilfordshire, that much was obvious, and they definitely hadn't wandered in off the streets from curiosity.

"We're from the English Antiques Society," one of the women said. She grinned with excitement. "Here for the Penrose Estate auction."

"We're thrilled to be here," a man beside her added. "I heard the house had a Victorian ottoman in every bedroom."

"That's right," Lacey said, her heart leaping with pride. "And they're all on sale today."

Getting the word out that they were selling items from the manor house had been the right call. Not only would it lure the murderer out of the shadows, but it had lured in other antiques dealers in the vicinity of Wilfordshire. She started to feel her nervousness for the upcoming event begin to channel itself toward excitement.

"Please, help yourself to refreshments," Lacey added.

"Refreshments? How delightful!"

The society members began babbling to one another as they selected pastries from the display and poured themselves mugs of tea.

Before Lacey even had a chance to show them into the auction room, she heard the bell above the door *ting-a-ling* again.

She turned, and was surprised to see some locals were entering the store. Her hairdresser. Carol from the B'n'B. Hester the librarian.

The door didn't even have time to close before they were followed inside by a group of curious tourists. Streaming right in after them was the vacationing Danish couple who'd been her store's first ever customers.

Hope blossomed in her chest. She had not known what to expect from today, but it certainly looked like she'd be holding a proper auction.

Which was the perfect time for Superintendent Turner to enter and ruin her mood.

Lacey tensed. The detective was with his partner, DCI Beth Lewis, and Lacey prepared herself from them to present her with a court document preventing the auction. But instead, Superintendent Turner kept his eyes averted and it was DCI Lewis who took the lead role.

"Lacey, we're here to observe your auction," Beth Lewis said. "We think it may be helpful for our investigation."

"Do you?" Lacey asked, frowning with suspicion at Karl Turner, who'd evidently had a change of heart and U-turned on the whole matter.

DCI Lewis looked at her superior as she spoke, in a strange role reversal. "Superintendent Turner wants to apologize. He's come to accept that it makes a lot of sense to hold the auction in order to lure the killer, and that it may indeed help in the investigation."

Superintendent Turner looked sheepish, like DCI Lewis was his mother getting him to apologize for some discretion. All of his usual bluster and bravado seemed to have drained out of him entirely.

"Karl?" Lacey said, deciding to address him by first name rather than the formal title that implied respect he most certainly had not gained. She waited expectantly, arms folded.

"If we could sit in on the auction that would be helpful," he mumbled.

"So it's not a ludicrous idea after all?" Lacey prodded.

"No. It's not ludicrous."

"Fantastic," Lacey said, smiling. "Then help yourselves to pastries."

She watched, feeling triumphant, as the two detectives selected treats from the counter and went inside the auction room to take their seats.

To Lacey's surprise, the place filled up quickly, so much so that the fifty chairs she'd rented weren't enough to seat everyone. Word must have spread that the items she was auctioning were very expensive, that perhaps as a novice she was likely to make mistakes that would earn some clever types some bargains. Lacey could hardly keep track of everyone entering, and was surprised to see all three of Iris's children had slipped in undetected and taken seats, separately, in the auction room. She wondered if they'd been forced to sit apart because of which seats had been taken when they arrived, or if it was out of choice. A sign of disharmony amongst the trio? None of them were eating the pastries either, she noted.

Just then, Nigel hobbled inside. It was the first time Lacey had seen him since he'd moved up, then back down, her list of suspects. She felt awkward, not knowing what to do or how to greet him. If he'd really backstabbed her and played her for a fool, she didn't think she could bear to carry on with the charade.

Luckily, there was a sea of people separating them. Nigel had no choice but to just wave to her over everyone's heads. Even returning that gesture made Lacey's stomach turn with the feeling of deceit.

She watched him closely as he took his seat. His limp was definitely more pronounced now, and Lacey twisted her lips as the feeling overcame her once more that Nigel was indeed the robber. Whether he was also a killer, though, remained to be seen.

Just then, the sound of Chester growling pulled Lacey out of her thoughts. She looked over to see Cruella de Taryn entering her store.

What's she doing here? Lacey thought, angrily, as she marched up to the woman.

"Lacey," Taryn said in her fake syrupy voice. "I thought I'd come and show some moral support."

Lacey narrowed her eyes with skepticism. Taryn was far more likely there to disrupt proceedings. "How kind of you," Lacey said.

"Isn't it good that my DIY work finished today?" she continued. "Just in time for your auction."

"Yes, what a wonderful coincidence," Lacey said through clenched teeth.

"I do hope Keith isn't too noisy in the garden, though," she added, punctuating the statement with her fake-friendly giggle.

Lacey narrowed her eyes. "What?"

"Oh, didn't I tell you?" Taryn said sweetly. "I'm getting Keith to remodel the garden. Those sheds I have out there are an eyesore, especially in comparison to your lovely garden. He's building some nice new wooden sheds to replace them."

If Lacey gritted her teeth any harder they'd crack. Of course, on the one day she needed to use the back room, Taryn had arranged for the noise to move from the adjoining wall to the adjoining garden! The noise would very easily travel into the auction room, and was absolutely going to interfere. Taryn was only here so she could have a front row seat to watch the whole thing go down.

"Doesn't Keith want to join in the fun?" Lacey asked.

Taryn looked amused by the suggestion. "Keith doesn't know the first thing about antiques. He's an all brawn, no brain type. Ooh, are these pastries made by Tom?"

She swirled off toward the counter, her upturned nose sniffing like a dog for a bone.

Speak of the devil, Tom entered next. He walked up to Lacey with his wicker basket radiating the smells of sugar and pastry.

"I brought reinforcements," he said, gesturing to his wicker basket of delights. "I saw everyone streaming in and thought there's no way I'd catered enough for everyone."

His sunny disposition instantly melted the frosty feeling that had seeped into Lacey's bones thanks to Taryn's presence.

"You don't have to cater for *anyone*," Lacey reminded him.

He looked at her like she was crazy. "What kind of friend would I be if I didn't support you on your first ever auction?"

Friend, Lacey thought. Had Tom given up on her dithering and decided to friend-zone her? She certainly hoped not.

As Tom stocked up the refreshments table with newly baked goodies, the smells of butter and sugar permeating the store, Lacey caught sight of the clock. It was auction time. She swallowed her nerves and entered the room.

So many eyes stared at Lacey as she took her position, she couldn't help but feel nervous. Amongst the people present she had her mean old boss, her nemesis, and a murderer. But scanning the audience and seeing Tom, as well as Gina, Ivan, Stephen, and Martha, helped to bolster her. Her allies outweighed her foes. And, of course, she had Percy Johnson for moral support, too.

Lacey began by presenting Iris's collection of Victorian vases. A coo of pleasure emanated from the English Antiques Society members and Lacey couldn't help but smile.

The bidding began, mainly taking place between the group, who seemed absurdly jovial and congratulatory to one another. It was a far cry from the New York auctions Lacey was accustomed too that were much more vicious and frantic. In fact, her auction had a very genteel atmosphere.

With the vases sold, Lacey moved onto the ottomans, removing the shoji screen behind which they were displayed.

Once again, the society members *oohed* and *ahhed* with appreciation. It was extremely endearing, and even the audience members seemed delighted by their antics.

But just as the bidding was being pushed up and up over the collection, the sound of hammering came from the garden.

Lacey felt instantly flustered. She began to stammer over her words.

Taryn smirked. Saskia looked at her watch and yawned. Superintendent Turner stood up and took his smoking tin from his pocket.

"You can't smoke in here," Lacey said, pausing the proceedings.

The detective shrugged, put a cigarette in his mouth, and crossed the floor for the garden, passing right in front of her as he went, with no regard for how impolite that was.

Lacey frowned. Determined not to let anyone or anything throw her off, she finished the bidding for the ottoman collection.

Next was the jewelry—the items in the acrylic boxes she'd first appraised. But just as she began, the banging from the garden stopped and was replaced by the sound of a chain saw! And on top of that, Lacey heard the sound of Chester barking furiously.

"Sorry," she said to the audience, finally giving in. "I have to see to this."

Percy stood. "Don't worry, Lacey. I've got this."

Lacey left the auction in his extremely capable hands and ran out into the garden.

There, she saw Superintendent Turner smoking, with his back resting against the greenhouse. Over the fence, in Taryn's lawn, Keith was working with a circular saw, cutting up bits of wood.

Between the two of them, barking loudly, was Chester.

Lacey had never heard Chester so wound up like this. It wasn't like him to bark. In fact, she'd only seen him become agitated once—when her store was being robbed.

That's when Lacey realized what was happening. Chester was trying to tell her something. Something important.

She looked over the fence at Keith to see his pant leg had ridden up. On the pale flesh of his ankle, red, raw, and as clear as day, was a set of puncture marks made by teeth.

Lacey gasped. Keith was her robber.

CHAPTER TWENTY SIX

Lacey took Chester by the collar to calm him down and looked over at Superintendent Turner.

"That's him!" she mouthed.

The detective frowned at first, but then when he looked over to where Lacey was frantically pointing, his eyes widened with understanding. He chucked his cigarette butt onto the grass and walked over to the fence.

"Excuse me," he called.

Keith powered down the chain saw. He looked a bit surprised to see a cop facing him. "What? I'm not doing nothing wrong."

"I wondered if you might be able to spare a minute. Just to have a chat."

"I don't chat with cops. Not without a lawyer."

"Then you'd better call your lawyer quick," the detective said. "Because if you don't answer my questions voluntarily, I'll have you arrested."

Keith looked instantly furious. "Arrested for what?!"

"Burglary."

"What?" Keith bellowed.

It was all getting a bit tense, and Lacey hoped the altercation couldn't be heard inside the auction room, though she suspected the tone of their angry voices would carry.

"Karl, please can you do this elsewhere?" Lacey pleaded with Superintendent Turner.

"Sure," the detective said. With a nonchalant shrug, he stepped over the fence into Taryn's garden and walked right up to Keith. "Come on, mate. Let's talk inside."

Lacey watched as the flabbergasted handyman was led inside the boutique.

Her mind felt scrambled. Taryn must've gotten Keith to break into her store. But then that meant the burglary and the murder weren't connected at all. Was her theory completely wrong?

Though Lacey's mind felt all over the place, she knew there was no time to dwell on it. She still had an auction going on inside.

She hurried back into the auction room to discover Percy had finished selling all the jewels and they were down to the final item. The grandfather clock itself!

Lacey took her position back at the podium. But her confidence that she was about to catch a killer had been shaken by the revelation of Keith being the robber. Perhaps the moment of clarity she was expecting from the sale of the clock wouldn't come after all.

"It's time for our final item," Lacey announced, hearing her own voice sound robotic as her mind reeled through everything at a mile a minute, desperate to make sense of it all.

She removed the screen to show the grandfather clock and an appreciative murmur went up around the audience.

"It's a one of a kind, handmade, eighteenth-century grandfather clock," she said on autopilot. "Made from fine burr walnut. The key is missing so the clock cannot be fixed, but it is beautiful as an objet d'art."

She scanned the audience with her eyes, looking from one sibling to the next. Before, she'd been so certain that whoever of them bid on the clock would be the murderer. But now, she didn't know what to believe.

"Let's start the bidding at ten thousand pounds."

The first bid was immediately put in by none other than Henry Archer.

Lacey looked at the youngest of the trio, doing her best to keep the suspicion from her eyes.

"Ten thousand," she said, pointing at him with affirmation. "Can I get ten thousand five hundred?"

"Here!"

The next voice belonged to Benjamin Archer.

Lacey snapped her gaze to him. So two of her three suspects were in on the bidding. But her third, Nigel, remained mute. He watched placidly, not making even a peep. If the dog bites on Keith's legs hadn't been enough evidence to exonerate Nigel in itself, well, his silence now was certainly enough. Nigel wasn't her guy. Not for the robbery. Not for the murder.

But was it one of the brothers? The two seemed intent on outbidding one another for the clock.

As the price was pushed up higher and higher, the battle passing back and forth between the two brothers, Lacey spotted something very curious. Between each pause after Henry made his bet and Benjamin countered it, the younger brother looked to Clarissa. It appeared to Lacey as if he was looking for some kind of assurance from her. Perhaps even instructions?

And then, while her focus was supposed to be on Benjamin during his bid, Lacey saw Clarissa give a small nod of the head.

"Thirty thousand," Henry announced.

Lacey could hardly stop herself from frowning. Henry and Clarissa were working *together*. They must've pooled their cash to outbid their elder brother.

Benjamin confidently bid thirty-five thousand five hundred pounds, his hand shooting up in the air, his gold wedding band flashing in the light. Lacey took the bid and turned to Henry, but she was starting to feel unreal, like her mind was filled with thick molasses. It was becoming hard to stay focused on the proceedings, because her mind was racing at a thousand miles a second.

Henry's hand shot up for the next amount. There was no glint on his wedding ring finger. No band. She heard Nigel's words echo in her mind. *"Since he found his wife and settled down and started his surfing business, he's been much calmer."*

He's divorcing! Lacey thought. *That's why he was visiting Clarissa in London. Have the two teamed up? Are they in this together?'*

But just as Lacey thought she may have found her answer, Clarissa gave Henry a small shake of the head. On his next turn to bid, Henry fell silent. He'd dropped out of the race.

In that one small gesture, Lacey's theory smashed into a thousand pieces around her.

She paused. Stumbled. Heard the keen silence that followed as the whole room seemed to draw in a breath. All eyes were on her, staring, blinking, waiting.

Lacey straightened up and turned her gaze to Benjamin. With a firm, confident voice, she announced, "Going, going, gone. Sold for thirty-five thousand five hundred pounds to Benjamin Archer."

She hit the gavel. The noise sounded like a bomb exploding in her ears.

Clarissa and Henry had indeed teamed up. But not to kill their mother. Because of sibling rivalry. Clarissa's failed business. Henry's failed marriage. And an older brother who had everything. Who rubbed it all in their face. Who'd succeeded where they'd failed. They'd been bidding on the clock not because they wanted what was hidden inside, but to get back at their older brother.

Their older brother who, in purchasing the clock, had moved back into the prime position on Lacey's list of suspects.

Was Benjamin Archer the murderer?

Lacey needed some air. Her mind was reeling. She staggered out into the garden, Chester nudging her with his nose as she bent over and tried to catch her breath.

Suddenly, Nigel was there.

"Lacey!" he exclaimed. "What's wrong?"

"Oh, Nigel," she said, throwing her arms around him. "I owe you an apology."

"What? Why?" Nigel asked, patting her back kindly.

"I...I thought you'd broken into my store," Lacey blurted. "That you'd stolen Iris's painting and hidden it in the clock, and then tried to steal it back but now I know I was wrong. Can you forgive me?"

There was a long pause. Lacey thought Nigel must be reeling from her accusation. He was probably so hurt that she could even accuse him he couldn't even look at her.

"There's nothing to forgive," Nigel said. "Because you're right."

Now it was Lacey's turned to be stunned into silence. "What? You...broke into my store? Why?"

"Lady Isabelle's painting. I hadn't been in Iris's room since her death. I couldn't. It was too painful. But that night, after I had you move her things to your store, I decided to. And I noticed the painting was missing right away. Besides me, there were only three other people who could possibly have known about its existence. Benjamin. Clarissa. Henry. It made me certain that one of the children was the murderer. That they'd killed their own mother, and my dearest friend, for a painting." His voice cracked as he spoke. "I saw red. I was overwhelmed with grief. I paced about for an hour working out what must've happened. I thought about the clock, and how incensed they'd been about it when they barged in here. It occurred to me that the key might not have been lost at all, that they may have hidden the painting inside, assuming the clock was amongst the handful of items they were set to inherit. I had to know for certain. I was mad with grief. I'm so sorry. So, so sorry."

Lacey paused, letting his words sink in. She'd been right about Nigel, but wrong about his motives. He'd acted out of grief, out of devastation that his best friend had been killed for a painting. And hadn't she, too, stood over that very same grandfather clock with a crowbar held over her head, ready to smash it up and find out whether *her* theory was correct? Perhaps she'd not gone as far as to actually damage anything, but she sure as heck was close to it. She could empathize with Nigel.

"But why didn't you bid for the clock?" she asked. "If you thought the painting was inside?"

"I have no money," Nigel replied.

"But you know that painting is worth millions. You'd easily earn enough for the clock from the eventual sale of the painting."

"Sell it?" Nigel exclaimed. "I don't want to sell it. Iris wanted the world to know the story of Lady Isabelle. She wanted the painting donated to a museum after her death. It's one of the reasons I was so distraught when we bumped into one another in the hallway. I had been sitting in Iris's room realizing I would never be able to fulfil her wish." His eyes welled up again with tears. "Then you showed me that photo. I don't know if you noticed, but Iris was wearing the clock's key on a pendant. It made me even more convinced the key wasn't lost, but that the children are in possession of it. I wanted to come clean to you right then, and then tell you my suspicions, but I couldn't bring myself to say the words." He looked at Lacey, eyes shining. "Please, I beg that you don't hand me in to the police."

Lacey suddenly remembered Keith, who was being questioned at this very moment. He must've gotten the dogs bites on his leg from some other event entirely. In her moment of stress, she'd made a rookie mistake and connected two unrelated things, building up a picture that was completely inaccurate.

"I won't," she told him. "They have their hands full with the wrong guy anyway..."

Nigel looked puzzled, but Lacey reached out and patted his arm.

"I understand what you were going through, and why you did what you did. I just wished you'd trusted me enough to tell me your theory."

"I'm sorry. But I was suspicious of you too."

"Me?"

"Yes. You appeared out of nowhere. I wasn't sure what you were all about at first."

"Huh," Lacey said, slightly stung. "Well, I thought *you* were the one who'd hidden the painting."

"Me?" Nigel exclaimed. "But I ... I *told* you about it!"

Lacey blushed. "I thought you were hiding in plain sight. That you were using me because I was naive. And I'm sorry I suspected you."

Nigel tutted and shook his head. "I can see how I made myself look suspicious. Please, let's move on from this whole debacle."

Lacey nodded.

With the robbery situation resolved and decoupled from the murder once and for all, Lacey's mind went back to the theory that she and Nigel had independently come to. That the painting was in the clock, and thus the murderer was Benjamin.

"We need to solve this once and for all," Lacey said with determination. "We need to break the clock."

If only she'd had the guts to have done that all along! If only she hadn't disturbed Nigel that night while he'd been attempting to do the same thing. If either of them had gone through with their plans and gotten confirmation that Lady Isabelle's painting was hidden inside the clock, then the murder would already be solved.

She looked up at Nigel, resolved. "It's the only way."

He nodded morosely. "Then let's do it."

They hurried back into the auction room. But Benjamin was already moving the clock.

"You can't do that!" Lacey cried, running over.

He turned, checkbook already in his hand. "I'm going to pay and take this away today," he told her with the firm authority of a CEO.

"That's not how it works, Mr. Archer," Lacey explained. "We require a ten percent deposit on the day to secure the item, the rest to be paid upon safe delivery."

Benjamin looked unflappable. "I will take it today whether you accept my payment or not."

"It's an insurance thing," Lacey tried to explain. She could hear the tremble in her voice, though. She was talking to a *murderer*. "To protect you and I both. We use special couriers, with their own protection, but anything outside of that puts us both in a legal quagmire."

"I don't care two hoots about your quagmires, young lady. Give me the name and number of your courier and I'll arrange it myself."

He was adamant, and not backing down, and Lacey felt herself starting to falter beneath his imposing demeanor. The sort of man who beat his own mother to death wasn't the sort of man she wanted to get into an altercation with, even if DCI Lewis was present, watching the interaction with a piercing, curious look.

Lacey glanced across at Nigel. He gave an almost imperceptible shake of the head, and she understood what he was communicating to her immediately. They had to back down. They weren't going to get their answers, not now anyway.

Lacey gave in. She provided Ben with the details. Without thanking her, he marched off to make his call and arrange for their main piece of evidence to be whisked away.

Lacey sagged with disappointment. She had taken two steps forward but one step back, and, for the time being, the mystery must remain unsolved. But she wasn't giving up. She'd come up with something, some way to expose Benjamin for his crime once and for all.

CHAPTER TWENTY SEVEN

Nigel and Lacey sat at the kitchen table. Through the windows, the sky was black. A thick mist had rolled in off the ocean. Hours had passed since they'd watched Benjamin take their only piece of evidence away, and neither had come up with a plan to catch him out yet.

A bottle of wine stood open between them—something to drown their sorrows.

Just then, Lacey heard a knocking on the door.

"Are you expecting anyone?" Nigel asked.

Lacey shook her head. Curious, she left Nigel in the company of Chester and another glass of Shiraz, and paced through the dark corridor to the front door. She pulled it open and saw Gina standing on her step holding a watering can.

"Great news, Lacey!" her neighbor exclaimed, stepping inside the cottage without waiting to be invited. "I've just got off the phone to the police. They arrested that loiterer. You'll never guess who it was!"

Lacey frowned, utterly at a loss. She looked at her cardigan-clad neighbor, dripping water onto the rug from her watering can. Her friend was clearly having a senior moment.

"I'm sorry, Gina, but what are you talking about?" Lacey asked, gently.

"The man!" Gina exclaimed, wide-eyed with excitement. "The man I saw snooping around the other night!" She paused and put a finger to her lips in contemplation. "Wait. Didn't I tell you about that? I told *someone*. Who was it? Honestly, sometimes I think I'm losing my marbles." She chuckled. "Oh, I remember. It was Ivan!

That's right! He was going to pass the message on to you but I guess he decided it best not to worry you."

Lacey shook her head, utterly dumbfounded. She was more than a little freaked out by what Gina was telling her, and the woman's absentmindedness was making things worse.

"Start from the beginning," Lacey urged her. "Someone was loitering around the cottage?"

Gina nodded. "It was the other night. I was out watering the plants. You know how they prefer to be watered under moonlight." She waved the watering can as if to prove some point. "Anyhoo, I saw this fellow. Big, burly guy, coming up the path toward the cottage. The sheep didn't like the look of him *at all*. They went lumbering off toward him, bleating blue murder!" She burst out laughing. "I've never seen a big man like that run so fast in all my life! He even tripped over and got nipped by a couple of them! Anyway, I told the police about it, and they just rang back to tell me the guy's in custody. It was—"

"—Keith," Lacey finished for her, her mind conjuring the memory of Keith in Taryn's garden with his pant leg rolled up to reveal bite marks on his ankle. Not bite marks from a dog, but bite marks from sheep!

Gina gave Lacey a perplexed look. "That's right. But how do you know who Wilfordshire's local scallywag is?"

"*Because,*" Lacey began, "Keith has been working as Taryn's handyman."

Gina gasped, as if the pieces had suddenly slotted together in her mind. "You don't think Taryn sent him up here, do you? To scare you? My goodness! What do you think she wanted him to do?"

Lacey shuddered. "I dread to think."

"That woman," Gina said, shaking her head. "Well, at least the police caught the guy. Identified him by the bite marks." She laughed. "So what are you up to?"

"Nigel and I are discussing what to do next, now that we know who killed Iris."

Gina nodded solemnly. "Would you like some help?"

"If you're willing to give it," Lacey said. "Three heads are better than two."

"Then count me in," Gina replied.

Lacey went to shut the door behind Gina when she heard a voice calling her from the darkness.

"Lace! Lace!"

She turned back and squinted to get a better look. Tom was hurrying up the drive. It was only then that Lacey realized he'd missed the auction, that after he'd returned back to his patisserie to bake more croissants, he hadn't returned.

"Tom?" she asked, surprised. "What happened to you?"

"Long story," he said, panting from the climb. "When I made it back to the patisserie, I discovered Paul had used baking powder instead of baking soda for tomorrow morning's pastry batch. I had to drive all the way to the Cash 'n' Carry to buy more, then make the whole lot again. By the time I got back to the auction, it was over and everyone had gone. So? What happened? Who bought the clock?"

"Ben," Lacey said.

"So it was Ben!" Tom exclaimed. "He's the killer? And the one who tried to burgle you?"

"Actually, the burglar was Nigel."

Tom frowned. "Were they working together?"

Lacey shook her head. "No. It's complicated. You should come in out of the cold."

Tom nodded and entered. As he followed Lacey and Chester along the corridor toward the kitchen, where the voices of Gina and Nigel grew louder, he suddenly paused and took Lacey's arm.

"He's here? Nigel?" he whispered. "The burglar?"

Lacey quickly explained. "When Nigel realized the painting was missing, he came to the same conclusion I did, that Iris was murdered for the painting, and that it had been hidden in the clock. He came here to break open the clock and prove his theory."

Tom pulled an expression of distaste. "Couldn't he have just called ahead and asked? Rather than breaking into your store with a crowbar and scaring the bejesus out of everyone!"

"Grief makes you crazy," Lacey said. "And he learned his lesson." She patted Chester's head, and he whined.

But Tom still didn't look convinced. He tipped his head to gaze into the kitchen, where Nigel was pouring Gina a wine. When he looked back at Lacey, his expression was serious.

"You're a more forgiving person than I am, Lace, to invite your self-confessed burglar into your home. Grief-stricken or not, it was a terrible thing for him to do to you."

Lacey paused. She'd noted the protective air in Tom's tone. He was looking out for her, and it made a warmth spread through her. Throughout the darkness of Iris's murder, Tom had always been her shining light.

They went inside the kitchen. Tom flashed Nigel a slightly reticent look, and accepted the glass of wine he poured for him with a slightly stiff "Thank you."

Together, they began strategizing on how to expose Benjamin. They talked everything through, from Lady Isabelle's painting to the clock, to the loophole in the will, to the history of male inheritance and Iris's final wishes.

"If only there was a way we could convince the police to look inside the clock," Lacey said. "Once they see the painting is in there, they'll have him."

"He'll be on his way back to South Africa by now, won't he?" Gina said. "Now he's got what he wanted, I can't imagine he'll want to hang around the scene of his crime any longer."

"He'll have caught the first plane, I'm certain," Nigel agreed.

"But what about the clock?" Tom asked. "A huge, heavy piece like that can't just be shoved in the undercarriage of a 737, can it?"

Lacey sat up straight. "That's a good point. Ben spent over thirty grand on that thing. He won't risk it being mishandled or damaged in transportation." But then she remembered the details she'd given him for the specialist removal's firm. They handled all kinds of aspects of delivering and moving large antique valuables. "That said, while it's not easy, it's not impossible for a wealthy CEO to pay his way out of the problem if he needs to."

She felt herself slump as the burst of adrenaline from her short-lived moment of hope left her.

"Okay, but where does he live?" Tom asked.

Lacey noticed his eyes were sparkling like he might have hit on a brain wave.

"Cape Town," she said. "Why?"

Tom held up a finger. "Give me a sec." He went on his phone, quickly tapping buttons. "Thought so!" he said, triumphantly.

"What?" Lacey questioned, curiosity making her impatient.

Tom grinned at her. "There's only one direct flight from London to Cape Town per day. All the rest involve connections and lengthy stopovers. A wealthy CEO isn't going to waste half a day sitting in a Moroccan airport for a connecting flight. He'll fly direct. Definitely."

"Your point?" Lacey asked.

"He missed today's flight," Tom said. "It was at four p.m. and the auction didn't finish until three. Unless he was rocket launched to Heathrow, there's no way he caught the flight. We have until four p.m. tomorrow to convince Superintendent Turner that your theory is right."

Hope blossomed in Lacey's chest again. Perhaps there was still a chance they could catch their killer.

"Hey, guys, look," Tom said, pointing to the clock on the wall. It was midnight. They'd been talking for hours. "It's Easter."

"You're right," Nigel said. He looked suddenly more depressed than ever. "Iris loved Easter. It was her favorite festival. She told me how every year she'd put on an egg hunt for the children, then they'd have an afternoon meal together, then take it in turns doing Bible readings." He dabbed at a tear in his eye. "Would anyone object to a prayer? In Iris's honor."

Lacey gave Nigel a sympathetic look. At times, she'd let herself forget there was a dead woman at the center of all of this. But Nigel had been her friend, her confidant, and he'd have to live the rest of his days knowing someone he cared for deeply had been taken from him before their time.

Gina patted Nigel's hand across the table. "Not at all, poppet. I think that would be lovely."

Tom and Lacey nodded as well, and they all bowed their heads as they listened to Nigel's poignant prayer of gratitude and forgiveness.

When he was finished, they all said a soft, "Amen."

But just as Lacey unclasped her hands and opened her eyes, something suddenly clicked in her mind.

Easter... Bible readings...

She leapt up and struck both her fists against the table. Everyone jumped in their seats and turned to her, blinking.

"Lacey?" Gina asked.

"What's wrong?" Tom added.

"We've got the wrong killer!" Lacey exclaimed.

"What?" Nigel said with a gasp. "But Ben bought the clock. It has to be him."

Lacey shook her head emphatically. "Trust me. It wasn't him. But I know who it was. And I know exactly how we're going to expose them."

Everyone around the table exchanged bewildered expressions as Lacey grabbed her phone.

"Who are you calling?" Tom appealed.

"Superintendent Turner," she replied. "He's going to want to be there when I catch a killer."

CHAPTER TWENTY EIGHT

Lacey strolled past the convoy of shiny black cars parked in the driveway of Penrose Manor and trotted up the steps to the door. As she wrapped her knuckles against it, she couldn't help but recall that moment all those days ago when the door had swung open beneath her fist and this whole nightmare had begun. Now, she'd come full circle, and she was here to finish, once and for all, what had started that terrible morning she'd found Iris Archer dead.

Though the sun was shining on her back, Lacey felt like a dark cloud was hanging over her head. Her breath seemed stuck in her lungs, she was so nervous about what she was about to do.

She looked down at Chester, her trusty companion. He wagged his tail at her; the doggie equivalent of a pat on the back.

Just then, the door was opened from the inside. Nigel stood in the doorway.

"They're here," Lacey said, nodding her head over her shoulder toward the cars in the drive.

"They are," he confirmed with a stiff nod.

He looks as stressed as I feel, Lacey thought as he let her inside.

She smelled the cooking right away, and headed for the kitchen. Inside, Tom was standing over the stove, working on the Easter meal. He gave her a tense grin as she entered. Even the unflappable Tom Forrester was nervous about their plan.

"How's it all going in here?" Lacey asked him.

His eyes flicked to the clock on the wall. "We're right on schedule."

"Great." She flashed him a smile, one she knew would betray her nerves. But she didn't need to pretend to be something she wasn't in front of Tom. She was about to confront a killer, after all.

Just then, the sound of squabbling came through the door that adjoined with the dining room. It was the three distinct voices of Benjamin, Henry, and Clarissa. Hearing them made Lacey's stomach turn even more. Her tongue felt suddenly like it was pasted to the roof of her mouth, as if her heightened anxiety had burned up all the water in her body.

"It's been like that since they got here," Tom explained, as she went to the faucet and poured herself a glass of fresh water.

"I'd expect no less," Lacey replied.

She downed the water and glanced over at the clock. It was show time.

"Let's do this," she said.

"Good luck," Tom told her.

She took a deep breath to steady herself, then pushed open the door into the dining room.

The scene Lacey entered into was exactly as she'd pictured it when she'd gone through the details of her plan last night with Gina, Nigel, and Tom. Laid out on the dressers that lined the perimeter of the dining table were all of the items from the playroom—tattered toys, dolls, books, and figurines that had seen better days. Each object had been labeled and itemized as per instructions. It reminded Lacey a little bit of a museum.

Walking around the perimeter of the room, peering at the items on display, were the three siblings. They kept jostling one another to get a better view, or to state their claim to whatever it was they were looking at. And beside each of Iris Archer's entitled children—wearing matching hawkish expressions—was a lawyer. They'd each brought one, to see over the proceedings. The whole thing made Lacey think of magpies stealing shiny objects from one another's nest.

"You cannot have my dolls!" Clarissa was wailing at Ben. "What do you even need them for?"

"My daughters will love them," the eldest brother replied haughtily.

"But they're *mine*!" She looked at her lawyer, her eyes round with childish indignance. "Isn't that obvious?"

"I'll put them onto the list of items you regard as your own, Miss Archer," her lawyer said dispassionately.

It was obvious the lawyers were hating every second of this. If there hadn't been a dead woman at the center of it all, Lacey might have seen the funny side.

"This is so unfair," Clarissa hissed. "He's already got the clock!"

"I paid for that, fair and square," Ben replied, smugly. "With money *I* earned from my business, might I add. Unlike yours, mine didn't fail!"

Lacey tensed. The claws were coming out. But she wasn't surprised. The children may have been putting on something of a united front before, but divvying up their items was always going to turn them against each other. And that's exactly how she needed them to be if she was going to extract the confession she needed.

Just then, the door swung shut behind Lacey with a dull thud. All eyes snapped to her. Lacey felt herself recoil under the anger in their eyes.

"What's she doing here?" Clarissa demanded, her glare so intense, Lacey felt like she'd been struck with a frozen laser beam.

Nigel replied coolly and calmly. "You know she was appointed to handle the items within the estate."

"But these aren't for sale!" Henry scoffed before Nigel had a chance to finish explaining.

Nigel pursed his lips with irritation. He managed to keep his cool as he explained, "She wants to be present when items are removed from the house. It's to legally protect her from any *claims* of theft that may be made."

Clarissa raised a thin eyebrow, clearly having successfully read between the lines and realized Nigel had insinuated that one of them might later claim Lacey took something from the house she shouldn't have.

Henry looked at his lawyer. He looked like a lost boy next to Benjamin in his sharply tailored black suit. The lawyer gave Henry a single confirmative nod of the head.

"Fine," Henry replied, folding his arms like a petulant child.

Clarissa looked nonplussed.

"Can we just get this Easter lunch over with?" Benjamin said to Nigel, in his abrupt manner. "I have a meeting in Johannesburg tomorrow morning. If I miss my flight I'll sue." He looked over at Lacey. "Both of you."

Nigel gestured to the dining table, which was laid out beautifully with fine china pieces that Lacey would one day be tasked with auctioning.

"Then please, let's sit."

His clipped tone made it evident to Lacey just how much he was struggling to stay composed in the face of Iris's murderer. She couldn't blame him. She was growing more tense by the second.

Ben beelined for the chair at the head of the table. Henry shot his brother a withering look as he was beaten to the seat.

"I don't know why we need to have this stupid meal anyway," he muttered.

"It's our last chance to say goodbye to Mother," Clarissa hissed as she took her. "You know how much she loved Easter. Always putting on those egg hunts for us."

Henry shrugged. "I don't remember any egg hunts. She must've given up by the time I was old enough to join in."

He slumped into his chair like a grumpy teenager. Lacey noted, once more, the missing wedding ring, the patch of white skin in his otherwise golden tan that indicated he had recently removed the band. Her theory became yet more solidified in her mind, and her confidence grew.

"Whether you remember or not," Benjamin said sharply to his younger brother, "this was our home, and this is our last chance to say goodbye before we're locked out of here forever."

He cast cold eyes at Nigel. A chill ran down Lacey's spine. Even though she'd worked out that Ben wasn't the killer, she still despised the man and his terrible attitude. She quickly took her seat at the other head of the table, opposite Ben. His siblings sat either side of him, and despite several feet worth of walnut wood stretching between her and them, it still felt too close for comfort.

Lacey looked at Nigel. He gave her a small nod of the head. Then the kitchen doors flew open and in came Tom, pushing a metal trolley. On the trolley were several silver cloched dishes, underneath which were all the various dishes for their meal. And lying next to them was the red leather-bound Bible she'd found in the guest room, with the empty compartment cut in the pages where Lacey had found the photograph of her father.

Tom began to lay the dishes out on the table, then handed the Bible to Lacey. He left.

"Am I right in thinking you used to read Bible passages together on Easter?" Lacey said. "Perhaps we ought to read some passages in honor of your mother. I found this Bible amongst her things."

She held it up. Just as she'd predicted, Clarissa's eyes snapped to it and widened. Her face began to drain of all color.

"Of course, it would've been amongst the auctionable items of your mother's," Lacey continued in a sing-songy tone. "A beautiful copy like this. Only it's been damaged." She opened it to show everyone at the table the cut pages.

"What is she blathering on about?" Benjamin asked with a scowl.

But Lacey's eyes were fixed on Clarissa, who appeared to be trembling. Despite her nerves, Lacey managed to keep her voice steady.

"There's a lovely passage in here I'd like to read," she said calmly. "Oh, unless *you'd* like to, Clarissa? Since it is your Bible, after all. Your special hiding place. The hiding place where you kept the key to the grandfather clock."

Henry and Ben both turned to look at Clarissa, who was becoming visibly stressed under the scrutiny of everyone's eyes. She tugged at the collar of her expensive-looking turtleneck.

"What is wrong with that woman?" Ben said, grabbing his fork, too impatient to wait for the reading. "She's a lunatic!" He began to shovel in his food.

"Do you want to tell them or should I?" Lacey said, her eyes now boring into Clarissa.

Clarissa squirmed. "I don't know what you're talking about."

"Yes, you do," Lacey returned without missing a beat. She had to put the pressure on. Turn up the heat. "You see, there's another reason I asked Nigel to gather you all here today, beyond finalizing the will. It's because I worked out who killed your mother. And the killer is sitting at this table." She looked at Clarissa again. "Why don't you tell them how you killed your mother, Clarissa?"

Ben spat out his mouthful of lamb. His fork clattered to the table. He looked at his sister. Then he tipped his head back and began to laugh.

He picked his fork back up and, pointing the grizzled bit of lamb on its tip toward Clarissa, pinned Lacey with his eyes.

"Her? Are you mad? Clarissa couldn't say boo to a fly without crying!" He shoved the lamb in his mouth and spoke through his mouthful. "I didn't know we were going to be treated to a comedy show over Easter dinner."

But Lacey stayed firm. She kept her eyes on Clarissa. The woman was looking awkward and Lacey decided to turn up the heat to get her to confess.

"Of course, you didn't harm her yourself," Lacey said. "You don't have it in you. But perhaps if you enlisted someone with a short fuse to help, someone who'd do the deed for you ... someone like your little brother, Henry."

Now Ben's shoulders began to shake with his mocking laughter. "Oh, this just gets better." He sneered at Lacey. "Let me guess, someone told you about the soup incident. About how Henry once lashed out at the chef? Well, perhaps if you'd been more thorough with your homework, you'd have found out that Henry hasn't had a violent outburst in years. That was only stress from his gambling addiction that made him act like that. But ever since he married Sheila and started his own thriving business, he's become a model citizen."

Ben went to tuck into his meal again. But Lacey was far from done. She didn't blame Benjamin for not wanting to face the truth, but she had to hold her ground in the face of his nasty condescending manner.

"So Henry hasn't told you about his divorce?" she asked Benjamin. "Or how his business has failed?"

Ben put his fork down again, this time more forcibly, clearly irritated. There was a spear of broccoli still on its tip that hadn't had the chance to make it all the way into his mouth.

He threw his napkin down and looked at Henry.

"Please tell this meddling American she's gotten completely the wrong end of the stick here," he barked, sounding like he reached the end of his patience. "That you and Sheila have a rock-solid marriage and a successful business."

But Henry didn't speak, and Lacey saw Ben's gaze flick down to his brother's left hand, to the space where his wedding band should be.

"Henry?" Ben said, the tone in his voice shifting.

His resolve was fading, and Lacey seized upon it.

"I'm afraid to say, your brother has indeed been under a lot of stress recently. His marriage ended. He came back to London, turning up on Clarissa's doorstep for help. That's when she concocted her devious plan. She saw the stress of the divorce had reignited something in Henry that hadn't been there in years, the wild, volatile side of him that had come out before during the years of his gambling addiction. She knew she could get him to lash out. One more time. At your mother. Clarissa set the whole thing up and—"

"ENOUGH!" Benjamin suddenly bellowed, thumping his fists onto the table. The gravy jug went flying, spraying thick brown globules onto the tablecloth. "Someone get this imbecile out of our home. She'd not welcome here with her spurious accusations."

But no one moved.

"Lacey can stay," Nigel said, in a quiet, solemn voice. He looked at Ben sympathetically. "And I think you ought to hear her out."

Ben shook his head furiously. He flew to his feet so abruptly his chair almost tipped over. "If she won't leave, I will."

He thundered for the dining room door. But at the exact same moment, the door flew open and Tom entered, flanked by Superintendent Turner and DCI Beth Lewis. Behind them, being wheeled in on a large trolley by some police officers, was the antique grandfather clock.

"What is that doing here?" Ben stammered, his fury transforming into confusion and disbelief. "That's supposed to be on a flight to South Africa!"

"I'm afraid we had to seize the clock as evidence in the murder of Iris Archer," Superintendent Turner said. He looked over at Clarissa and Henry, who were both looking down at their untouched dinner plates. "And we're ready to make our arrests."

Ben froze on the spot. He looked at his brother and sister.

"What is going on?" he demanded of them.

But neither spoke. They just sat there blinking at the tabletop as if it might provide some answers.

Something in Ben shifted, like reality was starting to dawn on him. Slowly, his face now devoid of all color, he returned to his seat. Like a balloon deflating, Benjamin sank back into it. All the fight had gone out of him.

He looked from his brother to his sister. "Is it true?"

Neither spoke.

Benjamin looked up at Lacey, wearing an expression of agony. "Tell me what happened. I need to know."

Lacey took a breath and began.

"All your lives, it was Ben and Henry against Clarissa. Even though your mother had said none of you would benefit from the will, you two boys were convinced you would. So Clarissa was alone. Always alone. Trying to bond with her mom through fashion, making jewelry out of bits of junk. The boys always damaged your creations, didn't they, so you took to hiding them. The Bible was just another place to keep your jewelry safe—not that it mattered, you never did quite achieve the bond you wanted with Iris, did you? Even when you studied business at the university and started your own fashion brand, it failed. I'm sure you thought your mother would help you keep the company afloat with a bailout, but she refused. She was sticking firm to her resolve to never give any of you handouts. The company folded and your bitterness grew."

Lacey turned her gaze to Henry. "So how do you come into it, Henry? All your life, you've been on the same team as Ben. The two boys united against their sister. Only, at my auction I saw you two working together, trying to outbid Ben for the clock. That's when I realized you'd switched allegiances. It wasn't Ben and Henry versus Clarissa anymore, it was Clarissa and Henry versus Ben. So what changed?"

She spread her hands onto the tabletop and answered her own question. "You see, I thought it was interesting that you both happened to be in England when your mother died. Only it wasn't a coincidence, was it? You'd come here specifically, hadn't you, Henry, because you were out of money? *Your* business had failed and you'd gambled away the profits. You couldn't face asking Ben to help you—he'd rub it in your face—but Clarissa had been through the same thing, hadn't she? Maybe she'd be able to help. You turned up on her doorstep and asked her what she'd done when she'd been facing destitution. And that's when Clarissa concocted her plan."

She looked again at the woman. "You lied to Henry, didn't you? You told him that your mother had helped you. That she'd supported you through your time of crisis and that if you went to the house together, you'd be able to persuade her to help Henry too. But all along you knew that she would refuse him because she'd already refused you. And you knew the second Henry heard his mother refuse him money at his time of desperation, it would push him over the edge. That he'd snap. You knew your mother was too frail to survive a fall, that it wouldn't take much to kill her. So why did you need her dead, if you weren't going to inherit any money from the will? Because of the painting."

She paused, giving everyone a moment to let what she'd said so far to sink in. "You'd sat on that couch in your mother's room enough times to notice Lady Isabelle's painting hidden amongst all the others. You knew the lore behind it, that its sale would set you up for life. And you knew you couldn't steal it, not while your mother was alive. But if she was dead, it would be added to the estate's ledger and sold to charity. The only way to get it out of the estate, legally, was to hide it. You'd been hiding things for years, to keep them safe from your brothers. There was that Bible, up in one of the third-floor guest bedrooms, where you'd hidden all your handmade jewelry. But that felt too risky. That's when you remembered the 'lost' key to the grandfather clock, the one you'd turned into a necklace just like you'd seen your mother wear." She held up the photo she'd found of Iris in the Bible. Clarissa must have been so inspired by her mother's glamor, she'd kept it, and had made her own necklace in an attempt to be just like her.

"The grandfather clock gave you the perfect set-up," Lacey continued. "It was from your playroom, which meant one of you would get it in the will. Then once it was out of the house, legally, you'd only need a brief moment alone with it to unlock the cabinet and retrieve the painting.

"With the plan in place, you just needed to set it in motion. But there was one problem. You were too much of a coward to kill your mother yourself. You admired her, after all. You even loved her, although she never made you feel loved in return. You're not a violent person. That's when Henry came in. You maneuvered him into the position. You set the whole thing up; persuading your desperate, volatile brother to ask for money when you knew he'd be refused, when you knew it would push him over the edge and make him strike his mother, just as you'd witnessed him do all those years before. You knew she was too frail to survive a fall. It hardly counted as murder in your mind, did it? Just a little shove with deadly consequences. When the deed was done, you left the room—under the pretense of shock, I presume—retrieved the key and hid the painting in the clock. You gave one another alibis for the time of the murder. And the key? Well, that left the house with you, Clarissa, on a chain around your neck."

Superintendent Turner stepped forward. "Let's not make this any harder than it has to be," he said to Clarissa. He held out his hand. "The key."

Clarissa paused. For a moment, it seemed as if she might refuse—and Lacey tensed, really not wanting to see an ugly scene with the police grappling the woman. But she must've done such a thorough job of exposing Clarissa, the woman finally let out a large sigh and reached for the nape of her neck.

"Miss Archer," her lawyer said, "I must advise you not to take any action right now."

"Oh, give it a rest, Gus," she snapped at him. "It's over."

She unfastened the latch behind her neck and removed a necklace from the myriad she was wearing. She held it up to the room. There, dangling like a pendant, was a small silver key. She dumped it into Superintendent Turner's outstretched palm.

The detective flashed Lacey a look that said, *You'd better be right about this.*

He went over to the clock and turned the key in the compartment at the bottom. The small door opened. There, nestled in the little space beside all the unworking cogs and mechanisms, was Lady Isabelle's infamous miniature painting.

All the air seemed to leave the room.

Ben turned pained eyes from one sibling to the next. "How could you?" he stammered.

Henry blew up. "I never had any fame to launch my business like YOU TWO! Mother kept me hidden from the press. No one even knew I existed! Do you know how much that held me back? She did *everything* she could to make me fail!"

Ben ground his teeth. "It wasn't Mother who made you waste all your money on slot machines! You had just as many opportunities as Clarissa and I did."

Superintendent Turner approached Henry and cuffed him. DCI Lewis did the same with Clarissa.

As the two siblings were led toward the door, Nigel broke down and shook his head.

"Iris only ever kept you out of the spotlight for your own protection," he said to Henry. "She had a whole account set up to pay for your rehab when you were ready."

Henry looked stunned.

As the detectives left, Superintendent Turner turned back over his shoulder to look at Lacey.

"Excellent job, Ms. Doyle. I'll make it known publicly that you didn't have anything to do with Iris's murder."

Lacey nodded, relieved.

It was over.

At the table, Ben began to weep.

Lacey had disliked the man from the second they'd met, but at this moment, she felt nothing but compassion toward him. His siblings had betrayed him. He'd lost his mother. Her heart ached for him.

She looked over at the painting wedged in the hidden compartment.

"What are you going to do with the painting?" Lacey asked Ben. "It's yours now. You bought it fair and square."

He looked up through tear-stained eyes. "I'll give it to the museum. That's what Mother wanted."

Nigel looked perplexed. "How do you know that?"

"Because Mother told me all about Lady Isabelle one night as my bedtime story. She read to me rarely, and it was the only time I ever felt loved by her. I savored every last detail of those stories. She told me how the woman was forbidden from painting by her husband, and how it drove her to insanity, and that all her art was burned. I thought it was make-believe, especially the twist at the

217

end about how Mother had found one single miniature that survived the blaze, and how the art world would be turned upside down when she donated it to a museum after her death." His voice trailed away. "I cherished those bedtime stories. Mother had a wonderful imagination..." His tears began anew.

Empathy aching in her chest, Lacey looked over at Nigel. He looked just as glum as she felt. They may have cracked the case, but there was nothing to celebrate.

EPILOGUE

"I still don't understand how you pieced it all together," Tom said, looking over at Lacey. "I'm thoroughly impressed."

"Thank you," Lacey said with a smile.

They were strolling along the beach, taking the languorous route to their respective stores, the morning following the exposé. It was so early in the day, the sun had barely risen over the ocean, and the whole world seemed bathed in blue.

Chester skipped across the sand ahead of them. He'd been delighted when Lacey had awoken him extra early with the news he was going on his walkies.

The coffee cup clutched between Lacey's hands warmed her from the early morning chilly air.

"Maybe you should switch professions," Tom suggested, in his usual jovial manner. "Become a detective."

"I think I'll stick with antiques," Lacey replied. "That is, if my store can ever recover from this."

She felt a tightening in her chest. Today was crunch time. If there were no signs of the store bouncing back by the end of today, she'd have to accept that it was time to give up on her dream.

"Didn't you make enough from the auction sale commission to keep it open?" Tom asked, sounding tense.

"That was a one-off," Lacey replied. "The bank needs to see a steady revenue. I need customers. If sales don't pick up today, then I guess I'll be on a flight back to New York City by the end of the week."

Silence fell between them. Then Tom stopped walking.

"You can't leave," he said, and Lacey felt her heart begin to race from the earnest expression in his eyes. "I don't know what I'd do with myself if you left Wilfordshire. I know it's only been a few weeks but I feel like you're a part of my life now. And I've only been waiting because of all the Iris stuff, but it's over now, so I think it's time I told you I think there's something special growing between us. I'd like us to have a real date. An actual date. Not a joke one at a vet's office, or elevenses across your counter with a teapot. I understand if it's too soon after your divorce, but I just had to—"

Lacey reached out and put a finger to his lips. "Shh. It's not too soon. And I'd like that too."

She kissed him gently.

They could see the crowd from the bottom end of the high street.

"I see you finished your new macaron display," Lacey said with a chuckle.

But Tom shook his head. "I already told you, I spent the whole evening last night making a new batch of pastry. It's not my display that crowd's there for. It's your store!"

Lacey did a double take. Tom was right. The crowd was mainly congregated around her storefront.

They hurried along the cobbles to see what was going on.

As they drew up outside the antiques store, Lacey saw a large sign had been stuck to her grating. The police insignia was in one corner and her face was right in the middle.

Wilfordshire Police would like to extend a huge and heartfelt thank you to Lacey Doyle, who volunteered her time and effort to help us solve two recent cases. Thanks to her perseverance, we have suspects in prison, and the residents of Wilfordshire can sleep soundly knowing their town is a safer place.

Lacey read the notice with disbelief, her cheeks growing warm.

The people around her started patting her on the back and congratulating her.

"Come on then, open up," Jane from the toy store said.

Lacey looked at her, mystified. The terror she'd seen in the woman's eyes that time had completely vanished.

"I've had my eye on a lamp for days," she explained.

"I've wanted to come in, too," another local said. "I just heard all the rumors. I'm sorry."

Lacey didn't need to hear apologies. All she cared about was the gaggle of customers eager to get inside her store.

Excitement making her fingers tremble, she fumbled to get the shutters up and unlock the door.

"Come in, come in," she exclaimed, wedging it open with the heavy door stop.

People poured in past her, rushing over to the displays for the items they'd been desperate to buy all this time.

Lacey was rushed off her feet trying to serve them all. But they were patient with her, and kind, and each person apologized for falling for the rumors as they handed their pound notes across the counter. By the time the initial rush of people had cleared out, Lacey's till was filled with stacks of money.

Just then, the door tinkled and Lacey looked up. It was Taryn.

She was about to tell her to leave, because she just didn't want anyone bringing her down right now, when Taryn launched into a monologue.

"About Keith. I just want you to know that I didn't tell him to go to your house or anything like that. He's an old school friend, just out of jail, and I was trying to help him get back on his feet by paying him to do some handywork. And well, I guess I shouldn't have been so generous because he took things way too far." She shrugged nonchalantly, barely making eye contact. "He must've heard the rumors about you and took matters into his own hands."

Lacey folded her arms, nonplussed by Taryn's rather overt attempt to cover her ass. "You mean the rumors you started?"

"I didn't start the fire, Lacey. I merely—"

"—stoked the flames?"

Taryn's lips formed a thin line. "I merely passed on what everyone around town was already saying."

Lacey replied, raising an eyebrow. "You know there's another term for that. Gossiping."

Taryn huffed. "Look, I'm trying to apologize here." Her tone was abrupt, and about as far away from apologetic as it could be.

"Are you?" Lacey. "Don't apologies usually contain the word 'sorry'?"

"I'm sorry, all right?" Taryn snapped. "Is that what you want?"

"It's a start."

The boutique store clerk narrowed her eyes, then turned on her heel and marched away.

Lacey watched her go, feeling like the feud between them was far from over, though perhaps they'd made the smallest of steps forward.

The bell over the door tinkled and a group of tourists crowded inside the store. All thoughts of Taryn vacated Lacey's mind instantly.

As Lacey helped her customers, she felt a swell of pride for her store, for the business she'd created on her own. Coming to Wilfordshire had been the best decision she'd ever made. Even if she hadn't gotten that far in discovering what had happened to her father, she was closer than she'd been before. The town had more clues to offer. There was no way she could leave this place.

During a lull, Lacey picked up her phone and called Ivan.

"Ivan, I want to buy Crag Cottage," she announced, the moment he picked up.

There was a moment of hesitation on the other end of the line. "You do?"

"Yes." Lacey tensed. Ivan sounded uncertain. But then he let out a huge exhalation.

"Oh, thank goodness. It's been such a handful keeping up with it all, I was going to sell it anyway but I didn't want to kick you out. I can give you a reduced rate and—"

"Ivan, let me stop you right there. I've earned commission from my auction, and there's more to come. My shop is full of customers again. We'll get the house valued properly and I'll pay you market rate, okay?"

Another pause. Then finally, Ivan said, "Oh, thank you, Lacey. I'm so relieved. Really, I'd bitten off more than I could chew with that place."

With a huge grin, Lacey ended the call.

There was one more piece of business she had to finalize before she was satisfied.

She dialed the number for the RSPCA.

"My name's Lacey," she said, when the phone was answered by an elderly-sounding woman. "I'm calling about my foster dog, Chester. I took him on a couple of weeks back and I'd like to adopt him fully now."

"Of course," the lady said, with a gentle voice. "We can do that for you. Hold on one moment, and I'll just get your details up. Lacey, did you say? That's quite an unusual name. But I can tell from your accent you're not British. American, are you?"

"That's right," Lacey said, as she listened to the sound of keys clacking onto a computer come through the earpiece. She gazed at Chester lovingly.

"Right, here you are. Lacey Doyle. Is that right?"

"Yes, that's right."

Suddenly, the woman's tone changed. "Oh," she said.

"What is it?" Lacey asked. Her mind began to race. Maybe Chester's owners weren't deceased after all. Maybe they wanted him back. "Has something happened? Am I not allowed to adopt Chester?"

"No, dear, it's not that," the woman said. "It's just...Well, this might sound like a very strange question, but you don't happen to be a relation of Frank Doyle's, do you?"

NOW AVAILABLE FOR PRE-ORDER!

DEATH AND A DOG
(A Lacey Doyle Cozy Mystery—Book 2)

DEATH AND A DOG (AN LACEY DOYLE COZY MYSTERY—BOOK 2) is book two in a charming new cozy mystery series by Fiona Grace.

Ella Rose, 39 years old and freshly divorced, has made a drastic change: she has walked away from the fast life of New York City and settled down in the quaint English seaside town of Wilfordshire.

Spring is in the air. With last month's murder mystery behind her, a new best friend in her English shepherd, and a budding relationship with the chef across the street, it seems like everything's finally settling into place. Ella is so excited for her first major auction, especially when a valuable, mystery artifact enters her catalogue.

All seems to go without a hitch, until two mysterious bidders arrive from out of town—and one of them winds up dead.

With the small village plunged into chaos, and with the reputation of her business at stake, can Ella and her trusty dog partner solve the crime and restore her name?

Book #3 in the series—CRIME IN THE CAFE—is also available for preorder!

DEATH AND A DOG
(A Lacey Doyle Cozy Mystery—Book 2)

Made in the USA
Middletown, DE
27 August 2021

47045958R00139